ADVANCE PRAISE FOR THE AWAKENER

"Helen Weaver's memoir is a riveting account of her love affair and friendship with Jack Kerouac. She is both clear-eyed and passionate about him, and writes with truly amazing grace."
—Ann Charters, author of *Kerouac: A Biography* and the editor of *Kerouac: Selected Letters 1940-1956* and *The Portable Jack Kerouac*

"A wonderful view of Jack Kerouac and, most of all, a classic coming of age story. Brilliant and very moving to read: honest, touching, funny, sad, and beautiful. I couldn't put it down."
—David Amram, author of *Offbeat: Collaborating with Kerouac*

"Helen Weaver's book was a revelation to me! Although I was a young woman in the fifties, I was there, but I wasn't *there*! This is the most graphic, honest, shameless, and moving documentary of what the newly liberated women in cities got up to—how they lived, loved, and created. Who knew? It is time they did! And here's how."
—Carolyn Cassady, author of *Off the Road: My Years with Cassady, Kerouac, and Ginsberg*

"Firsthand witness to the Beat literary movement, Weaver (*Antonin Artaud: Selected Writings*) pays homage to the man and the writer Jack Kerouac, whom she met and fell in love with in 1956. Befriending Kerouac, Allen Ginsberg and comic Lenny Bruce, she makes these iconic counterculture figures tangible and captures New York's Greenwich Village of the '50s and '60s. The memoir reveals the author's own awakening—from discovering rock and roll through her personal sexual revolution to Buddhism. A lover of words and language, Weaver—immortalized in Kerouac's

Desolation Angels as Ruth Heaper—writes this book 'as an act of atonement' to Kerouac: 'I rejected him for the same reason America rejected him: he woke us up in the middle of the night in the long dream of the fifties. He interfered with our sleep.' She moves from translator to writer, but states she is 'uncertain whether it was the story of my own life or the story of the remarkable people I had known.' Ultimately, it's both."

—*Publishers Weekly*

THE AWAKENER

THE AWAKENER

A Memoir of Kerouac and the Fifties

Helen Weaver

City Lights Books
San Francisco, California

10 9 8 7 6 5 4 3 2 1

Cover design: em dash
Book design and composition: Linda Ronan

Front cover photograph: Jack Kerouac and Helen Weaver in Greenwich
Village, ca. 1963. Photographer unknown.

The names of some people have been changed to protect their privacy.

Excerpts from *Jack Kerouac: Selected Letters 1940-1956* reprinted
by permission of SLL/Sterling Lord Literistic, Inc. Copyright © by the
Estate of Jack Kerouac.

Although every effort has been made to contact and trace copyright
holders, in a few instances this has not been possible. If notified, the
publishers will be pleased to rectify any omission in future editions.

Library of Congress Cataloging-in-Publication Data
Weaver, Helen.
 The awakener : a memoir of Kerouac and the fifties / Helen Weaver.
    p. cm.
 ISBN 978-0-87286-505-1
 1. Beat generation. 2. Weaver, Helen. 3. Kerouac, Jack, 1922-1969.
 4. New York (N.Y.)—History—1951- 5. Ginsberg, Allen, 1926-1997.
 6. Bruce, Lenny. 7. Authors, American—20th century—Biography. I.
 Title.
 PS228.B6W43 2009
 813'.54—dc22
 [B]
                                          2009026896

Visit our website: www.citylights.com

City Lights Books are published at the City Lights Bookstore,
261 Columbus Avenue, San Francisco, CA 94133

for Helen Loring Elliott (1931-2004)
"the other Helen"

CONTENTS

one PROLOGUE

Sunday Morning *11*

two THE VILLAGE

Sullivan Street *21*
Watchstraps Forever *33*
Farrar, Straus *37*
The Odd Couple *43*

three JACK

A Heap of Wheat *53*
Just in Time *57*
Two Dinners *63*
Season's Greetings *69*
Happy New Year *79*
Can't We Be Friends? *91*
A Room of my Own *99*

four LENNY

From Beat to Hip *107*
Free Speech *121*
Webster's Unabridged *137*
The Real Obscenity *143*

five CHANGES

Endings *153*
My Claim to Fame *163*
A Visit to a Poet *171*

The City of Spindles *177*
It's All A Dream *187*
Reunion *199*
Impermanence *211*
An American Classic *221*

six EPILOGUE

Jack's Voice *235*

APPENDIX

The Dictionary of Hip *241*
An Astrological Appendix *243*

Acknowledgments *257*

one PROLOGUE

SUNDAY MORNING

*The American bards shall be marked for generosity and
affection and for encouraging competitors. . . . The great poets
are also to be known by the absence in them of tricks and by
the justification of perfect personal candor. . . . How beautiful
is candor! All faults may be forgiven of him who has perfect
candor.*

—Walt Whitman, preface to *Leaves of Grass*

I was sitting on the john in my pajamas when the buzzer rang. It
was seven o'clock on a Sunday morning in November 1956 and
Helen and I—my roommate had the same name as me—didn't
have any plans for the day. Neither one of us had gone to church
in years. As far as I knew it was going to be just another boring
Sunday in Greenwich Village.

Who the hell could be ringing our bell at this ungodly hour?
To see who it was you had to look out my bedroom window,
which looked onto the flagstone courtyard on West 11th Street
below. To let somebody in you had to throw down the key in a
sock, because the buzzer only worked one way.

As I splashed water on my face I could hear Helen rummag-
ing around in her room. Then her door opened and I heard her
pad across the living room and into my bedroom.

"It's Allen and Jack!" she yelled, sounding wide awake and
very excited. I knew who she meant right away. She had told me
all about the two writers she used to hang out with at the West
End Bar when she was a student at Barnard College and they were
at Columbia.

I joined her at the window and looked out. There, looking up at us, were not two but four young men with big backpacks sitting beside them on the ground. The first snow of winter had frosted the little courtyard like a Christmas cookie and more snow was falling on their bare and tousled heads.

Helen and the one with the horn-rimmed glasses had been shouting at each other and now as I stared at this dreamlike apparition, she went for the sock.

Pretty soon I heard the tramp, tramp, tramp of four pairs of feet on the stairs and into our living room came four of the most amazing-looking men I'd ever seen.

A raggletaggle band they were: unshaven, in clothes that looked as if they'd been slept in for a week—which, in fact, turned out to be the case, for they had been hitchhiking nonstop from Mexico—and each carrying a beat-up canvas rucksack on his back.

Suddenly our tiny and rather barren living room was teeming with life. The studious-looking one in the horn-rimmed glasses with the dark curly hair, whom Helen introduced to me as Allen Ginsberg, was obviously the leader. He introduced in turn the beautiful young man with the sad Russian face as his lover, Peter Orlovsky; Peter's tall, silent brother, Lafcadio; and the not very tall but dark and absurdly handsome one, Jack Kerouac.

Allen said they were all poets, and the deep respect with which he uttered the word "poet" indicated that being a poet was a passport to anywhere. They were exhausted, having traveled all night. Yet the energy around them, the energy they brought into our room—that odd room with the four doors and no windows, like a stage set that had finally found its play—was electric, was tangible. These grubby characters were somehow magnetic, dramatic, even glamorous, in a non-Hollywood, off-Broadway way.

And Jack, the little man with the peculiar name (I remembered now, Helen used to call him "Jack Caraway Seed"), the one in the lumberjack shirt who looked like he had just gotten off the deck of a ship, was handsome enough to be a movie star in spite of his five o'clock shadow and rumpled clothes.

In high school any boy that good-looking would have scared

Allen Ginsberg, ca. 1958.

*Jack Kerouac in
San Francisco, 1952.*

me to death, but for some reason this man immediately put me at my ease. He didn't seem to be aware of his good looks and besides, he looked familiar, the way strangers sometimes do, as if I'd met him before somewhere and didn't have to start from zero. It was as if the minute he walked in the door a movie started and I was in it, we were all in it, and wonder of wonders, I knew my lines.

While Allen and Helen started yakking away over by the coffee table and Peter wandered around the apartment examining all of our books and Lafcadio took up a position by the bathroom door as if he were guarding it, Jack zeroed in on me.

I was certainly far from glamorous. Helen and I hadn't even thought about getting dressed. She had slipped a nylon peignoir over her nightgown and I was still in my flannel pajamas. The boyish haircut I had worn when I thought I was gay had grown out to something midway between a pixie and a twenties bob. Back at Oberlin they used to call me Flapper Weaver.

Jack had on a black-and-blue plaid shirt with the tail out over his baggy black pants. There was something incongruous and even comical about his good looks—literally comical, for he had the classic rugged profile of Dick Tracy in the comic strip of the thirties. He had a high forehead with a lock of hair that fell over it, a deep furrow between his eyebrows, and a kind of perpetual squint, as if too much light was coming into his eyes.

The boys had taken off their heavy backpacks and set them against the wall beside Lafcadio, the dour Russian caryatid by the bathroom door. All except Jack, who had opened his up and started unpacking it. He and I were sitting on the floor in the middle of the room.

"I'm a writer," he said proudly, taking out manuscripts and handing them to me one by one. They had strange titles: *Tristessa* and *Mexico City Blues* and *Angels of Desolation*. I thought they all sounded sad.

"I wrote this," he said, handing me a dog-eared hardcover book: *The Town and the City*, by John Kerouac. Wow—he was a published author! I was impressed. I turned the book over. In the photograph on the back of the dust jacket I saw a younger, tamer Jack, his hair combed, in a jacket, a shirt, and a tie, looking pensive with downcast eyes.

"Guy made me look like a fag!" Jack said of Arni, the photographer, shaking his head ruefully.

But he perked up immediately. "It's like Thomas Wolfe," he said, with an intense gleam in his very blue eyes. Yes, he did look like a writer. I used to love Thomas Wolfe. As a student at Scarsdale High School I had read all of his books, had copied "O lost and by the wind grieved, O ghost, return again" into my diary. I'd even made both of my parents read *Look Homeward, Angel*. But since college I'd been on a Henry James kick. I felt that I had outgrown Wolfe.

In his course on the American novel at Oberlin, Andy Hoover had talked about the two schools of writing, which he called the Leaver Outers and the Putter Inners. Wolfe, of course, was the Putter Inner par excellence.

So I said, "Yes, I like Thomas Wolfe, but he would have been a better writer if he'd written less. He lacked discipline. He was lucky he had Maxwell Perkins for an editor. Now, take Henry James, for example. . . ."

Well, this was like waving a red flag in front of a bull.

We took up the debate of the Leaver Outers vs. the Putter Inners, and the battle was joined. Jack insisted that a good writer didn't need editing. "Writing should be spontaneous, like *jazz!*" (I noticed he had a way of italicizing certain words.) "Writing comes from *God.* Once you put it down, it's a *sin* to go back and change it!" He assured me that when his next book was published no editor was going to change a single word.

Jack Kerouac, 1950. For the dust jacket of The Town and the City.

And he leaped to the defense of his idol, Thomas Wolfe. We sat there on the floor surrounded by manuscripts, me in my pajamas and Jack in his rumpled clothes, and proceeded to debate the relative merits of Thomas Wolfe and Henry James, for all the world like two old friends who had known each other for years.

We both felt strongly about what we were saying and yet there wasn't a trace of animosity in our debate. Even as I played devil's advocate I was secretly checking him out on a nonverbal level, gently testing the waters of attraction: *Yes, he is really good looking; he talks funny, but I like it; he looks like he sleeps outdoors. He looks like he's been everywhere. He looks like a movie star—but he likes me! I can tell.* Our eyes locked, our mouths kept talking, our minds sparred. And yet it was comfortable, as if we had already been intimate.

There was something so natural and unpretentious about this man, even while he was telling me that he and Allen were both great writers. He said that they had discovered a whole new way of writing, and that they were going to be famous. The way he spoke, it sounded like a mission. It was their duty—and their destiny—to lead a revolution in American literature, to save it from the deathlike grip of the academy and return it to the flow of natural speech.

Jack's own speech pattern was utterly unique. He told me he had been born in Lowell, Massachusetts, of French-Canadian parents; he had spoken French until he was six years old. So there were not only the twangy vowel sounds of Massachusetts, so northern and laid-back in harsh Manhattan, but also the breath of Little Canada and his French-speaking family. And then there was this strange mixture of italicizing enthusiasm and world-weary sadness, as if he were already an old man seeing everything from a great distance.

He was a wild card foreigner who had shipped out on freighters and traveled the length and breadth of the land and looked it. His handsome squinting face had seen all weathers and he seemed to have brought all weathers with him when he walked in the door. He had frozen in the Arctic and fried in the jungles of Mexico. He carried his head low, or a little to one side, with a kind of sheepish, humble expression. Even his smiles were sad, and his laugh when it came was not a full-blown belly laugh, but more of a wistful, bemused chuckle.

I told Jack I wanted to be a writer, too, and he didn't laugh. He said, "That's great!" and smiled his approval.

"This is how you do it," he said. He pulled a little brown pad out of his shirt pocket and handed it to me, explaining that he always took one of these with him wherever he went. In these little nickel pads he jotted down impressions of everything that struck him, like an artist with a sketch pad, and used them later on in his books. He even called it sketching.

The boys were taking turns cleaning up in the bathroom. As Jack headed for the shower I listened as Allen described their adventures in San Francisco the previous summer. At a poetry reading at the Six Gallery Allen had given the first public reading of a long poem called *Howl*. As he declaimed his poem Jack had started shouting "Go!" in cadence and beating out the rhythm on a gallon jug of wine. Allen recited the opening lines for us, starting with "I saw the best minds of my generation destroyed by madness, starving hysterical naked," and I immediately recognized this poem as an electrifying manifesto. Helen and I applauded. I could picture the scene.

Allen told us that the day after this reading, Lawrence Ferlinghetti, founder of City Lights Books, had sent him a telegram that quoted what Ralph Waldo Emerson said to Walt Whitman after reading *Leaves of Grass*: "I greet you at the beginning of a great career." Ferlinghetti had added, "When do I get the manuscript?" City Lights had published *Howl* and it was already selling well, thanks partly to another reading in Venice at which Allen had caused a sensation by removing all of his clothes.

Allen had dedicated *Howl* to "Jack Kerouac, new Buddha of American prose, who spit forth intelligence into eleven books . . . creating a spontaneous bop prosody and original classic literature," as well as to his other mentors, William Burroughs and Neal Cassady. Allen said we had to meet Burroughs. It was a name I had never heard before but the way he said it Burroughs was synonymous with God.

I noticed that Allen's way of speaking was similar to Jack's. They both had beautiful voices and a distinctive lilting, hypnotic, almost singsong, way of speaking that I had never heard before. Allen said that when he read a long poem he would get carried away and begin chanting like a cantor. He had a habit of waving his index finger in the air like a modern-day Hebrew prophet. He looked like a Jewish intellectual but he sounded like Moses come down from the mountain.

And it was with a kind of maternal pride free from any trace of competitiveness that Allen reported on the latest developments in Jack's career. Grove Press had accepted an excerpt from Jack's novel *The Subterraneans* for publication in *Evergreen Review* and was interested in others of his unpublished works. The two men stood confident on the threshold of their fame.

That Sunday morning was a little like the scene in *The Wizard of Oz* where Dorothy steps out of the black-and-white world of Kansas into the technicolor land over the rainbow. I had the definite sense that Helen and I weren't in Kansas any more.

She and I had always accepted the fact that we were on the

fringes of the New York art and literary world, but suddenly I felt a part of it all. Looking from Jack to Allen, who was equally charismatic in a different way, and sensing their enormous vitality, their enthusiasm for literature and life, their steadfast belief in each other and in their destiny, mesmerized by their beautiful voices and the incantatory style of their speech, I did not doubt for a moment that they would be famous. It was just a matter of time. Such energy and charm and purpose could not be denied. They would beat down the doors of the publishing houses—beat down the walls, if necessary. They were a force of nature.

Now the force of nature was hungry and wanted breakfast. We were low on food, so a collection was taken up and Jack volunteered to go down to the deli on the corner of 11th and Hudson and buy bacon, eggs, and English muffins.

I came from a small family—just me and my brother and our parents. I'd never made scrambled eggs for six people before. I still remember how those twelve raw eggs looked in my mother's Pyrex bowl.

After breakfast the boys felt the fatigue of their marathon journey. Allen asked politely if they might take a nap and we were happy to oblige, as we were tired too. The boys dug their sleeping bags out of their rucksacks and lined them up on the living room floor and Helen and I retired to our rooms. As I drifted off to sleep, acutely aware of all of that young male energy on the other side of my door, a funny image flashed into my mind.

At our cottage at Candlewood Lake Club one summer a mouse had four babies in my father's sock drawer. The way those four poets were lying side by side in their warm cocoons reminded me of those little pink sacs, thin-skinned and quivering with life, huddled together in Dad's top drawer. As soon as we discovered them the mother mouse lost no time in whisking them all away to a safer location. Now it was as if some giant mother mouse had laid her babies in our living room, each in its separate sack.

What was going to happen to the warm bodies on our living room floor? What did destiny have in store for them?

two THE VILLAGE

SULLIVAN STREET

Those friends thou hast, and their adoption tried,
Grapple them unto thy soul with hoops of steel.

—William Shakespeare, *Hamlet*

I'm not sure I believe in "destiny," but I've often pondered the irony of someone like me, a girl from Scarsdale with a strict and even repressive middle-class upbringing, ending up with these wild characters who represented the opposite of everything Scarsdale stood for: rebellion, art, sex, drugs, jazz, racial equality: in a word, freedom.

Looking back, I think it was the very fact that they were so different from everything I'd grown up with that explained their appeal.

I hadn't much cared for Scarsdale anyway. It was all about what does your father do and do you have the right clothes and do you belong to the Scarsdale Golf Club, which in those days wouldn't dream of admitting Jews, let alone "Negroes." I think there was one lone black girl in my class at Scarsdale High.

When I fell in love with the boy across the street at age eight and I told my mother that we had decided to get married, she said I couldn't marry Willie because he was a Jew. And I wasn't allowed to play with a girl who lived on the wrong side of town, whose house didn't have any furniture or rugs on the floor. Poverty, Jewishness—anything forbidden—became exotic and therefore desirable.

As an adolescent I was a shy, sickly "brain" who wrote poetry and lived for books and movies, didn't go to dances or football games, and whose one date in high school was a disaster. When I graduated from Scarsdale High in 1948 the caption under my picture in the yearbook read "No genius without a little madness."

I decided to go to Oberlin because, unlike the eastern colleges most of my classmates would attend, it did not have sororities and fraternities, and because it was as far away from Scarsdale as possible. Oberlin was full of bright kids, many of whom were social misfits like me. I felt right at home.

I had no idea what I was going to do with myself after I graduated from college. In my short life I had known nothing but school. I was terrified of the open space that suddenly loomed before me. At Oberlin I even dated, and I decided to marry the boy I was dating my senior year, an art history major from Brooklyn.

Three weeks after the wedding Charles was drafted into the army and sent to Camp Kilmer, New Jersey, for basic training. It was 1952 and the Korean War.

I signed up for a secretarial course in White Plains. By the time I had learned Gregg shorthand and could type sixty words a minute Charles had wangled a job in the mail room at Fort Dix along with permission to live off base. We found an apartment in the home of a young Irish family in Mount Holly, New Jersey, and I got a job as a secretary at the Campbell Soup Company in Camden, the home of Walt Whitman and an incredibly dreary place.

Inscribed on the granite facade of the post office building near where I got off the bus every morning were the words "Where there is no vision, the people perish." This always struck me as a pretty good description of Camden.

To get to work on time I had to catch a bus that left at 6:55 a.m. By the time I got home it was almost seven and I was always exhausted. On weekends I cleaned, did the laundry, and went grocery shopping.

I remember waking up one Saturday morning and thinking, *Is this it? Is this all there is?*

I also remember lying in bed with my husband and feeling nothing at all: staring at the ceiling and wondering what was wrong with me. Gradually I lost all desire for sex.

I started to wonder whether I was gay—a word I had just learned from my Oberlin friend Lili Chan, whom I visited a few times in her apartment in Greenwich Village.

Back at Oberlin, Chan had had a very intense friendship with a girl that I suspected was more like a love affair. I had been attracted to this girl, too—I'll call her Eva Di Angelo—but since she was a piano major in the Conservatory, our classes met in different buildings. Then I became involved with Charles and soon Di Angelo became a shadowy figure in the back of my consciousness, mysterious and unattainable.

But one day at Campbell's, I got a phone call from Di Angelo. She was right around the corner, asking if I was free for lunch.

I walked out of the office and there she was on a street corner in Camden, looking like a boy in an Italian movie, tossing away a cigarette and giving me a crooked smile.

That was the beginning of the end of my marriage.

Nothing much happened in Mount Holly, but that summer, after the U.S. Army gave Charles an honorable discharge and I quit my job at Campbell's, I spent two weeks with Chan and Di Angelo in a cabin in Ogunquit, Massachusetts, and ended up in Di Angelo's bed.

The discovery that I could be attracted to a woman was mind-altering, life-changing. The whole notion of competing with women for attention from men was turned on its head, but it went beyond that. If women had suddenly been transformed from rivals to the objects of my desire, then all of my previous conditioning went out the window. The world was a far larger and more complex place than I had imagined. I felt my life cracking open. And of course the fact that homosexuality, in the fifties, was socially unacceptable only added to its appeal.

I felt that loving a woman had made me a better person, a more truly human being: *nihil humanum mihi alienum est* (nothing human is foreign to me), as the Romans used to say.

It did not, however, bring me any closer to solving the mystery of the orgasm.

In the fall Charles and I went back to Oberlin. He got a job as

Helen Weaver in Oberlin, summer 1955

a graduate assistant in the art department. I took literature courses and sat in the stacks reading the poetry of George Herbert and trying to come up with an idea for a master's thesis.

I met an undergraduate English Literature major named Benjamin and realized I wasn't a lesbian after all.

In the spring of 1955 Charles and I separated. My new friend Ben wanted to marry me, but this time I knew I wasn't ready. I had been afraid of freedom. Now I wanted it.

My marriage was over. My love affair had backfired. I had given up on my master's thesis. I should have felt like a complete failure, but for some reason I didn't.

That summer I stayed in Oberlin in order to fulfill the residency requirement for an Ohio divorce. I spent the summer waiting on tables at the Oberlin Inn and hanging out at a local greasy spoon that had "Rock Around the Clock" on the jukebox.

I played that song over and over. Somehow I knew it wasn't just another song: it was a manifesto. That new sound that suddenly appeared that summer was the sound of freedom. I wasn't the only person in America who was being reborn. It was the summer of 1955 and the birth of rock 'n' roll.

When I got back to New York after my divorce came through there was never any question that Greenwich Village was where I wanted to be.

As a young woman with a B.A. in English literature, I had two choices: teaching and publishing. Although my parents had both been teachers, I didn't really have the calling or the stamina, so publishing it was. And even if New York City hadn't been the publishing capital of the world I would have ended up there anyway. As Dan Wakefield points out in *New York in the Fifties*, if you were a young person from the provinces with literary or artistic aspirations there just wasn't any other place to be. And Greenwich Village, known to those who lived there simply as the Village, was the hottest place in New York.

Chan had an apartment on Sullivan Street. When I was living in Mount Holly and working at Campbell's I had taken the bus to the city and visited her a few times. Chan had introduced me to the gay underworld in the city by taking me to the Bagatelle on University Place and the Page Three on Seventh Avenue. By contrast with my life as a housewife and secretary in New Jersey Chan's life in Greenwich Village with its *louche* nightlife and great shops and restaurants took on an irresistibly compelling aura of mystery and charm. She had talked her way into a job in the production department of Viking Press. What could be better—a job in publishing and an apartment in the Village?

I'd spent a week with Ben in a basement apartment on Charles Street so I already had some sense of the lay of the land. The Village was a patchwork crazy quilt, totally different from the foursquare grid of uptown New York. Most of the streets had names instead of numbers; or if they did have numbers they sometimes intersected in impossible, illogical ways. How could there be a corner of Fourth Street and 10th Street? But there was.

Lying as it did down near the southern end of the island and teeming as it was with artists, would-be artists, and oddballs like myself, the Village seemed to represent the repressed unconscious—even the repressed sexuality—of Manhattan. I used to joke that we Villagers were like certain species of fish that can only survive at the bottom of the ocean. If we went above 14th Street, we would explode.

As someone who had been on the bottom rung of the social ladder at Scarsdale High I felt right at home on the bottom of the island. Like many a would-be bohemian, I had a classic case of *la nostalgie de la boue*. To the overprotected little girl from Scarsdale that I was, the very dirt of the streets and the subways and the stairs of tenements was exciting. It represented freedom: freedom from everything I had escaped: parents, marriage, academia. Downtown was where it was at. It was be there or be square.

My first Village apartment was a third-floor walkup on Sullivan Street just a few blocks south of Chan's. After I got settled I found a job as a "gal Friday" for Paradigm Books, a very small book publishing company that has long since bitten the dust.

My father said this was the wrong way to go about it: I should find a job first, and then look for an apartment; but since he gave me the money for the first month's rent plus the month's security anyway, I did it my way. That was Dad: forever telling me that money didn't grow on trees, or on him, and then undermining his own argument by his never-failing generosity.

E. B. White wrote that New York City bestows "the gift of privacy, the jewel of loneliness." That first apartment was a magical place for me because it was there that I learned the art— and the joy—of solitude.

Chan was a great teacher, for she knew how to live on nothing and she had an artist's eye. She told me you could get great furniture at the Salvation Army, and how to make an elegant, inexpensive bookcase out of bricks and boards. As for that luminous Japanese Noguchi lamp that gave a subtle oriental flavor to her little room, it was cheap too, and still available at the Museum of Modern Art. It was she who had helped me find my apartment by getting the *Villager* the first thing Thursday morning.

She was also a great source of information on clothes. Now that I was a Villager I had to look the part, and that meant looking like a ballerina: long skirts, Capezio ballet shoes, and black stockings. Above all, black stockings. It was the New Look all over again. A shop on 8th Street called Fred Braun sold leather goods of extraordinary sensuality. Their specialty was a wildly expensive flat shoe, a kind of elfin desert boot that was as far from loafers with pennies in them as Greenwich Village was from Scarsdale. Chan and I lusted after these objects that had the power to make daily life magical.

In *Minor Characters* Joyce Johnson talks about a certain pair of dangling copper earrings that she never wore uptown in front of her parents but kept in her purse for those times when she secretly took the subway down to Greenwich Village. These objects and these clothes identified us as members of a radical underground. They breathed a whole new way of life that was subversive, forbidden, earthy, as revolutionary as art itself.

And they were not just symbolic; they were beautiful. That was part of the secret of living alone: make your space and everything around you so beautiful that loneliness simply doesn't occur.

On Saturday night I would get dressed up in my dyke costume— black slacks, white shirt, black-and-white checked tie (very short and "feminine," it scared me to look too butch), black jacket, newly washed hair slicked back, dark glasses, Fred Braun shoes and drawstring bag—and walk up Sullivan Street to Chan's apartment. The old Italian men sitting on their front steps would stare at me as I went by. I used to imagine that they, like the Italian barber who cut my hair, wondered why this pretty girl would want to dress up like a boy.

Chan was pretty too. An artist and a serious student of modern dance, she had a catlike grace and long black hair that fell down like rain. Her prominent cheekbones gave her a Native American look, but she had once told me proudly that she was a full-blooded Chinese.

I would pick up Chan and we would have dinner at the Grand Ticino or the Dragon Inn. After that we would go to the movies or, if we were feeling brave, we might go and sit in the Bagatelle and have sweet vermouth on the rocks with a twist of lemon and watch these cute collegiate dykes slow drag to "Oh Yeah, She's My Baby" and "You've Got the Magic Touch." I was careful not to make eye contact with the ones who looked like they drove trucks, terrified that one of them might ask me to dance. When we got enough of a buzz on we would get up and shuffle together for a while before we called it a night. I guess we thought we were pretty hip just being there at all. It was very innocent and actually rather boring because although there was so much sexual energy in the room you could cut it with a knife, we weren't getting any.

There were times when I woke up in the middle of the night in this little cell in this building in which I knew not one single person and felt the metallic coldness of the city air.

Sometimes a strange phone call would come in the middle of the night: a breather, a telephone stalker who for all you knew knew exactly where you lived and was coming to get you. Being a newcomer I hadn't known enough not to put my first name in the phone book.

There was a guy who used to call me at 3 a.m. on a Saturday night and say in a deep black voice, "I was told you could give me some information." And when I said nothing: "I was told you could tell me about . . . *phallic endive*." No, it was not a dream. Old Phallic Endive called me maybe half a dozen times before he decided he was never going to get the information he needed and stopped calling.

I must have met Richard Howard shortly after I moved to the city because he's inseparable from those prehistoric days when I was working at Paradigm Books and learning the art of solitude. I met him through Ed Stringham, the son of some friends of my parents who worked for the *New Yorker* magazine. The whole function of this evening with a family friend was to connect me up with Richard, so that the rest of my life could begin.

There are certain people in life with whom, the moment you first lay eyes on them, there is a sort of click of recognition, and it's *Oh, there you are—now we can begin.* There are people you fall in love with not as lovers, but as friends. Richard was one of those people. Helen—the Helen who would become my roommate—was another.

Even though Richard was gay and I was female and not gay—at least, not totally—he courted me. There's no other word for it. That was Richard's style, and mine too, come to think of it. When you're a bit of a misfit like me there is a thrill to finding a major new friend that is so intense it's almost sexual, and there's also the sense that you have to make up for lost time.

As of today, Richard has published eleven books of poetry, one of which won the Pulitzer Prize. He has translated more than

150 books from the French, a body of work that reads like a list of France's leading writers. His is a distinguished career covered with honors too numerous to mention.

Back in 1955 when I met him Richard was working for Funk & Wagnalls as a lexicographer. In other words, he was writing encyclopedias: expanding at a geometric rate the already formidable amount of knowledge that was crammed into that vast Henry Jamesian brow. Picture, if you can, Bruce Willis made up to play Henry James, and you'll have a pretty good idea what Richard looked like in those days. Like me, he had been writing poetry for years, but unlike me, he was really good at it.

We would meet after work at our respective publishing houses and he would take me on a carefully orchestrated itinerary: first home to his flat to feed and walk his bulldog, Max; then maybe to his favorite new restaurant in the Village, where while waiting for the entree he would read me his latest poem; then on to the Museum of Modern Art for a new exhibit or a French movie I had to see or to a concert by his handsome pianist friend Alvin Novak, who had studied in Paris with Nadia Boulanger, or uptown to meet his mother, on a visit from Cleveland, or downtown to the Theater de Lys, where *The Threepenny Opera* had begun its seven-year run and the divine Lotte Lenya was still on board. Richard told me what books to read and what music to listen to.

He even took me to Boston to visit Robert Lowell and Elizabeth Hardwick. Lowell wasn't my favorite poet, but he was famous, and I greatly admired her essays in *Partisan Review*.

This was royalty, and I was nervous. But Richard assured me that they would love me, and besides, "A cat may look at a king." This was one of his favorite expressions, and he lived by it. Richard was fearless, unstoppable, and yes—ambitious. Churchill is supposed to have said, "Greatness knows itself," and Richard was—or knew he was going to be—great.

The visit was a disaster. Oh, they had a grand time, but I uttered not a word, sat there like a little vegetable that had just been shipped from the Midwest, trying to look intelligent as these three geniuses discussed writers I had never heard of and books I hadn't read and picked apart the latest issue of *Partisan Review*.

Then there was the literary gossip, all delivered with wit and panache. I might as well have wandered into a salon with Dr. Johnson, Oscar Wilde, and Madame de Staël. I remember not one scrap of the brilliant talk that flew over my head.

I do remember, however, exactly what I was wearing that day. It was a dress I had bought at Fred Leighton's, a shop on 8th Street that sold Mexican imports, and I had bought it on time because it was far too expensive for my secretary's salary. It was of a blue and white heavy homespun cotton in the Mother Hubbard style: high Victorian collar with a tiny ruffle, long sleeves with a tiny ruffle at the cuff, and a square yoke to which were stitched a deeply satisfying number of tiny pleats and from which the dress fell in luxurious fullness to midcalf, with a self belt tied with a bow in the back. A fabulous dress I wish I had today. This dress had to make up for my inability to speak, and perhaps it did.

I was no dummy, mind you. Richard wouldn't have bothered to take me under his wing if I'd been stupid. But Richard Howard was another order of magnitude, one of those rare beings who aspire to universal knowledge and almost achieve it, who attack life with an energy that radiates from them like splendor lines from the sun and attracts a whole solar system of lesser lights.

And he was funny! He and the poet John Hollander—another of the Columbia geniuses he or Helen introduced me to—were clowns who egged each other on ("Faster! Funnier!") and came up with gems like John's "Mandrill Ramble:"

I saw a monkey in the zoo,
As fair as me, as fair as you,
And something glittered there like polished brass.
He turned around three times three
And Oh he was a sight to see
That monkey had an iridescent ass!
It shines—it glows—just like—a rose—
I thought I'd scream when I saw it gleam
Oh ain't they fine those monkeyshines
That monkey with the iridescent ass!

which Richard sang to me with arched brows in his sonorous, slightly nasal voice.

And Richard, the great intellectual, liked to talk about sex. He probably thought more highly of me because I had had a lesbian affair and had been to gay bars and danced with women. I'm not sure if it was Richard or one of the other Columbia wags who came up with the term "HD."

"HD" stood for "Homosexual Dread," or the fear that straight people, in those pre-Stonewall, pre–coming out days, had of homosexuality and of anybody who might be gay. Today we call it homophobia. Of course, in those days the word "gay" was a code word, known only to denizens of what Di Angelo called "the shadow world." I first heard it from Chan, and believe me, back in the fifties, the very word "gay" had a wild, sexy, forbidden, magical resonance that it has since completely lost. It's been taken over and sanitized and is now printed in the *New York Times* and spoken aloud in the U.S. Congress, for God's sake. And all this is good and long overdue. But the word has also lost its power, or maybe it has a different kind of power—political rather than sexual.

But back then, most straight people were terrified of homosexuality: hence, Homosexual Dread, or HD. But since in those days many homosexuals were equally terrified of straight people, Helen and I decided that depending on the context, HD could also stand for "Heterosexual Dread," and this extended meaning was accepted into the canon. As in, "He may be queer as a nine-dollar bill, Mary, but he doesn't have HD."

Richard and Helen and I prided ourselves on not having either form of HD. We had been around the block, we were hip, and we could talk about anything. I remember Helen telling me, "I had dinner with Dick Howard. He was in one of his great moods and we stayed up for hours and talked about everything. We talked about Going Down."

I first laid eyes on Helen at Dale's, a luncheonette on the corner of Fifth Avenue and 17th Street, down the street from Paradigm Books. It was one of those places where you sat around a counter,

Helen Elliott, ca. 1956.

à la Chock Full o' Nuts. Helen used to come there after seeing her shrink, whose office was around the corner, and I noticed her right away.

She was striking: a tall brunette with soulful brown eyes, an overbite, and a showgirl figure that was something of a Village legend. In spite of her height she had a waiflike quality that always reminded me of Judy Garland, and it turned out she had a voice like Garland's too.

I always ordered a BLT down, heavy on the mayo, and I could tell she had also noticed me. One day we found ourselves sitting side by side and we struck up a conversation. She told me she worked at the MCA talent agency on Broadway, where she met a lot of stars, and she was taking singing lessons herself. She was from Omaha, which was also, she was proud to say, the home of Marlon Brando, who was her all-time top favorite movie star. I loved Brando too but my real hero was Elvis Presley, that new sensation whom the adults looked down on but the teenagers all adored. Helen and I soon discovered what was perhaps our greatest bond. Unlike most of our contemporaries, we were both crazy nuts (as Helen would put it) about rock 'n' roll.

Helen had taken classes at Barnard and she knew all the bright lights from Columbia, including Richard Howard. She decided I was somebody she wanted to know, so she called Richard and told him he had to invite us both to dinner.

Did I mention that Richard was a fabulous cook? The dinner was a success and after that we were all three great friends.

Richard advised me to "grapple her unto my soul with hoops of steel," and that's exactly what I did.

WATCHSTRAPS FOREVER

When the mode of the music changes, the walls of the city shake.

—Plato

Although we had both been born in the Midwest, Helen and I had come from very different homes.

My parents had met as students at the University of Wisconsin in Madison. Our family moved East when my mathematician father was invited to head the division of natural sciences at Rockefeller Foundation in New York City. Though far from rich by Scarsdale standards, we were comfortable and my brother and I grew up in a beautiful book-filled home. Helen's father had to struggle to make a living as a traveling salesman for Mutual of Omaha.

Yet I thought I'd had a lousy childhood until I heard about hers. A year younger than my classmates (I'd skipped second grade when I finished my workbook on the first day of school) I was bullied unmercifully by my "best friend," victimized by a gang of sadistic older girls, and spanked with a hairbrush or a yardstick for what I considered ridiculous reasons by my parents, who belonged to the "spare the rod and spoil the child" school of child raising. As for my standard tortured adolescence, the less said about that, the better.

But all this was nothing compared to Helen's start in life. Her father loved her, but he was seldom around, and when he was home he and her mother fought constantly about his drinking. When Helen started dating and going to jazz clubs her mother called her a whore and threw her out of the house. And when her mother died, she left Helen one dollar in her will.

In the state of Nebraska it was against the law to leave nothing to a daughter. Helen had framed the dollar bill and hung it on the wall of her bedroom.

She hated birthdays, changed the date on her birth certificate, and lied about her age for so long that she finally got confused about it herself.

From her point of view I, with my loving, stable, and overprotective parents, was either very lucky or very spoiled, depending on her mood. And she had her moods, and we had our differences, as you will see. But our very different backgrounds had made us both rebels. We were still in the honeymoon phase of our friendship when we were discovering our similarities.

We both loved show tunes and we knew the soundtrack from *My Fair Lady* by heart. On Saturday mornings I would put on my weekend drag (in those days women weren't allowed to wear pants to the office) and I would walk west through the Village over to Helen's apartment on Jane Street. When I turned down her street I would start singing "On the Street Where You Live" pretty loud and I would keep it up all the way to her front window. To this day I can't hear that song without thinking of her.

Sometimes when I turned down Jane Street Helen would be out walking her black-and-tan German shepherd, Treff, and we would sing together. Once she and Treff spent the night in my apartment on Sullivan Street. I can still hear his toenails clicking on the bare floor as he paced restlessly in the night.

We called each other "H." We cut our hair short and wore men's watches on our wrists. We smoked Viceroys, drank Rheingold beer, and wore dark glasses at night.

We probably didn't even know that hipsters and jazz musicians wore "shades" at night to protect and conceal their dilated pupils when they smoked marijuana. We just knew it was hip. We didn't smoke marijuana yet, but we talked as if we did. We peppered our conversation with hip talk, kept lists of hip expressions, and even planned to write a dictionary of hip.

We had both been rock 'n' roll fans ever since Bill Haley and the Comets came out with "Rock Around the Clock" the summer of '55. Chuck Berry, Little Richard, the Everly Brothers, the Five Satins, the Del-Vikings, "In the Still of the Night," "Come Go With Me"—all that stuff was mother's milk to us after the thin watery gruel of Tin Pan Alley. ("Deliver me from the days of old!")

I had loved some of those songs of the thirties and forties: "Long Ago and Far Away," "Over the Rainbow," "When You Wish Upon a Star," "The Dreamer," "If You Are But a Dream;" but that was when I had to live on dreams. That was then, this was now.

We listened to the Top Forty, bought all of Elvis's records, and saw every one of his awful movies as soon as they came out, sitting in the balcony of the beautiful old Loew's Sheridan Theater that used to be on the corner of Seventh Avenue and Greenwich Avenue before they tore it down. When Screamin' Jay Hawkins came out with a wild side called "I Put a Spell on You" we dug it so much that when he came to the Paramount Theater we took the subway all the way to Brooklyn and sat through a movie about steeplejacks with a fear of heights, surrounded by screaming teenagers who rocked the balcony. But it was worth it to watch Screamin' Jay crawl across the stage in an Arab headdress and belt out his classic tune.

We were in our mid-twenties and supposed to be too old for rock. Incredible as it may seem today, in the fifties to be over twenty-one and to actually admit you liked rock 'n' roll was tantamount to an act of political subversion that required real courage. Rock 'n' roll was for teenagers. The ridicule we faced from our peers was almost monolithic. Only a few members of the New York intelligentsia—Bob Gottlieb and Dan Wakefield come to mind—understood that this music was truly revolutionary, that it was real music, that it was the wave of the future.

Bob Gottlieb wrote later in *Mademoiselle:*

*By the time of Haley's "Rock Around the Clock" and [Elvis's]
"Heartbreak Hotel," I knew that something great had happened.
The real music of Country and Blues had pushed its way out
of the underground and was blowing all the fakery away. I
remember trying to share with bewildered friends my feeling*

about the special qualities of Elvis's voice, his musicianship, the
excitement of, say, "I Want You, I Need You, I Love You."

Everyone else heard doo-wah-diddy, saw teenagers in leather
jackets and greasy pompadours and Elvis shaking his pelvis, and
thought it was all too anti-intellectual and lower class for words.
Right!

It was with Elvis as it had been with Sinatra (and as it would
be with the Beatles): the teenagers were the first to *get* it. "Love
Me Tender" was to Elvis what "Ole Man River" was to Sinatra: It
proved he had a voice and now even the adults had to admit that
he could sing.

Helen and I had fifties nostalgia—in the fifties. Rock was a
great bond for two women who were really very different.

Richard Howard did not share Helen's and my enthusiasm
for the new sound. When we were all invited to a costume party
at a swanky uptown apartment, I got myself a cowboy hat and a
bolo tie on 42nd Street and borrowed a friend's guitar and went as
Elvis Presley. Richard came as my other hero, Marcel Proust. When
Richard's boyfriend Sandy, who came as Harpo Marx, introduced
us: "Monsieur Proust—Monsieur Presley!" Elvis was appropri-
ately inarticulate (like, who was this cat with the monocle?). As
for Marcel, he peered down his nose at this barbarian, raised a
supercilious eyebrow, gave a Gallic shrug, and turned away.

The way Helen and I walked around arm in arm in men's
shirts, blue jeans, boyish haircuts, big Timex watches, and shades,
some people who didn't know us (and even some who did) took
us for lovers. We didn't give a rat's ass what people thought. We
actually liked it that people were confused about us. We loved
each other, but we weren't lovers. *Au contraire,* we were just
trying to look like our heroes, Brando, Dean, and Presley and any
teenagers who vaguely resembled them.

We hung out together to the point where one of us would
say what the other was thinking. Once when this happened we
spontaneously clicked our watches together and said in unison,
"Watchstraps forever!" It became our motto.

We decided to look for an apartment.

FARRAR, STRAUS

Work, for the night is coming!

—Anna L. Coghill, 1854

My job at Paradigm Books wasn't going so well. It was an interesting job, on the face of it: theoretically, working for a very small publishing house should have given me an opportunity to learn every aspect of the business. I liked the authors, the freelance people, and the other employees—the junior in-house editor, the bookkeeper, and the other "girl." I got to read manuscripts. The list was mostly foreign writers and a lot of it was really good. The problem was, I couldn't stand the owners, Mr. and Mrs. S.

He wasn't so bad: a rather pathetic little man who couldn't dictate a letter to save his soul. All of his letters had to go through several drafts, and I always ended up writing them myself, which I rather enjoyed. But she was a holy terror. If I made a mistake she was nasty and if I did something well she was jealous. She made the bookkeeper sit all day on a wooden library chair. Every time this older woman complained that her back hurt and said she needed a chair with back support, Mrs. S. assured her that a new chair for her was "on order." It was "on order" the whole six months I worked there.

It got so I couldn't stand answering the phone and saying the same dumb thing every time: "Good morning, Paradigm Books, Miss Weaver speaking, how may I help you?" I'll admit it, I had an attitude. One morning when Mrs. S. asked me if I had inspected the new stationery, Miss Smart Aleck said, "Well, I didn't look at every sheet." I somehow managed to lose a sample chapter of a book that turned out to be the author's only copy. How he could have been stupid enough to submit an only copy I can't fathom, but it was still a major goof on my part.

Eventually Mrs. S. hired a girl to replace me and had me teach her my job. The S's were too cheap to fire me because they might have had to spring for unemployment, so instead they made my life so unpleasant that I quit.

The job hunt that followed was an interesting experience. I had a good interview at Dover Publications down on Varick Street. The editor-in-chief there was about to hire me and asked me to step out of the office for a moment while he made a phone call. I had given Mr. S. as a reference. When the Dover man called me back in he had a funny look on his face. He said, "Don't ever give that man as a reference. After what he told me, I can't hire you."

It seems that Mr. S. had said, among other things, that I had "a cavalier attitude toward detail." I had to laugh because if anything, I am hung up on details—a borderline case of obsessive-compulsive disorder. But the man at Dover did me a big favor by telling me the truth: I was being blackballed by Paradigm Books.

My next interview was for a job in the production department at Farrar, Straus and Cudahy, right across Fifth Avenue from Paradigm. The personnel director there happened to be the father-in-law of my senior year college roommate. Maybe Curti told him I was a smart girl and a responsible person (only a slight exaggeration), because when I walked in with my résumé and my revised list of references he didn't beat around the bush. He looked me in the eye and said, "So what happened over there? Did you make a boo-boo?"

I told him exactly what happened, and Bob Wohlforth, bless his heart, decided to trust me, and gave me the job.

I had lucked out. Now I was working for a real publishing company run by a very smart man who loved his work, the legendary Roger W. Straus Jr., a firm that to this day is one of the very best in the business. And because my new boss, Harold Vursell, was managing editor and children's book editor as well as production manager, I really did learn the business this time, from the submitted manuscript to the finished book.

I was Hal's "second girl:" the assistant production manager, a tall handsome woman named Dorris, was my other boss. They both welcomed me into the fold and treated me like family from the start.

A tall, well-spoken man whose suits were made in England and who peered at the world through little half-glasses at the end of his nose, Hal managed to be elegant and unpretentious at the same time. When he died, much too young, the summer of 1976, Bob Giroux called him "a good bookman." He could sit down with a messy manuscript, make a few phone calls, scratch a few figures on a pad, and half an hour later give Roger a per-copy manufacturing cost that was invariably right on the money.

Hal was full of colorful expressions he had picked up on his travels and from his churchgoing parents back in Illinois: "Work, for the night is coming!" "No rest for the wicked!" and "Shut up, he explained." If a place was remote and hard to find it was "where God lost his shoes." If he needed to express incredulity or dismay in the face of some new development, it was "O God O God O Montreal!" (I've never understood that one, but it's singularly satisfying.)

What was it Pasternak said? "You in others: this is your soul." I keep Hal alive by quoting his droll sayings and can only hope he's forgiven me for my chronic lateness, frequent hangovers, long lunch hours, and the foul mood I was in for the last two years I worked for him. But the first three were fun, because I was learning new things and working with people I loved.

Roger's enthusiasm for his work was infectious. He popped into our office every day on his rounds, making us laugh with his wisecracks and keeping track of everything that was going on.

I managed to worm my way into the editorial meetings by offering to take notes and type up minutes. It was here that I first learned that from a publisher's point of view the author is a necessary evil: a sort of un-housebroken, hypersensitive *enfant terrible* who needs to be nursed along, ignores deadlines, and makes impossible demands, and that it would be a whole lot easier and more efficient to publish books without having to deal with them—except for the inconvenient fact that you need them in order to have books to publish. When an author was actually physically present in the house there was a sense of excitement and almost of danger in the air, as if a wild animal were loose in the halls.

Authors often failed to deliver their manuscripts until long past the promised date, a condition that Roger always referred to as being "egg-bound," as in: "Edmund Wilson is egg-bound, and under heavy sedation." The image of Edmund Wilson, who resembled a bulldog, sitting on a nest like a hen who couldn't produce her egg, reduced me to giggles.

If Roger had a date with a tiresome author or agent it was, "I have to have lunch with so-and-so, for my sins." But there was no one better at spotting a new talent or landing a paperback deal, and we all knew that he loved the whole crazy game.

Selling books was a whole lot harder than selling soup, because every book that came out was a brand new product, often totally unknown. Back at Campbell's Reginald M. Budd, the head of the advertising department, used to talk about reaching "the people in the row houses" and "the great unwashed." At Farrar, Straus, Roger talked about reaching people who lived way out in Bad Breath, Arkansas or Chewing Gum on the Bedpost. His definition of a *quid pro quo* was "You scratch my back, I'll scratch yours" or (to the horror of the religious book editor) "You blow me, I'll blow you."

Roger had enough energy for several ordinary men, and although he wasn't exactly handsome—his features were coarse— he was sexy. He was a big Jewish wolf who though devoted to his gorgeous wife, Dorothea, liked to flirt with the "girls," even those (like me) who looked like they might be "a little dykey around the edges." In those days I showed up in some outrageous costumes, generally black, and he used to call me Blackie. When his father died the coarseness disappeared and for a week Roger W. Straus Jr. looked like a boy. We all noticed it.

And then there was Robert Giroux, the star editor, whom

Roger had lured from Harcourt, Brace and who had brought with him an astonishing list of authors, including T. S. Eliot, Edmund Wilson, Thomas Merton, Flannery O'Connor, Elizabeth Bishop, Hermann Hesse, Aleksandr Solzhenitsyn, Pablo Neruda, Czeslaw Milosz, Bernard Malamud, and Isaac Singer.

I was in awe of this great man who resembled a big white-haired teddy bear and who, in spite of his greatness, was unfailingly kind to a lowly editorial and production assistant like me.

It was the summer after I found my way to Farrar, Straus that Helen and I decided to live together.

THE ODD COUPLE

Each of us carries a room within ourselves, waiting to be furnished and peopled, and if you listen closely—you may need to silence everything in your own room—you can hear the sounds of that other room inside your head.

—Susan Sontag, *In America*

307 West 11th Street is an old brownstone with a small paved courtyard just west of Hudson Street and kitty-corner from the White Horse Tavern of Dylan Thomas fame. Our apartment was on the third floor and consisted of two small bedrooms, a narrow bathroom with an old-fashioned clawfoot tub, and a middle room with a kitchenette. We called this middle room the living room but really it was just some space that was left over when they chopped up the top floor to make it into a two-bedroom apartment. It didn't have any windows. Instead, it had four doors leading to the two bedrooms, the bathroom, and the outside world.

It was more like a stage set, a place to make exits or entrances, than an actual room. Of course, we hung out there, but it always had a temporary, bus station feeling to it. No matter where you sat in that room your back was to a door, and you couldn't look out a window unless Helen or I had left our bedroom door open, which we didn't usually do. A feng shui disaster.

Helen moved in a few days after me so I spent the first night in our new apartment alone. The movers came to Sullivan Street and picked up my stuff and carted it up the stairs of the new place and dumped it in that middle room. A bunch of Helen's stuff was already there too and the room was so crammed with furniture and boxes that you could hardly turn around.

My rule for moving day is: always make the bed first so at least you have some place to collapse when you run out of energy. After I'd fixed the bed I found I needed a cup of tea, so I dug out a saucepan, found a rag to clean off the top of the stove, and went to run some water.

I was looking around for the kitchen sink when it slowly dawned on me that there wasn't any kitchen sink. The only sink in the apartment at 307 West 11th Street was a small washbasin in the bathroom. It was so small you couldn't get a medium-size saucepan, let alone a teakettle, under the faucet. The only way you could run water into a pot was in the bathtub. How the hell were we going to do the dishes?

The real estate agent hadn't bothered to point out this feature of the apartment. Welcome to Greenwich Village. Our apartment had everything but the kitchen sink!

After this fact sank in I sat down on the floor in front of the dirty stove and cried. It was not an auspicious beginning.

On Sunday night Helen arrived and eventually the place began to take shape. But the floor of the living room was covered with an ugly linoleum that had seen better days. I knew the room would look better if it had a decent floor so one weekend when Helen was out of town I decided to paint the linoleum. I got some black porch and deck enamel and moved my sling chairs and Helen's coffee table into the bedrooms and went to work.

In choosing black for the color of our living room floor I may or may not have been influenced by Helen's and my favorite John Cheever story, "Country Husband." The man in the story lives in a snooty suburb called Shady Hill that might as well be Scarsdale. While he is standing on the platform waiting for the commuter train that will take him to the city he runs into a garrulous neighbor who goes on and on about her decorating problems. What in the world is she going to do about her odd-size windows? The man is not having a good morning and finally he tells her, "Why don't you just shut up and paint them black?"

Helen and I took to saying "paint it black" as a synonym

for "get off it," "enough already." But come to think of it, black was my favorite color long before I read that story. Black was "bad" (i.e., "good"): was everything forbidden, subversive, off-beat, starting with the black stockings and black ballet slippers I wore in high school when everyone else was wearing white bobby socks and loafers.

So black it was. I thought Helen would be pleased.

We were having a muggy spell and the paint didn't dry right away.

Sunday evening I had dinner with Chan. When I got home there was a note pinned to the door of our apartment in Helen's handwriting. The note said:

Helen—I hope you can find it in your heart to forgive me for what I've done to the floor. I put newspaper down and then took it up again. Please prepare yourself as it is not an invigorating sight.

With love, Helen

When I opened the door, I gasped. My gleaming black floor was gone and in its place was an angry abstract expressionist collage, a sort of Robert Rauschenberg effect. I couldn't blame Helen for not wanting to walk on the tacky floor, but I wasn't happy. It seemed that this apartment was destined to not look good. Looking good was not its thing.

One day we paid a brief visit to the woman who had the ground floor apartment in our building. What a shock! She had exactly the same space we had, but instead of its being chopped up into three separate rooms, she had a floor through, and instead of our black linoleum and newspaper collage the floor consisted of these lovely old wide pine boards polished to a fare-thee-well. The sun shone through her windows onto a small garden of green plants. It was exactly the same space as ours but instead of a funky stage set she had an elegant Greenwich Village home. I didn't know it at the time, but I was looking at the future.

One night as we were coming out of the movies at the Loew's Sheridan a guy was up on a ladder changing the billing on the marquee. There were some black wrought iron letters leaning against the side of the building. I grabbed an H and Helen and I looked at each other and ran. The guy probably didn't care, but we were jubilant, because we were the H's and now we had this big groovy H for our front door.

We were friendly with the local teenagers. Any kid who had a duck's ass haircut and a black leather jacket or looked vaguely like Jimmy Dean or Marlon Brando was invited up to our pad to drink beer and listen to our 45 and 33 rpm rock 'n' roll records. The kids thought it was cool that we called each other "H." Pretty soon Meatball, Billy, and Tommy started calling each other "M" and "B" and "T" in the sincerest form of flattery.

Some of these boys actually turned out to be hoods, with tattoos, needle marks, and records (not the kind you could play on a phonograph). Others were aspiring method actors. It was hard to tell the difference. God, or our innocence, protected us.

Helen didn't think it was such a big deal to have to do the dishes in the bathtub. It turned out she was right. It was not such a big deal for her, because she didn't do the dishes that often. At least that's the way it seemed to me back then. I was beginning to discover our differences.

In the first place, she was a lot more assertive than I was. She met famous people all the time at her job and she would go up to anyone or call them on the phone and ask them over for a drink, and nine times out of ten, they would come. Unlike me, Helen was a night person. She would call up all-night radio show hosts like Gene Shepherd and Long John Nebel and talk to them on the telephone for hours and they would become friends.

She had been into jazz since the age of fourteen. I didn't start liking jazz until a few years later, when I was introduced to marijuana. In those days, all that restless energy reminded me of my own unsuccessful attempts to achieve orgasm, or maybe somebody else's climax that didn't include me. Helen could sit in the Five Spot or the Half Note until the wee hours nursing a drink, whereas I got bored after a few sets and wished I was in bed with a book. On those rare occasions when we went to a bar or nightclub together I always wanted to leave before she did.

Worst of all for the future of our living arrangement, she could put up with a lot more disorder than I could. I probably have one of the lowest chaos thresholds in the universe, whereas Helen—well, let's just say we were at opposite ends of the neatness continuum. In our particular version of The Odd Couple, I was Jack Lemmon to her Walter Matthau (or Tony Randall to her Jack Klugman in the TV version). When I got up to go to work in the morning I did not want to see last night's dishes sitting in the bathtub. So I ended up doing the dishes even when it wasn't "my turn." I resented it, but I did it anyway. I hated the feeling of resentment that was building up inside me but I hated waking up to messes even more, so I knelt on the bathroom floor and did a slow burn. Have you ever washed dishes in the bathtub? It's hard on the knees, even if you're young and don't have arthritis.

Once when I was mad at Helen for something or other—one of the rare occasions when I actually expressed my anger—I tried to explain to her that I got madder at her than at other people because I expected more from her. I quoted the Shakespeare sonnet that goes, "For sweetest things turn sourest by their deeds; / Lilies that fester smell far worse than weeds." This did not go over very well. Not surprisingly, Helen did not appreciate being compared to lilies that fester.

I felt like I did more than my share of the cooking too. We were both good cooks, but I probably wanted my dinner at a certain time while she was much more relaxed about the whole thing.

Helen told me a joke about two guys living in a mining camp in Alaska who both hate to cook. They have an agreement that one of them will do all the cooking until the other one complains, at which point the one who complains has to take over the job. One particularly severe winter they have eaten up all their supplies and the only thing left to eat is moose shit. The one who is doing the cooking has made moose shit soup, moose shit stew, moose shit croquettes, etc. Finally one night, at his wits' end, he serves moose shit pie. This is the last straw, and his friend takes a bite, throws down his fork in disgust, and says, "Arrrrrgh! This is moose shit pie! . . . *but good!*"

"Moose shit pie—but good!" became another one of our sayings. Helen could always make me laugh, and that is probably what kept us together for so long.

That, and the liberating effect she had on my life.

I had told Helen about my mother's Sex Lecture (or lack thereof). Granted, I was probably too young to be told the Facts of Life, but the answer I got at age five was the only one I ever got.

When I asked her the inevitable "Where did I come from?" my mother, who was sitting at her dressing table at the time, put down her hairbrush, looked me in the eye, placed her right index finger on her lips, and with her left hand pointed with a jabbing motion to her crotch. That was it! You came from There, and we will not discuss it again.

My mother and father were both born in the nineteenth century to devout churchgoing parents and their ideas about sex were Victorian, to say the least. Except for a few practical facts about menstruation, that was all the information I got.

A shrink I told this story to said, "Well, at least she pointed you in the right direction!"

And years later, when I told it to Mother herself, she said, "At least I didn't tell you you came in the doctor's satchel!"

My freshman year at Oberlin when I brought my first boyfriend home to meet my parents, my father told us we were not allowed to speak to each other on the second floor of the house—presumably, because that's where the bedrooms were.

I don't necessarily hold my parents responsible for the long delay in my ability to have orgasms. They were just passing on what they'd been taught, and even as late as the fifties sexual repression was in the very air of the times; but their attitude certainly didn't help.

But Helen's did. I think Helen saw me as someone who had been sexually repressed by my parents and had unconsciously incorporated a lot of their puritanism and guilt. She always encouraged me to become more sexually active. Living with her I sometimes felt guilty for *not* having sex more often, a perfect reversal of the values I had been brought up with. The more I drank, the later I stayed up, the more men I had in my life, the better she liked me—up to a point, and as long as they weren't *her* men.

Everyone called us "the two Helens" or just "the Helens." To my friends, she was "the other Helen." To her friends, *I* was "the other Helen." To the many friends we had in common, it was a toss-up. There were times when I felt so overwhelmed by the force of Helen's personality that I used to think of myself, with bitter irony, as The Other Helen. I became aware of this—of the degree of my alienation—only when it started to change, when I started to know who I was, and what I wanted, and to believe that I was entitled to it. But that didn't happen until the sixties.

three JACK

A HEAP OF WHEAT

It's the Garden of Eden and anything goes.

—Jack Kerouac, *Desolation Angels*

"Follow the master of traffic!" Jack commanded as he took my hand and led me across Seventh Avenue against the light.

It was the afternoon of that Sunday in November when the boys had landed on our doorstep. Peter and Lafcadio had gone off somewhere. Jack and Allen and Helen and I were walking through the Village on our way to visit Lucien Carr, an old boyfriend of Helen's whom they all knew from their days at Columbia.

The boys were already celebrities in the Village: "Witless Madcaps Come Home to Roost," the *Village Voice* announced a few weeks later, heralding their arrival from San Francisco. As we walked across town to Lucien's there were scenes of recognition all along the way. It seemed as if on every street corner there was a poet or a musician just waiting to clap Allen or Jack on the back and insist we all go for coffee at the Riviera.

Helen had already filled me in on Lucien's lurid past. He had spent two years in prison for the manslaughter slaying of a homosexual admirer who had been stalking him for years, but she had assured me that Lucien had acted in self-defense. Now Allen was explaining, in his quiet, excited voice, that it was Lucien who had brought him, Kerouac, and Burroughs together at Columbia back in 1944, before the murder took place. The whole story was in *The Town and the City*, that book that Jack had handed me that morning, except that the names had all been changed to protect everyone's privacy. So it was really a *roman à clef*.

When we finally reached the apartment on Grove Street where Lucien lived with his wife Cessa and their two little boys, I saw another incredibly handsome man. Lucien Carr was a blond beauty with slanting green eyes and high cheekbones—no wonder men and women were both attracted to him and Helen had a soft spot in her heart for Lucien.

He was charming, too—witty, sarcastic, a brilliant talker and a devout drinker and hell-raiser whose Bible was Rimbaud's *Une Saison en enfer*. In short, a devil. Cessa was very gracious, but I could see that she was not particularly thrilled that Jack was back in town. From the tales Jack and Lucien told of their past escapades, I could see why. While Lucien had cleaned up his act to the extent of holding down a steady job at the wire service United Press International, he still had a wild streak and Jack and he had a way of egging each other on to greater and greater excess, as I was soon to discover. With two small children to take care of—Caleb Carr (who later became a writer of historical mysteries) was crawling around on the floor, and his brother Simon was still a toddler—Cessa had her hands full holding it all together.

After a raucous spaghetti supper with lots of red wine we found ourselves on the street again. Helen and the boys were all for heading on to the Five Spot or the Half Note and Lucien knew of a bar where we could get drinks even on a Sunday. But I had had enough partying and was ready to go home. It was starting to snow again and I wanted to be alone with Jack. I took him aside and told him that what he and I should do was go back and finish listening to my record of *My Fair Lady*. To my relief, and somewhat to my surprise—I could see that he really loved drinking with Lucien—he agreed.

We said goodbye to the others and walked back to West 11th Street in the falling snow.

The record player my father had given me when I went to college was on the floor of my bedroom. I didn't have much furniture, so once again Jack and I found ourselves sitting on the floor, but this time we were alone.

Jack loved *My Fair Lady* as much as I did—partly, I think, because it is about the English language, which was the great love of his life. Since he had grown up in a French-Canadian neighborhood English was a second language for him. He had had to learn to speak it just as Liza Doolittle did. But instead of Professor Higgins, his teacher was English literature—above all, Shakespeare and the King James version of the Bible. Unlike many Catholics of his generation, he had read and reread the Bible and knew many passages by heart. He told me how as a high school student in Lowell he used to pin long lists of vocabulary words on the wall of his room.

And I told him how on Sunday afternoons when my friends were outside playing, my mother would sit me down and make me memorize the Sermon on the Mount, which takes up three whole chapters of the gospel according to St. Matthew. I didn't appreciate it at the time, but even then I had to admit that the language was beautiful.

We sat entranced by the music and the words and sang along with "Wouldn't It Be Loverly," and I heard for the first time that beautiful Sinatra-like singing voice of his. Soon we were holding hands and before I knew it we were enjoying the kiss we had been waiting for ever since we had met that morning. And if Jack's breath was redolent of all the wine he had drunk at Lucien's I don't remember minding it at all.

Soon we were falling diagonally across the little space between the record player and the bed. Laughing, we picked ourselves up and climbed into my bed at last.

That was fifty years ago, but I still remember how gentle he was. And I can still hear the way he muttered "perfect breasts" under his breath, as if he were talking to himself or taking notes in one of his little nickel pads. Given my lack of confidence in my modest charms and my tendency to compare myself with Helen, that was music to my ears.

As was the way he talked to me in French. Not being French myself, I didn't laugh at his French-Canadian accent. In fact, I loved it and the Old French–sounding dialect that went with it. Although I'd never heard *joual* before I somehow understood it. His Canuck patois became the language of our love.

And he was so beautiful! At thirty-four he still had the body of an athlete. And he made love like a natural man: spontaneous, tender, sensual, and enthusiastic.

Even though it was our first time together, he wanted to do everything. And even things that I didn't particularly like I went along with because I was so attracted to him and because he approached everything in a spirit of play. "Let's play sixty-nine!" he whispered, as if it were a game, as if we were just pretending to do it, like children in a sandbox. It made it sound so innocent.

He quoted poetry to me, from *The Song of Songs*, no less: "Thy navel is like a round goblet, which wanteth not liquor; thy belly is like an heap of wheat set about with lilies," and so on. Well, nobody had ever talked to me that way before, and I never forgot it.

Jack, of course, remembered everything that ever happened to him: that was his gift and his burden. In *Desolation Angels* he calls me Ruth Heaper, in reference to that "heap of wheat" that my belly used to be, and he says it best:

. . . we mortified Mars with our exchanges of hard & soft—With a few extra tricks, politely in Vienna—that led to a breathless timeless night of sheer lovely delight, ending with sleep.

JUST IN TIME

*Isn't Heaven Buddha's nirvana? . . . I felt suppressed by this
schism we have about separating Buddhism from Christianity, East from West, what the hell difference does it make?
We're all in Heaven now, ain't we?*

—Jack Kerouac, *The Dharma Bums*

"Don't open your eyes—catch your *dreams!*" Jack said when I
woke up next to him in the morning.

So I kept my eyes closed, but I couldn't remember my dream,
so Jack told me his. He had dreamed that he had hopped a ride
on the Midnight Ghost, a freight train that ran between Santa
Barbara and San Francisco. He sang me a mournful little song
about it he had made up: "Gonna ride the Midnight Ghost. . . ."

Then I remembered my dream: I was back at the Campbell
Soup Company, but instead of being a lowly secretary, my job
now was to sing the V-8 jingle for the French-Canadian market. I
still knew this jingle by heart and I sang it for Jack.

Jack was amazed at my French which, thanks to a very unusual high school teacher named Charles L. Reid Jr., was without
a trace of an American accent. And I loved Jack's non-Parisian
version of the language. The French-Canadians, I noticed, did
their r's on the tongue instead of in the gullet the way Mr. Reid
had taught us. Jack was such a good audience that I sang him a
couple of the little French folk songs that I had learned from my
mother's friend Mollie.

Thus began our morning tradition of catching our dreams

57

together and "starting each day with a song," as Jimmy Durante used to sing.

But it was Monday morning and I had to get dressed and go to work.

Jack knew I worked at Farrar, Straus, and he said to be sure and give his regards to Bob Giroux. When Harcourt, Brace had published *The Town and the City*, Giroux had been his editor. He said that Giroux was a sweet man, but he no longer believed in editors. He repeated his belief that writing was a sacred act and that henceforth no editor was going to change a word he had written.

"I'm a recording angel. We're all angels! . . . We're all in heaven *now*!" he said.

"We are?"

"This is all a *dream*!" He waved his arm around the room. "None of it is *real*!"

When I looked dubious he kissed me and got out of bed. He dug a dog-eared brown book out of his rucksack and began reading to me:

All the mind's arbitrary conceptions of matter, phenomena, and of all conditioning factors and all conceptions and ideas relating thereto are like a dream, a phantasm, a bubble, a shadow, the evanescent dew, the lightning's flash. Every true disciple should thus look upon all phenomena and upon all the activities of the mind, and keep his mind empty and self-less and tranquil.

Jack showed me the book: Dwight Goddard's *Buddhist Bible*. He said he took it with him everywhere.

"You oughta read it! It'll open your eyes!"

Jack put the book on my desk and cleared a space next to the wall. He said that if I didn't mind, he was going to stand on his head.

"Sorry?"

"I do it every morning. It cured the phlebitis in my legs! I learned it from a railroad bum I met in L.A. a year ago, a Jewish ex-marine from Paterson, New Jersey. He said it cured his arthritis.

This bum carried a little piece of paper with a quotation from the words of the Buddha. He was a *bhikku*, like me."

"What's a bickoo?"

"A holy wanderer. They travel around praying for everybody and begging for food. If you're a Buddhist, it's no disgrace to be a bum!"

Jack assured me that if I stood on my head for five minutes a day it would cure my allergies and I would live a long life. He had noticed that I sometimes had a hard time breathing through my nose.

He upended himself in a yoga headstand while I headed for the bathroom. As I stood in the shower we had rigged up over the tub I thought to myself that Jack's philosophy was a funny mixture of Catholicism and Buddhism. The passage he had read to me was very poetic, but the idea that nothing was real didn't appeal to me. It sounded too much like the Christian Science my sister-in-law was trying to pound into my head. Mary Baker Eddy also believed that the physical world did not exist—a world with which I was just beginning to make my peace.

When I came back from the bathroom Jack was sitting on the floor of my room reorganizing the contents of his rucksack. He was taking things out and arranging them neatly in piles, separating out all the dirty clothes to take to the laundry.

He handed me a snapshot. "My wife says this kid is my daughter, but she's not." I saw a pretty little girl, about four years old, her face the image of Jack's. Why was he denying his paternity? I wondered. As if in answer to my unspoken question he said, "It's a *sin* to bring children into the world. *Life is suffering!*"

I was not easily shocked, but that seemed very extreme. At the First Congregational Church of Scarsdale that our family attended, sin was hardly ever mentioned. It was not a word I was used to hearing. Sin was a Catholic word, but the Catholics certainly believed in having children, as long as you were married. This must be his Buddhism again, I decided. I remembered hearing that the first noble truth of the Buddha was that life was suffering. Jack seemed to have combined the worst of both worlds: Paul's emphasis on original sin and the Buddha's on suffering. I was beginning to see that there was a very dark side to his personality.

I was twenty-five. I did not know that I would never have children and that my childlessness would be a choice I would never regret. Ten years later Jack's attitude might have been no big deal, but at the time, it upset me. What I heard him saying was not only that life was suffering, but also that life had no value. He didn't believe that, but that's what I heard.

Jack was telling me that his wife Joan was a liar. He said that she had been unfaithful to him and now she was trying to hit him up for child support. I asked him why he didn't divorce her if he no longer loved her. He said he was afraid if he got divorced he might get married again. Staying married was insurance against remarrying. All this was quite confusing to me.

At the office that day I told Bob Giroux I had met a friend of his over the weekend. When I told him who it was, he chuckled fondly and shook his head. He described how Kerouac had come into his office at Harcourt, Brace with a huge scroll of paper containing the text of a book called *On the Road* and with a great flourish, had flung it across the floor.

"I told him, how the hell can a printer work from this? I'm afraid I offended him, but really, it was impossible.

"After we published *The Town and the City* we used to get phone calls from two sets of lawyers hired by two different wives."

So he'd already been married twice! My new boyfriend was a character, to say the least. But I was still aglow from my night of love and I simply filed the less appealing aspects of his personality away and refused to let them undermine my happiness.

During my lunch hour, remembering the pitiful state of his clothes, I went down to Klein's, the big department store on 14th Street, and proudly bought a couple of pairs of blue boxer shorts and a plaid flannel shirt for "my man."

Allen had found Peter, Lafcadio, and himself other places to stay in the city (they had spent the first few nights on Richard Howard's floor), but there was never any question that Jack would stay with us. We never discussed it, it just happened. Helen was delighted. She had quit her job at MCA and she loved having Jack around to keep her company during the day. There was a party almost every night, with drinking and listening to records and dancing to Elvis. But Jack's and my songs were Ella Fitzgerald on *Beautiful Friendship* and Tony Bennett on *Just in Time*.

In the morning after these late nights Helen and Jack could sleep in and have a leisurely breakfast before he buckled down to his daily stint of writing, but I had to get up and drag myself across town to the office. I'm a person who doesn't do well if I don't get enough sleep. But for those first days the excitement and the music and the poetry—and above all, Jack's tender lovemaking—carried me through in spite of my fatigue, and I still woke up singing.

TWO DINNERS

I'm sentimental, so I walk in the rain
I've got some habits even I can't explain
Could start for the corner and turn up in Spain
But why try to change me now?
                    —Cy Coleman and Joseph McCarthy Jr.

My parents were anxious to meet this new boyfriend who was a published author.

They had sold the house in Scarsdale and had built their dream house in New Milford, Connecticut, but my father had a few more years to go before retiring from his job at Rockefeller. They had taken a little apartment in Hartsdale, an easy walk from the train station.

They invited Jack and me to dinner. So one night after I got out of work I found myself waiting for him in Grand Central Station. We were supposed to get the 5:49 to Hartsdale.

I was nervous. In the few weeks that Jack had been living with Helen and me he had proved to be extremely unreliable about time. When he was out drinking with Allen or Lucien—especially with Lucien—it was not unusual for him to arrive three hours late for dinner, and a few times he hadn't shown up at all until the next day.

Helen didn't seem to mind the crazy schedule, but I had been raised to be punctual and this sort of thing tended to drive me crazy. When I tried to talk to Jack about it his eyes would glaze over and he would just shrug and say, "Nothing *matters*—it's all a *dream*!"

His Buddhism again! I was beginning to feel that his Buddhism was just one big philosophical rationalization for doing whatever he wanted.

But he could always charm me out of my bad humor by singing to me, in his perfect imitation of Frank Sinatra, a little-known tune that might as well have been his theme song, "Why Try to Change Me Now?"

I can see myself standing there in Grand Central by the gate to the commuter train to White Plains, wondering if Jack will show up at all. The minute hand on the big clock on the information booth is clicking on toward 5:49, and I'm getting more anxious by the minute. The conductor has opened the gate and people are starting down the ramp.

Where the hell is he? We're going to miss the train! We'll be late for dinner. My mother will hate that.

Suddenly I see him coming around the information booth, walking fast in his lumberjack shirt, looking like he belongs in the Maine woods instead of the lower level of Grand Central Station. As he comes closer I see that he's carrying something in a brown paper bag. He sends me a guilty reassuring smile that crinkles up his eyes and turns into a sheepish grin as he says, "See, I made it—you worry too much."

His dark hair is wet and slicked back and I'm pleased to note that he's put on a clean shirt under the lumberjack one. But I can smell liquor on his breath. "What's that in the bag?"

"It's a present for your father. You said he liked Kentucky Bourbon. It's Jack Daniels, the best! And I got some White Owl Cigars for me."

But if the bottle is a present for my father, why is the seal broken?

In the diary I started after New Year's I refer somewhere to the "Grand Central Premonition." Apparently it was when I was standing there waiting to take Jack home to meet my parents and he showed up at the very last minute with alcohol on his breath that I got my first whiff of a realization that this relationship wasn't going to work.

I had had plenty of warning signals but I was too young to

pay attention. Besides, I had married Charles, a proper profes-
sorial type, for practical reasons, without love, and that hadn't
worked. Now, without making a conscious decision, I was trying
the opposite: I was risking everything for love. Of course I ignored
the signals. I was in love with Jack. And after all, he did show
up, didn't he? And the bottle inside the brown paper bag he was
carrying was a present for my father, wasn't it?

Maybe the seal wasn't broken. Maybe Jack had stopped at
a bar on the upper level and that's why I smelled alcohol on his
breath. All I know for sure is that we were both nervous. Jack was
intimidated by places like Scarsdale, by parents who could afford
to send me to college. At the last minute he got cold feet and I had
trouble getting him on the train.

"What's your father gonna think of me?"

I assured him that my parents were very kind, down-to-earth
people.

"They'll love you!"

But in truth, I wasn't so sure myself. I had picked a man
who was as unlike my father as possible—a penniless writer, twice
married, and a deadbeat father who was probably a hopeless
alcoholic. A rebel, a wild man, a man who was as far from Scarsdale
as I could hope to find—and yet, I wanted to take him home to
meet my parents. I wanted to rebel and be accepted at the same
time. I was intimidated by Scarsdale, too. I loved Jack because he
was the opposite of everything I had been surrounded by growing
up there. He was the exotic other, the poor Catholic, the sexy
foreigner, the boy from the wrong side of the tracks: everything
lower class, romantic, and forbidden. And best of all, a writer—
which was what I wanted to be myself.

What, indeed, was my father going to think of him?

Against all the odds, the evening was a success.

No sooner had we walked in the door—no sooner had I
introduced Jack to my parents, than he asked them whether they
believed in God. It was almost, "How do you do, Mr. and Mrs.
Weaver, do you believe in God?" They may have been startled, but
they were also impressed by his seriousness, and this was a subject
close to both of their hearts. While my mother took the silverware

out of the sideboard and began setting the table, she began to answer Jack's question.

She probably told him that she didn't think God was an old man with a long white beard who lived up in the sky and watched everything we did. And that she didn't believe everything in the Bible: that she cared more for the ethics of Jesus than for the miracles that had been ascribed to him. She probably quoted him her favorite passage from G. K. Chesterton: "The Christian ideal has not been tried and found wanting; it has been found difficult, and left untried."

My father was delighted with Jack's gift. If the bottle had been opened he pretended not to notice, and went off to the kitchenette at once to make Old Fashioneds for Jack and himself, Mother and I abstaining.

Soon Jack and my mother were engrossed in conversation about their religious beliefs while Dad and he proceeded to pay their respects to the Jack Daniels. Warmed by the liquor, my father temporarily forgot his distaste for the bohemian life and his anxiety about his daughter's being mixed up with this unusual person.

Jack and he had both grown up in small towns in America with fathers who had trouble making a living. They were both shy, sensitive, and ambitious men who loved the books of Joseph Conrad and the sea and music—and me. Somehow, the vice president of Rockefeller Foundation and the self-styled Dharma bum managed to bypass their differences and focus on the things they had in common. Jack forgot his nervousness and my parents were completely disarmed. I had been right: they loved him.

On the train back to Grand Central that night Jack told me how much he had liked my parents, especially my father. He had picked up on how much my father doted on me.

"You should fall on your knees and worship him! He's your *giant secret lover!*"

Shortly after our trip to Hartsdale Jack and I received another dinner invitation, this time from his old friend and fellow Frenchman, Henri Cru. Jack and Henri had met at Horace Mann, a prep school Jack had got a scholarship to in Riverdale, New York, and it was Henri who had introduced Jack to his first wife, Edie Parker. Henri was living in a walkup apartment on West 13th Street just off Hudson Street. He was a rather dashing young Frenchman who treated Jack with a kind of affectionate raillery similar to Lucien's. He was also a gourmet cook.

The apartment was one big room, but Henri had divided it up and made it into a kind of maze by hanging floor-to-ceiling curtains that gave it a dreamlike quality. He had set a beautiful table with a really good wine instead of the cheap stuff Jack usually drank and he had made an exquisite *coq au vin* in his little tenement kitchen.

A memorable dinner in a Village hideaway within walking distance of ours, Jack sharing his past with me: it should have been a lovely evening, but for some reason Jack went into a deep depression. He stopped talking to us and just sat there drumming on the table and scat singing to himself, something he was really good at, but there was no joy in it that night. He was a one-man jazz band lost in a world of his own. He didn't touch the wonderful dinner Henri had prepared but guzzled the expensive French wine and called for more.

In the end he just sat there singing "Gonna ride the Midnight Ghost" over and over. My handsome lover had disappeared and in his place I saw an old wino with haunted eyes.

I had had intimations of Jack's alcoholism before that evening. I had seen the sadness in his eyes and had pretended it was poetry. Now I looked into his eyes and saw not poetry but despair. They were the eyes of a man looking down a road that led nowhere but the grave.

Jack had pulled himself together for my father, but with his old friend he let me see who he really was, and the sight froze my heart. After Henri took my plate away I put my head down on the table and wept.

SEASON'S GREETINGS

What is this Christmas you profess, in this void? . . . in this nebulous cloud?

—Jack Kerouac, *Lonesome Traveler*

For Christmas that year my father gave me a little red portable black-and-white TV. When the messenger from the Rockefeller Foundation brought it up our stairs wrapped in cheery poinsettia paper and I unwrapped it, Helen and I laughed. TV was square and my father just didn't get it. We were too hip or intellectual to have such a bourgeois item in our beat pad.

Jack, whose father could not have afforded to give him such an expensive present, was shocked at our ingratitude, and I don't blame him. Granted, we were two hipper-than-thou chicks who wore shades at night and painted the floor black and slept with poets and didn't believe in anything but rock 'n' roll Jimmy Dean Marlon Brando and Elvis Presley—but will you please tell me how we could have watched Elvis on the Ed Sullivan show without that TV?

We sneered at the TV, but we kept it.

Jack left to spend the holidays with his mother at his sister's home in Orlando, Florida, so Helen and I were on our own again. We spent Christmas Eve in Johnny Romero's bar drinking Seven and Sevens and listening to Harry Belafonte sing calypso on the juke box. Belafonte had a calypso Christmas carol, "Mary's Boy Child," that we played over and over. "Long time ago in Bethlehem, so the holy Bible say" was black enough to be acceptable.

Although we both missed Jack it was a relief for me to have him out of the house for a while.

I had been getting more and more bugged with his drinking. He didn't usually begin drinking early in the day, although he did love a shot of whiskey in his morning coffee, his *café royale*; but he needed alcohol on a daily basis and when he drank he lost all track of time. I hated never knowing when or if he was going to show up, and the late nights and the lack of sleep when he was home were taking their toll on my nerves. It was getting so even after we all went to bed and the house was finally quiet, I still couldn't sleep.

Seeing the way I dragged myself into the office in the morning with dark circles under my eyes, my boss Hal gave me Seconal for my insomnia. Jack did not approve.

"Don't take those *goof balls*! They're *bad* for you!"

He prescribed an old French-Canadian remedy of his mother's: hot milk with honey, and even fixed it for me himself. But what I really needed he couldn't give me: a boyfriend who didn't need to dull his senses with alcohol in order to function in the world.

One morning a few days after the dinner with Henri Cru I woke up with an angry red rash all over my body. Those red bumps itched something awful. I tried antihistamines, various ointments, oatmeal baths, all to no avail. Whether the bumps were a reaction to the "goof balls" or to the stress of living with Jack, I couldn't get rid of the damn things. Before I met Kerouac I had never even heard the word "hives." I missed a whole week of work and was terrified I was going to lose my job.

But Jack came up with another of his French-Canadian remedies. He went out and bought Epsom salts, heated up water on the stove, got a washcloth, and brought all this into our bedroom. He made me take off all my clothes and stand in a basin while he slathered hot Epsom salts all over my body. It felt wonderful and in the morning my rash was gone. Jack said it was the Epsom salts, they never failed, but Helen just smiled. Later she told me my rash went away because Jack had paid some attention to me, and I knew that she was right.

By the time Jack left for Orlando I was ready for a break.

On the evenings Helen and I didn't go to Romero's I went to bed early with *The Town and the City*. At last I had time to read Jack's novel, and it *was* like Thomas Wolfe and it was really good. Rested and refreshed, I was free to savor Jack's best qualities—his sweetness, his intensity, his eloquence—on the printed page, in the safety and comfort of my solitude, and to remember why I loved him.

But the best thing about his absence was our letters. I kept his, of course. I kept everything he ever gave me: the drawings, the "magic Buddha stone"—the beautiful butterscotch onyx with one rough side and one smooth side that he claimed had been polished by the thumbs of generations of meditating monks—and everything he ever wrote, even little notes like "I am trapped with Treff in the White Horse / come rescue / Jack XX" and one precious one that says simply, "Dear Helen / I love you and I want you to know that I love you, " and is signed with a little heart.

But now, inspired by our first separation and by the heightened emotional state that always, for good or ill, accompanies the approach of Christmas, we got to write each other genuine love letters.

(Note: Al was a hoodlum with dark and gloomy looks, needle tracks, and tattoos whom I slept with a few times before I met Jack. He had a French last name.)

Little bird singing in the morning letter:

Dear Jean-Louis,

I woke up early this morning (i.e. 10:00 but that is early considering that I read The Town and the City til nearly 2:00 last night) and am so full of plans and energy I can't go back to sleep. Since I started on the Kerouac heat treatments I am so much better it is unbelievable—long nights of sleep uninterrupted by scratching, and even my eye is beginning to show some of its former lustre. In short, to quote Shirley and Lee, I feel good. (Which reminds me—last night H and I saw Frankie Lymon & the Teenagers on TV and it was absolutely breathtaking.)

In addition to the TV we now also have a Christmas tree—

a small but real one which we bought from some teenagers on the block (not the egg-throwers, or so we choose to believe). There are five of them and they all came up last night, flipped in their furtive teenage fashion over us & our apartment & manner of living, were extremely impressed that we called each other "H." and started calling each other "J," "T," "M," etc. They took some beer bottles away for us and when hearing a lot of dangerous-sounding rattling I peered out the window & warned them to take it easy I was greeted by a barrage of "OK, H," "Right, H," from five separate 15 year old throats.

We have more or less severed relations with Al since he had become something of a nuisance, calling up at 2 AM and expecting us to jump out of bed to welcome him—the same at early hours of the new day—also asking for money with shady promises of repayment but no mention of your $5—(don't worry, I'll get it)—casually making long distance calls—these are probably not the real reasons but anyway we are fed up and intend to lower his suitcases to him on a string when next he rings our bell.

I talked to my bosses yesterday and was almost ashamed of their generosity—they are paying me for the whole week I was out, my desk is covered with presents, etc. etc. it's almost too much. I am overjoyed because in the next two weeks I only have to work 6 days and have two beautiful 4-day weekends.

I am sorry you are not going to be here for New Year's Eve—perhaps you will change your mind & come back a little earlier. One of my chief concerns is to nurse my skin back to its customary smoothness before your arrival. I think in another week it will be almost as good as ever.

Convalescence always fills me with love of life and makes me want to hurl my knitting self into every activity. Today I plan to do extensive cleaning including the stove and the ice box (defrost & weed out)—buy presents for my mother & father, Helen, and you, and possibly a party dress for myself, since the only one I possess is a lugubrious black sheath— sophisticated NYer style. There are also the Xmas tree ornaments to be bought.

Dick Howard was over here last night for a flying dinner

and he intimated that you were a make-out artist. Naturally this made me furious (though I didn't show it) & also made me wonder how much you care for me. I guess there's no point in discussing it like this. Well anyway, I love you, Jack—I feel like quoting great passages of your own writing to you to prove to yourself how good you are, but fear it would have much the same effect as telling you how beautiful you are. Poor Jack, let me help you count your gold.

Erase doubts from your mind, je vais rester fidèle à toi parce que je suis HUNG UP: je n'ai pas de choix. I kissed Allen because he reminded me of you. MORE LATER. Hope you can read the dread scrawl of

Helen

Meanwhile, Jack had a letter in his typewriter down in Orlando which I got a few days after Christmas. It was a very affectionate letter, calling me "Lovey Dovey" and ending "mange mon bec which means, eat my kiss, which means, love ya" and signed with his French name, "Jean-Louis / Amant de toi." I liked all of it except the part where he said that "women must be guided by men," which sounded too much like the Bible to me, although he did soften it by adding "and my advice is Love Me Tender Love Me True." He had bought his nephew Paul an Elvis Presley album for Christmas.

He said he was busy getting his books ready for the printer: "I'm bringing back to NY 4 huge other Manuscripts, my greatest . . . but O my God so much is written in this world I would as lief quit and stop griming pages with the printer's ink. . . ."

In the relative peace and quiet of his sister's home Jack spent twelve days typing up his notes from his last trip to Mexico.

Up in New York, I went a little wild in his absence. Although I loved him dearly I was beginning to realize that he wasn't the answer to my prayers and that he would probably never be able to give me what I needed. I had chosen him for his wildness but I was discovering that he was a little too wild for me. I had chosen him because he was as unlike my loving but overprotective father as possible and now, with an irony that was probably lost on me at the time, I wanted him to be *more* like my father and to take care of me. I was angry with him for not being the hero in the story of my life.

At any rate, when Gregory Corso arrived in town and Allen introduced him to Helen and me, I went to bed with him. I did it partly because I was pissed off at Jack and partly because he reminded me of Jack. Talk about ambivalence! A little dark-haired streetwise urchin, another of those "bantam" types Helen and I favored, Gregory looked more Slavic than Italian with his gypsy face and prominent cheekbones. He was a poet who had been in prison and he had that same slightly singsong voice and *sprechstimme* way of talking that Allen and Jack had, with a daffy clownishness that was all his own. If Allen was Prospero and Jack Ariel in this Tempest that had entered our lives, then Gregory was a finer sort of Caliban. Like Allen and unlike Jack, who was physically modest, Gregory was a great believer in nakedness. He cracked Helen and me up by asking us wistfully on more than one occasion, "Want to see Gregory's body?"

When I cheated on Jack with Gregory I had no idea that they had a past history of competing for the same "chick." I only did it once, for although Gregory was cute and an enthusiastic lover, I didn't love him, and I immediately realized that I had made a mistake. Gregory stayed with us for a few days before he found a place of his own but I made him sleep in the living room in a big leather chair we had picked up at the Salvation Army.

To salve my conscience, I sent Jack a box of White Owl Cigars for Christmas, and finally got around to answering his letter:

Wednesday [January 2, 1957] (at FSC)

Dearest Jack

I have been trying to save a peaceful hour for you ever since I got your dear letter in the mail Friday morning—so I have snuck into a warm office after hours (ours is an ice box). NY is freezing cold today and yesterday—you will feel it next week.

I soaked in eagerly more news of you from Allen's letter— Washington sounds great—amazing that your bag was found

you are charmed. I'm dying to see you in your new coat & hat—
imagine them to be like Gregory's, whom I met last week. Before
I forget, Allen says to tell you all your financial arrangements
are fine with him—and to the same end, since you are in a hurry
to leave these shores and this mad nervous city I enclose your
passport pictures—tho I hate to do anything to hasten that
departure from my warm embrace. . . . but since you must I will
simply wait and hope your memory is as strong as mine.

Xmas was wild—H. gave me 2 Elvis records—Don
McGovern came over to see her, which made her very happy,
naturally—an old love called me up & we had a wonderful
time—wish he could meet you & come under your vital
influence, since he seems to be dying in narrow straits, who
was once a wild Jack Kerouac with wild hair and a big hooded
jacket, now drawn in a velvet collared coat—a sad sweet boy
(mais tout simplement un ami).

Highlight of last week was parents coming for dinner,
meeting Helen & seeing apt. for the first time—a howling success.
They adored Treff & my father flipped over Screamin' Jay on I
Put A Spell on You which I sent him the next day—it made me
love them the way I did when I took you home for dinner.

Friday nite Dick Howard took H. and me, Al & Peter out
to dinner (!) to an expensive Italian restaurant where we had
a big feed & tried unsuccessfully to get Pete to drink Martinis.
After that we went to Village & bumped into Gregory in Anton's
Print & Frame Shop. He tugged at my heart because he seemed
so much like you face, gestures, etc. He has been very good to
me & we are great friends. Yesterday we went to Museum of
Modern Art & then to see La Sorcière beautiful movie with a
fantastic Green Mansions girl you must see it. The Frenchman
who was the hero reminded me painfully of you also—New
Year's Eve was very pleasant, at Lucien and Cess's with Allen,
Peter, Gregory, the Hollanders, Donald Cook & Linda.

Everyone kissed nearly everyone at 12:00 but no one got
really drunk although Allen pretended to. Sunday H and I went
to Brooklyn and saw the Rock & Roll Show at the Paramount
and then after eating at Howard Johnson's went to Giant—

*a strange 3-hour epic where J. Dean ends up looking like Lucien
Carr behind glasses & moustache. It had some great moments—
i.e. when Jimmy stakes out his land in the beginning & a drunk
scene at the end. A lot of crap too.*

*Al is out of the picture—he was terrible to me one afternoon
& since he's left town we don't expect to see him again. He's a
strange person. I guess your $5 is gone forever.*

*Everyone misses you but no one so much as I. I wish you
had told me you decided to go to Europe after all—but I guess
you had to wait until you knew about money from Al.*

*Do you want me to love you Jack? Silly of me to ask since
I hardly have a choice in the matter—Please hurry back. The
nights are so cold!*

*Scarcely what one could call a love letter—but the best I
can do in these sterile surroundings. I miss you, darling. Will
read* Town & City *tonight & think of you. And don't think I'm
getting maudlin, chum, or you'll feel the back of my hand—*

Love—Helen

When I got home that night there was another letter waiting
for me, postmarked New Year's Eve.

Jack was pleased with the White Owl cigars and waxed poetic
about how much he missed me but continued to lecture me about
being too aggressive. He wanted me to be a sweet little flower and
he warned me, "Tho life is a dream, there'll be a continuation
of the nightmare, if you dont do as I say and follow me now, to
heaven."

His letter was full of dots which he said were all kisses. He
said again that he was working on four different books at once
and he assured me that they were going to make us rich.

He thought he'd be back in New York by Tuesday, January 8
and he went into all sorts of loving detail about what he was
going to do to me then. But the sentence that really impressed
me, in spite of its grandiosity, was "I will lead schools, be exiled,
scoffed at, I prophesy it, and I will lead schools." I believed him.

He signed off with more kisses and more of his French
Canadian love.

I had time to write him one last letter before his return:

Thursday [January 3, 1957]
One more love note for Jean-Louis from Helen before he
appears at her door leather-clad, bearing four shapely 'scripts,
and (she hopes) smiling—Helen's happy, reading your book,
menstruating after a little anxiety about the wisdom of child-
bearing right now, and delighted to be on such a convenient
schedule! She loves you and is content to be your angel, will
follow if you'll look back always, wants you to be with her
always, in USA and Europe, indoors and out, prays for your
beautiful soul and yearns for your beautiful body every day
and night with a growing or full constant light—
HURRY UP!!!!!

Donne's poem "A Lecture Upon The Shadow" ends: "Love is
a growing or full constant light, / And his first minute after noone,
is night."

HAPPY NEW YEAR

Try it then yourself, living with a genius, see what it is like and how easy it is.

—Frieda Lawrence, in a letter to Mabel Dodge

On January 1, 1957, I started keeping a journal:

I'm twenty five years old and I've had a pretty lousy life all told—miserable childhood & adolescence worse, so-so college days, actually that's the best part with long talks in the dormitories at night with my girl friends, listening to music and rubbing each other's backs and lying in the sun in the spring and using some of my youthful energy in pleasure, though not all, not all—but then a long lean grim dry spell of niggardly marriage, hagglings with my father, stuffed up noses, guilt and tension, poverty, cold, winter, city night loneliness, the arid excitement of being on the town with the girls who hack their hair off & dress with a vengeance—and by god I'm sick & tired of not being happy, of being cold and bored and a prisoner and working, doing somebody else's nowhere work, WAITING, all the time waiting for the sweet sunshine of love, and suffering dismally as it comes and goes, never stays, never can I really rest by a fire secure in the arms of a providing strength—and I want it, why shouldn't I have it, I'm still stubbornly young, strong, I love my poor demented self in spite of myself, my mind is still eager and I love life for what it can be and because I am alive, and I want to see it all and have the things I want to have—I want to lie on Mediterranean beaches and dine beautifully, hell around with the

greatest people going, make mad love with Jack Kerouac, meet
everyone, drink in beauty, be mad when I feel like it and at peace
when I need that—why can't I?

A somewhat different tone from my letter to Jack where I'm
willing to follow him anywhere as long as he agrees to look back
like a rebellious Orpheus at his Eurydice. There was someone
inside me who was not satisfied with the role he wanted to assign
me, he who believed that "women must be guided by men" and
who warned me to "stay sweet" and not be "aggressive" or there
would be "a continuation of the nightmare."

I had forgotten how therapeutic it was to let off steam by
writing down what was bothering me. Maybe I made a New Year's
resolution to keep a journal. Maybe it was Jack's idea. Whatever
the reason, now that the honeymoon was over I started the Jack
Kerouac Journal. And looking into myself with the aid of this
mirror, I decided I needed help.

When I said that Helen and I didn't believe in anything but
rock 'n' roll Jimmy Dean Marlon Brando and Elvis Presley, I lied.
We believed—oh, how we believed—in the gospel according to
Sigmund Freud.

Psychoanalysis was the religion of the fifties. Almost
everyone we knew had the two A's—Anxiety, whether specific or
free-floating, and an Analyst to help them deal with it. Everyone
talked about their analyst and we all believed that they could help
us. Even though it took forever and cost the moon, analysis was
our only hope of ultimate salvation.

Right after I came to the city I had made a few attempts at
finding an analyst. My marriage had failed and every other relationship had ended, as in my beloved Proust, in either boredom
or heartbreak.

I had had a few sessions with a shrink I found through Chan.
After I told him about my one and only love affair with a woman, he had commented, "Is that *all?*" He was probably trying to
reassure me that I wasn't gay but instead he belittled an experience
that had shaken me to the core and changed my life. That was the
end of him.

I always wondered—how were you supposed to choose a good one, anyway? It was a Catch-22 situation. You're neurotic, you can't really trust your instincts, and yet you're supposed to find someone to make you healthy.

Then there was the money.

Helen told me a funny story about a friend of hers who was looking for a shrink. Peggy met with a man whose hourly rate, multiplied by the five times a week he recommended for her case, amounted to a little more than her weekly salary. When she told him this he said, "Sometimes in life it is necessary to make sacrifices."

There was no way I could afford to pay for psychoanalysis on my secretary's salary. In the hope that my father would agree to help me, I started making phone calls.

And so it was that one Saturday in January, after a raucous afternoon with Helen and Gregory at a bar on Eighth Avenue where Gregory had wangled a gig painting a "murial," I made my way uptown to the office of Jacob Levin, M. D.

I'll never forget my first glimpse of Dr. Levin. I was walking up Park Avenue from the 34th Street crosstown bus, a little drunk, and I happened to look up at the building on the corner of 35th and Park. There, gazing out a second-story window with a vacant expression on his face, was a little man with a beard smoking a pipe who looked exactly like a *New Yorker* cartoon of an analyst. I went in the building, up the elevator, found the door, sat in the waiting room, the inside door opened, and out walked the same little guy! I should have turned around right then and walked out. I should have known he wasn't real.

He never smiled, and he was expensive—$25 an hour was a lot of money in those days—but I decided to give him a try. At least he looked like a shrink.

I knew that Jack would not approve. He seemed to have some sort of phobia about analysis, as if it were the enemy of art.

That Sunday Elvis was on the Ed Sullivan show. Gregory made a big spaghetti dinner and Helen, Allen, Peter, Gregory, and I put the little red TV on the kitchen table and drew up chairs and sat

Photograph by Helen Elliott

Gregory Corso, Allen Ginsberg, and Helen Weaver, January, 1957.

in front of it as if it were an altar. But to our disgust Ed Sullivan had instructed the cameraman to shoot Elvis "waist up only" because the famous gyrating pelvis would offend the family audience. In my journal I wrote, "Elvis lovely, Ed a Westchester snob."

As an adolescent I had hated the dancing lessons my mother made me take at Hitchcock Memorial Church in Scarsdale, and the one dance I attended at the Scarsdale Golf Club was the worst night of my life. But Elvis and his pelvis had cured me of my fear of dancing and set my own hips awhirl. The way he moved got us all moving the lower half of our bodies.

Elvis really started the sexual revolution of the sixties. He was doing the Twist (with a twist) *before* the Twist. He was considered vulgar, animalistic, lewd, and obscene. He was accused of moving like a black person; rock 'n' roll was "nigger music." But when Ed told the audience that Elvis was "a decent, fine boy," something did start to change.

On Monday I saw Dr. Levin again. He said he didn't think I was ready for deep analysis, i.e., five times a week. He recommended that I begin with psychotherapy—see him twice a week. I felt rejected. I didn't know whether I could trust him. Yet he seemed the best I had seen so far.

When I got home I found a postcard from Jack en route.

He said he'd probably be home on Wednesday, said he'd received my "gone letter:"

Glad to hear of various good times you had Xmas & NY's eve. . . . Funny about yr. dad digging Screamin Jay. . . . Tho I'm sposed to be a lazy bum I havent done anything for the last 12 days but rattle this typewriter day and night tryna catch up with my wild handscripts writ in desolation & solitude. . . . money in the future bank for logs on the fire and scotch & soda and the late show and you in my fleecy arms. . . .

Jack said we were invited along with Allen and Peter to a weekend in Old Saybrook, Connecticut with John and Shirley Holmes, and to save a January weekend for that. He ended the card with "I hope yr. 33 speed is fixt, I'm bringing back Chet Baker LOVE N'craint pas. . . . Je t'aime . . . Oui . . . XXX Jean."

Jack arrived Tuesday afternoon. He had an appointment with Malcolm Cowley at Viking Press about his unpublished novel, *On the Road.* Allen told me later that Jack was so nervous he

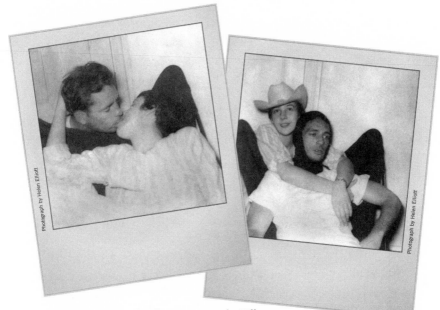

Jack Kerouac and Helen Weaver in the Village, January, 1957.

consumed a pint of bourbon in the elevator. After seeing Cowley he met Allen, Peter, and Gregory in the Village for more drinks and got so wasted that he was ashamed to call me. It was Gregory who finally dialed the phone and put Jack on.

And so, my journal says, "I sighed and sorrowed and welcomed the battered lost man back into my arms that love him, love his every corner and contour and concavity." We exchanged Christmas presents. He had brought me jazz records, Charlie Parker and Chet Baker; I had bought him a beautiful red plaid flannel shirt. He immediately took off his old blue one and gave it to me. I had bought 45 rpm records of "our" songs, "Just in Time" and "Beautiful Friendship." I put them on the phonograph and we danced.

He said that we must never be demonstrative in public and kissed me all evening in front of a party of ten. He told me I was too good for him. He told me I must always let him get drunk when he wanted to. I wrote in my journal:

His guilt about his drunken arrival was pitiful; he couldn't leave the subject alone. I told him (a lie, of course) that my only concern was what it would do to our lovemaking, a concern which proved, alas, to be justified. But at least we were together. We slept together and woke up together, which is after all one of the few joys of living.

But the pity of it—he says who we are is "a minor matter, a minor matter." He says again that he is old. I know he loves me as much or more than he has anyone. He thinks I don't believe he does because he knows women want more than the simple knowledge, that they need a care which he can't give now.

"Now": Both Jack and I were still clinging to the illusion that someday he would be able to support me, that his books would make us rich, that we would live happily ever after in a home with hot toddies and logs on the fire.

One of the strangest remarks was, "Don't be like Cess" (in the matter of Lucien's drinking), as if she were the epitome of a nagging wife. I thought she had achieved a pitch of control and subtlety that I could never reach.

The saddest love I have ever known. I suffered more with Di Angelo, to be sure; she was an artist of cruelty as only a woman can be; but the trapped greatness here gets you.

The February issue of *Mademoiselle* was out with a piece entitled "The Lively Arts in San Francisco." It included a photograph of a bearded Allen and a tousled Jack. Gregory, who had attended the shoot, had mussed up Jack's hair to make him look more like the wild man the media required. Gregory was right: it was an image of Jack that was reprinted many times.

The text by Michael Grieg described Allen as "a kind of cross between Whitman, Rimbaud and bop pioneer Charlie Parker" and "the *enfant terrible* of San Francisco letters," and declared, "his poetry, like his way of life, is pungent and violent." As for "John Kerouac," Malcolm Cowley had called him "the greatest unknown young writer in America."

There was more good news. The day after he arrived Jack wrote a letter to his friend John Clellon Holmes from my "Hawthornian room" that looked out on the White Horse tavern, telling him that tomorrow he would be signing a contract with Viking Press for the publication of *On the Road*. He quoted the Diamond Sutra: "Keep your mind free and all-penetrating and calm" but admitted, "Tonight I drink with Lucien, alone in a blizzard. . . ."

While Jack was writing Holmes in my Hawthornian room I was having a drink with my father at the Algonquin Hotel of literary fame. I had screwed up my courage and made a date to meet him after work. I was planning to ask him to help pay for psychotherapy with Dr. Levin.

I was nervous. I truly believed that my "neurosis," if that's what it was, was largely the fault of my repressive upbringing, and it seemed very strange to be asking my father to pay to undo the damage he and Mother had done. The current thinking was that analysis was more likely to be successful if you paid for it yourself, but I didn't feel I had a choice.

So I swallowed, took a deep breath, and told him, "I can't have a healthy relationship with a man. I need professional help."

To my amazement he agreed to help me. He wanted, of course, to know Dr. Levin's credentials—where he had studied, what degrees he had, and so forth. The truth, which I should have known by then, was that it was almost impossible for my father to refuse me anything I really wanted. Although I sometimes had to listen to the same little speech about how money didn't grow on trees I don't remember ever asking him for anything important that he didn't eventually give me.

But this was a breakthrough for us, because although the word "sex" was never mentioned, on some level my father was acknowledging my sexuality. I felt as if I'd grown an inch.

Years later I learned that the Rockefeller Foundation had underwritten Alfred Kinsey's research into the sexuality of the human male. The Foundation had continued to support Kinsey throughout the furor created by his book *Sexual Behavior in the Human Male* (1948) but had cut off his funding when he turned his attention to the supposedly virtuous American female. Kinsey published those results in 1953 in *Sexual Behavior in the Human Female*. I doubt that my father's was the decisive vote in either decision, but as director of natural sciences of the Foundation from 1932 to 1959, he surely had a say in the matter.

But he did agree to underwrite my research into my own sexuality, and considering his Victorian attitude toward sex, I think he was amazingly generous.

That night Jack went over to Lucien's and Helen was off somewhere on a late date. I went to bed early for a change, but was too excited about my talk with my father to sleep.

In the middle of the night Jack and Lucien reeled in, drunk as lords, yelling at each other and crashing into the furniture. My Victrola was in the living room now. They put *My Fair Lady* on the machine at top volume and started singing along with Stanley

Holloway at the top of their lungs on "Just a Little Bit of Luck" and "Get Me to the Church on Time."

This was too much for me. I had to get up and go to work the next day and I was at the end of my rope after a week of short hours. Something inside of me snapped, and I lost it completely.

I got out of bed, ran into the living room, and started pounding Jack with my fists. I actually tore out a chunk of his hair. As soon as I realized what I had done I burst into tears. I screamed at them to get the hell out. They refused. At last I got them to go into Helen's room and closed the door. I went back to bed and lay rigid while they caroused and bumped around wildly. Finally, about 3 a.m., they left, taking Treff with them, as I discovered to my horror after they were gone.

I was still awake when Helen came home at five. Out of her mind with worry over her dog, Helen phoned Cessa, who assured her that Treff, miraculously, was safe and sound in their apartment. She said Jack had fallen off their fire escape toward dawn and cut his head. He and Lucien were sneaking out to find more liquor. Cessa told her that Lucien (who previously thought I was a wimp) had revised his opinion and was now referring to me admiringly as "Slugger."

Helen and I talked until six, when I went back to bed to lie awake until time for work. I wrote Jack a note and left it on our bed:

Friday morning

Dear Jean-Louis,

I'm sorry I hit you & I hear you took an even worse beating from a fire escape, so you must be quite a sight today. Poor bruised face—I long to wash it with hot boric acid (???). Anyway, I want to nurse you to life.

That's my whole point. To hell with all this escapism— alcohol or Buddhism, it's all just one great deadener of your vitality—when I hit you darling it was because I wanted to make you feel something, to admit the pain driving you, and when you said it didn't make any difference, in Jesus-meek pardon, that

*you didn't care, it was like the end of the world. I wanted to hurt
you so you would see and feel—instead of cutting everything
out. Lucien was right when he said you won't give. Even he
understood my loneliness last night.*

*You'll probably go to your grave insisting that women (I)
never want you to Have Fun. If it were only fun—that state
you seek is death, annihilation, the end of your art, it makes
your beautiful face that I love better than any, ugly, brutal, &
unresponsive. I can't take it—no woman can. I want to warm
you to the core so you won't need these nowhere escapes but I
can't wait forever.*

*And I have to hold together meantime—so dear one,
you must find an alternate place to stay on week nights, thus,
before Sunday. Because you brought Lucien here (which I very
emphatically requested that you not do) I have to go put in a full
day's work after a completely sleepless night (ask Helen). I'm not
putting you down Baby—I want you and love you but I wish
you would imitate me this year. All my battered baggy-eyed love*
    Helen

I spent that night at Chan's apartment, sleeping around the
clock. When I got home Saturday afternoon I found the wounded
warrior subdued, sheepish, and humbled, wanting only peace. We
spent a quiet, sad, loving time never discussing "problems." We
went to bed in the middle of the afternoon and watched TV and
later I cooked a big dinner for the three of us. Gregory came and
spent the night on the floor.

On Sunday Jack and Gregory went to Salvador Dalí's for
dinner. Dalí had met Jack and Allen in the Russian Tea Room
shortly after they got to New York. Allen had told Dalí he wanted
to meet Marlon Brando, whereupon Dalí looked at Jack and said,
"He is more beautiful than Brando!"

On Monday Jack was supposed to call me at noon and let me
know if he would be home for supper or go to Paterson with Allen
to see William Carlos Williams, but as usual he forgot.

In *Desolation Angels*, Jack writes that his love Ruth (he calls me

"Ruth Heaper" in that book) tells him to leave on the advice of her psychoanalyst. "This asshole wants to screw you himself!" Jack fumes—in the book.

Just for the record, that analyst said no such thing. That son of a bitch never opened his mouth. Well, hardly ever.

Dr. Levin belonged to the school that the analyst's job is to sit there and take notes while you free associate. If you happen to forget the rules and ask him a question, he throws it back at you with "Why do you ask?" Your basic orthodox Freudian wall.

Remember the old joke about the two analysts who have offices in the same building and keep seeing each other in the elevator? As the years go by, one gets fat and rich and happy and the other one gets thin and poor and miserable. When finally the poor one asks the rich one the secret of his success, the rich one shrugs and says, "Who listens?"

Well, with a few exceptions—he always perked up when I talked about sex—Dr. Levin belonged to the Who listens? school of psychotherapy. From my position on the couch I often heard him yawn and once or twice I actually caught him snoring. At twenty-five bucks an hour.

It was perfectly true that he disapproved of Jack. He made that clear with an occasional question like, "Who pays the rent?" or "Why do you put up with this?" His disgust at Jack's freeloading was stronger than his Freudian vow of silence. He made it clear that he disapproved of me as well.

In my journal I wrote, "I feel that he puts me down, is judge rather than scientist. But perhaps it is wrong of me to expect otherwise."

But nasty as he was, he (along with my journal) did provide a mirror in which I saw that living with Jack was making me crazy. It was undermining my health and possibly even my job. The fact that Jack contributed little or nothing financially bothered me, too.

It was bad enough living with Helen, who thought book-keeping was a bore and refused to keep accurate accounts of the money she spent on food and other household necessities, so that I never knew where we stood financially. Of the three of us, I was the only one who had to hold down a job, and though it was certainly not true that I was supporting the whole operation, in my state of nervous exhaustion it sometimes felt that way.

I knew I had to ask Jack to find a place of his own, but where was I going to find the strength to do it? I couldn't turn to Helen for help; she liked having him with us.

There was growing tension between her and me as well. She had admitted to me that she found herself punishing me for treating Jack the way her mother had treated her alcoholic father. She said she knew it was really none of her business but sometimes she couldn't help herself.

In my naïveté I imagined that Jack could find himself a room somewhere and we could go on seeing each other and he could stay with me on weekends. But Jack didn't see it that way.

On the evening of Monday, January 14, I asked Jack to leave.

I hated myself for doing it—felt pompous and self-righteous and ached for his dazed face that couldn't look in mine. He hung his head and sang to himself, "Unrequited love's a bore." I felt as if he deliberately misunderstood me, acted as if I was saying I never wanted to see him again. He left immediately, taking his keys of access to me, lurching out into the snowy winter cold, stumbling under his huge pack containing all he owned, carrying his cheap suitcase of manuscripts.

Our last words were "We'll see each other again" and "I love you."

Peace descended on me. I thought of him drinking in the White Horse and almost went down there but didn't. I slept well.

Which brings me to the real reason I asked Jack to leave.

While it was perfectly obvious that my analyst had nothing but contempt for Jack and his art in his tiny bourgeois locked-up lecherous orthodox Freudian soul—Jack was right about that— nevertheless it was also true that in the end it was my decision. I asked Jack to leave not because my analyst told me to and not because of some proto-feminist declaration of independence on my part. I rejected him for the same reason America rejected him: he woke us up in the middle of the night in the long dream of the fifties. He interfered with our sleep.

CAN'T WE BE FRIENDS?

Maybe I'm too "wild" for protracted love affairs. It's the world I need most. . . . I want to live . . . and see more of the world, and God knows why, and a woman's love is only one of many wild loves.

—Jack Kerouac, *Windblown World*

After Jack moved out things were very different in ways I didn't expect.

In the first place, as soon as I caught up on my sleep I started to miss him terribly. I told my journal that I felt "a throbbing emptiness—as after a radical extraction of a living part of me, the anaesthetic the doctor used wearing off."

But with Jack, I soon discovered, it was all or nothing, and he made it very clear that he wanted nothing to do with me.

Helen, whom I also loved, was angry with me for asking him to leave, and some of the old issues that Jack's presence had distracted us from—whose turn it was to cook dinner or do the dishes, who owed who for groceries, and so on—began to surface again.

On the other hand Dr. Levin, whom I didn't even like, was obviously pleased with me and even began speaking to me now and then.

Since Jack didn't want to see me I was suddenly out of the loop. I spent more and more time with Chan, often sleeping over to avoid the tensions at home. Helen in turn was hanging out at Lucien and Cessa's, where she could continue to see Jack.

I began to wonder if I had done the right thing. I hated the thought that I had hurt him and at the same time I was angry

Helen Weaver, Helen Elliott, and Treff at the Weaver home in New Milford, Connecticut, January, 1957.

at him for *not* being hurt—or at least, not showing it. I was too young to understand that his avoiding me was proof of his love.

To try and bridge the growing distance between Helen and me I invited her to my parents' home in Connecticut for the weekend. Before we left I saw Jack's keys on the coffee table. He had given them to Helen to return to me.

We made it, tugging Treff into cabs and across Grand Central to the train for Danbury and she and the dog riding in the baggage car with a coffin. I had to leave them, as only one person was permitted to stay with the dog. The weekend was physically relaxing but relations with Helen continued to be strained and neither one of us was inclined to discuss our problems.

Jack had also gone to Connecticut with Allen to see John Clellon Holmes, a visit that turned into a drunken orgy Holmes describes in *Visitor: Jack Kerouac in Old Saybrook.*

On Monday Malcolm Cowley called Helen to ask where Jack was. It seems they weren't answering the phone in Old Saybrook.

Sterling Lord, Jack's agent, was all excited: Jack and Allen were written up in the *New York Times*.

A week after I asked Jack to leave I wrote him a long, rambling letter:

January 21, 1957

Jack my love I miss you very much you said we would see each other again but we haven't and I'm beginning to fear we never will—I would hate that. I feel a fool to have been so pompous & awkward & moralistic in the way I talked the last time we were together. I still believe that was the right thing to do, but I wish I could have done it with more grace and humor so you wouldn't have felt I was casually (or callously) giving you your walking papers.

Helen said that when she told you I sent you my love you answered that I use that word pretty loosely. It's all very well for you to say that but you know in your heart that I do love you, and for you to pretend that I don't simply absolves you from the responsibility of doing anything about it.

There followed a long pompous and moralistic lecture about how love is not simple and a relationship demands effort and that's why he prefers the company of men, blah blah blah—I'm sure I didn't realize that I sounded exactly like my mother.

Yet conversely, a solid relationship with a woman could give you a great peace and fill a terrible void inside of you that all the friendship in the world can never fill. Perhaps nothing can fill that void inside of you. I doubt that your love affair with God can do it, because you are too filled with feelings of guilt and self-loathing to rest at peace in the arms of a western personal god, and you're too painfully alive, too aggressive & too sensible to really swallow this Buddhist crap and look yourself in the eye. . . .

I told you I wanted this change in the arrangements for our sake—but you let that be the death stroke. I never intended it as

such, and you know that. I may have been clumsy in the way I
went about it, but I was not deliberately cruel. I cannot cut off
my feelings. I miss your company so much that I hope you will
want to see me even if you feel you can't make any commitment
at all. . . .

I didn't send this letter.

Nor did I find the courage to express my pent-up resentments to Helen. When I brought them up in therapy Dr. Levin, in a rare burst of communication, advised me to bring them out in the open.

Dreading confrontation with Helen, who had a short fuse and a way of blowing me out of the water, I left her a note implying that she was not doing her share of the housework. Since the issue, though ongoing, was seldom acknowledged, she professed to be shocked. We did manage to discuss our differences and the upshot was that Helen said that since I was suffering from anxiety and feelings of persecution, maybe I would be better off living alone. I decided she was probably right.

I had moved three times in a year and a half. The idea of moving again was both daunting and tempting.

At Oberlin I had always done better with a room of my own. I was still too young to know (much less to accept) that I am one of those people who are destined to live alone and like it.

I asked my journal, "Does living alone necessarily mean isolation? First I kicked Jack out—now I leave Helen—am I doing this so I won't have any emotional life, i.e., material to analyze?"

When Jack got back from Connecticut he came to see Helen, calling first to make sure I wasn't there. He told her he didn't want to "run into" me, that he didn't want to see me "for a while," words that gave me both hope and fear. He was holing up in a room on Houston Street, had told Lucien and Cess that he wouldn't see them for a few days, that he wanted to write and think.

I threw myself into work, both at the office and at home. I cleaned the apartment compulsively, getting exhausted and then holding it against Helen, knowing it was crazy but unable to stop myself. I was in pain over Jack's refusal to see me and creating order out of chaos helped to soothe my mind. I started looking for an apartment, feeling guilty toward Helen even though it was her idea that I leave.

I was tempted to visit Jack in his retreat—Helen now thought he was at the Marlton, a seedy hotel on West Eighth Street—but managed to control the impulse.

One day at the office I was writing Jack another of those letters I never sent when Bob Giroux came in. We got to talking about Jack. Giroux had heard that Viking Press was going to publish *On the Road*, the book he had rejected six years before when he was back at Harcourt, Brace.

Once again he recalled getting all those calls from lawyers when Jack was being pursued by his wives. Somehow this made it easier for me to stick to my guns and not try to contact him.

"But," I told my journal, "I miss the sight and touch of his unequaled beauty—his rackingly sad face, his noble profile, beautiful mouth, soft fine hair, fleecy arms, etc. etc. etc. I'm sure he could have me for the asking."

In the end I wrote him a note asking him to a party Helen and I had been invited to. I told him that I loved him and wanted to see him. I took the note to the Marlton and waited all day, but he didn't call. Helen finally tracked him down at Lucien's and asked him if he intended to do anything about my note. He said, "Oh, I don't know. . . ." and did nothing.

"Which brings me," I wrote, "to the limit of my patience, though not the extreme bound of my love. That still lingers on but anger all but drowns it out. Anyway, it's the end, I feel, and there is a peace in that."

I saw other friends. Helen was job-hunting. Relations with her were better.

Then one day after my therapy session I decided to stop in at Lucien's, knowing that Jack might be there. When I arrived Helen looked horrified. Lucien and Cess were deep in conversation. Only Allen spoke to me—to say that Jack had gone out to pick up Joyce Glassman. He was living with her.

I felt as if somebody had punched me in the stomach.

Mumbling some excuse, I left. I walked home along Bleecker Street, retracing the route from Grove Street to West 11th Street that I had taken with Jack the day I met him back in November.

I couldn't believe that Jack was living with Joyce Glassman. She was a friend of Helen's from Barnard whom I had met a few times and found perfectly innocuous. Now, all at once, she was the enemy. A little round blonde person with a faraway look in her heavy-lidded blue eyes and a kind of perpetual pout on her face that I supposed some people found sexy, she was the exact opposite of me. What on earth did Jack see in her?

And everyone knew about it except me. My humiliation was complete.

After I got home Helen called from Lucien's to apologize for my reception. I knew that Jack was there and I asked to speak with him.

It was a strange conversation. I asked him if Joyce minded his drinking, for which he had no reply. He sounded nervous, said he was meaning to write, that he would call me. I knew he wouldn't, unless he got desperate to have his copy of *The Town and the City* back.

I hated Joyce Glassman from the bottom of my broken heart. All my anger at Jack got transferred onto her: she was the temptress who had lured him away from me. I had fantasies that some day I would walk in my front door and see her sitting in my living room, with or without Jack, and I would have to leave or else I'd kill her.

In my journal I prayed to a God I didn't believe in that Jack would be impotent with Joyce, as he had been with me a few times at the end:

Put him down, God, as you did with me so even our last meetings were full of fear and sorrow. Oh, make him remember our first beautiful nights together and his groans of delight and discovery—let him not forget my beauty in the arms of that nowhere chick!

One night in early February I was cooking dinner for Helen and me when the phone rang.

It was Jack. He was down in the White Horse and he wanted to pick up his copy of *The Town and the City*. I said fine.

When he came in I was strangely calm and even able to eat my dinner with him sitting there. After dinner Helen left us alone for a while and he told me he had missed me. He

Jack Kerouac on the beach in Tangier, spring 1957

said we were not through. He confessed that he had tried to make love to Helen one time when he was drunk but that he couldn't go through with it.

He seemed to want to confess about Joyce, too. He said she was a sweet simple girl with a country face and that she had something that I didn't have: kindness. This cut me to the quick. Even though I told myself that all it meant was that she was willing to put up with more bad behavior on his part, I knew that on some level it was true.

I knew that I must be a selfish person. Helen was always telling me so, not to mention my parents, but I also knew that I'd been good to Jack, as good as I could be, and although I finally refused to take care of him, I did care for him. I felt he was the one who had let me down.

I had a date with a friend who lived on 13th Street, so I had to leave Jack in the apartment watching TV with Helen. When I came home I found a note on the door. Jack was in the White Horse and wanted to see me, so I went to pick him up.

He came back up and we sat in my room and talked. I found that I felt no sexual desire for him. He seemed, as I wrote in my journal that night, "such a pitiful unmanned incoherent mess—and yet so fundamentally wise to his plight."

He still smarted from my beating him and from the time he saw me kissing Al. He claimed that when I tore out that chunk of his hair it was the beginning of the end of his looks. He said the hair had never grown back and that he had to wear a cap to cover the empty spot.

He wanted to come back tomorrow night and see me when he wasn't drunk. He said he would call me. I hoped he would call instead of just appearing and taking me by surprise. Although I was calm on the surface, I still loved him and it was painful for me to be with him.

At around midnight he called Joyce to report why he had not shown up when he said he would. Half an hour later Joyce called back—I remember hearing her voice on the phone and marveling at her courage—and gave him her ultimatum. She said she would pick him up at the White Horse in half an hour, and if he wasn't there when she got there, that was the end, she was through with him. She took a cab from where she lived way up on West 113th Street down to the Village at one a.m., and she had to work the next day, too. This was more than I would do and I thought, I guess she really loves him.

After Jack left Helen told me, "Jack still loves you. He told me so."

A few days later I came home to find Helen in tears. Jack had come by with Allen and Gregory and she had to tell them they couldn't come up because I didn't want to see Jack. Gregory had shouted, "Fuck you!" at the top of his lungs.

On February 15 Jack sailed for Tangier on a Yugoslavian freighter.

A ROOM OF MY OWN

> *"On the Road" is the second novel by Jack Kerouac, and its publication is a historic occasion. . . . [it] is the most beautifully executed, the clearest and the most important utterance yet made by the generation Kerouac himself named years ago as "beat," and whose principal avatar he is. Just as more than any other novel of the Twenties, "The Sun Also Rises" came to be regarded as the testament of the "Lost Generation," so it seems certain that "On the Road" will come to be known as that of the "Beat Generation."*
>
> —Gilbert Millstein, *The New York Times*

By the end of March, at Helen's request, I had moved out of the apartment on West 11th Street and was commuting to my job from Hartsdale while looking for a place of my own.

Also by that time, in a bizarre twist of fate, Joyce Glassman had started working at Farrar, Straus, first as John Farrar's secretary and later as an editorial assistant to Bob Giroux. My bosses, Hal and Dorris, both knew the whole story and like the true friends they were, pretended to dislike Joyce out of loyalty to me. Hal started calling her unflattering names like Pudding Face and The Unbaked Muffin.

At first Joyce and I were as tense around each other as two female cats. But I often had to deliver memoranda and jacket art and so on from my boss to hers. We were always polite, and gradually I found myself almost liking her. There was a determined set to her head, an attitude that seemed compounded of amusement, resignation, pugnacity, and intellectual distance. Far from being the dumb blonde I had imagined her to be, I discovered that she was both intelligent and articulate, and was writing a novel.

Once after work I was on my way uptown to buy Capezio shoes at a place on upper Broadway, and Joyce and I found ourselves riding side by side on the Fifth Avenue bus. We managed to make small talk all the way to 59th Street. I was even able to ask after Jack, who was writing to her from Tangier and Paris. I found myself wishing we could have a real conversation—after all, we had a lot in common—but it was not yet our time.

Later that spring I found my own apartment through Jack's friend Henri Cru. It was a few doors down from his place on West 13th Street, in a building that was next-door to the Salvation Army. A four-flight walkup and incredibly cheap, it had a good-sized living room with a kitchenette that did include a sink this time, a tiny separate bedroom, and a tiny bathroom with a clawfoot tub. Best of all, it was the only apartment in the building that had casement windows, with windowsills so big you could sit on them and watch the kids shooting baskets in the playground across the street. For $54.50 a month it was mine, all mine. I was alone and in control again, but unlike the Sullivan Street apartment, it had charm. And because the building was owned by the Catholic Church, which had the option of using it for a convent, I didn't have to sign a lease.

Henri insisted on carrying all of my worldly possessions up the four flights of stairs on his broad French-Canadian back and refused to take a penny for his labors. Years later he complained that I should have bought him a bottle of wine, but I was too stupid to know that at the time.

Helen and I were friends again and working on our dictionary of hip.

In September *On the Road* was published and Jack became famous overnight.

Because the regular reviewer, Orville Prescott (he who had pronounced Nabokov's *Lolita* "dull, dull, dull") was on vacation, the job of reviewing the book for the daily *New York Times* fell to a young journalist and jazz critic named Gilbert Millstein. It was an extraordinary review, the kind every writer dreams about, though in Jack's case the instant attention it brought him became something more like a nightmare. Millstein was one of the few critics of Kerouac's generation to recognize the spiritual hunger underlying the Beats' "frenzied pursuit of every possible sensory impression."

In December the *New York Post* had a piece entitled "The Beat Generation—Beaten?" The media were already capitalizing—and capitalizing on—the term. Jack, who had returned to town in September to promote his book, did a one-week stint at a Greenwich Village nightclub called the Vanguard, reading his work in front of a jazz pianist for three shows a night. The *Post* reporter, Alfred G. Aronowitz, ridiculed Jack's performance. When asked who had been the first to recite poetry to music Jack answered, "Carl Sandburg . . . Homer."

Some time that fall I saw Jack at a party. He was with Joyce and very drunk and we didn't get a chance to talk but the brief glimpse made me realize how much I missed him.

As the first anniversary of our meeting approached I relived the events of the previous year. I knew he was in Orlando again and I decided to surprise him with a box of White Owl Cigars.

Jack wrote back right away. He said that when he saw the Farrar, Straus label on the package (I mailed the cigars from the office) he thought Bob Giroux was sending him a book. "When I saw the cigars I laughed and knew who it was–it was very sweet of you and they're damn good cigars." He went on:

When I saw you at Bob Merims' party I wanted to talk to you alone, even go off with you, but J. was watching me like a hawk and I didnt want to maker cry. I dont wanta hurt anybody. You hurt me when you took that damn psychoanalyst's advice and said I couldnt stay, it should have made no difference to you. But I also understood your point of view. You'd do a whole lot better goin to confession than going to those fakes, and confession is free. Ho ho. I'm not tryna proselytyze you, I dont even go to confession myself. But can I see you when I come back to N.Y.? I know where you live from Henri Cru showing me your door.

We can sing My Fair Lady again. . .I'll sing you my new version of Sinatra's Chicago.

Jack was concerned that *On the Road* was slipping off the bestseller list: "Steinbeck, Mailer, Jones, were all raging bestsellers I guess I'm really made to be a poor Zen lunatic, which is alright with me. But I do want to sell the book to the movies. . ." Apparently there was some possibility of him playing himself in a movie version that never came off, even though Marlon Brando's father, who was also his manager, was interested, and had called Jack's agent about it. Jack went on:

You looked lovely that night at Merims'–in that lost generation dress. I was very drunk. I was sposed to appear on further tv shoes shows but was too tired from drinking. . .I wonder if I screwed up my chances of making it a bestseller. . .well, trying to get as much as you can is infinite perturbation. . .I like poetry better than nervous wealth.

He said he'd be in New York some time after New Years and would call me. He was going to stay with his mother in his aunt's house in Brooklyn.

Jack never called.

But one night I was roused from sleep by a long blast of my buzzer. It was a weeknight and I had to go to work the next day. I staggered into the living room and opened the casement window so I could see who it was in the street down below.

There was Jack, so drunk he could hardly walk, looking up at me with a sheepish grin and doing a kind of soft shoe dance on and off the sidewalk, like Gene Kelly in *Singin' in the Rain*.

"Are you Helen who wove the web of Troy?" he called up to me, swaying.

Homer, indeed.

And then, when I didn't answer, "Ring the thing! . . . Ring the thing!" And he repeated his little Gene Kelly dance, just for me.

No man had ever shouted poetry to me from the street

like some Falstaffian Romeo and my heart ached for him, but somehow I resisted.

I shouted down to him to call me tomorrow, we'd make a date.

He didn't, of course. It was years before I saw him again.

The Sunday *New York Times* was not as enthusiastic about *On the Road* as the daily *Times* had been. The weekend review by David Dempsey was entitled "In Pursuit of 'Kicks.'" It wasn't a bad review, though not in the same class with Gilbert Millstein's astonishing panegyric in the daily *Times*, but it did speak of "depravity," "Bohemianism," and "the hot pursuit of pleasure." Dempsey concluded, "one reads [the book] in the same mood that he might visit a sideshow—the freaks are fascinating, although they are hardly part of our lives."

When my father read this review he forgot how much he had liked Jack in person. He forgot the kind, serious, if eccentric, man who had charmed and disarmed him on that bourbon-soaked evening in Hartsdale. Like the rest of America, he bought the Jack created by the media, a Jack who was endowed with all the least attractive traits of the book's hero, Dean Moriarty, the car-stealing, womanizing reform-school graduate who was a thinly disguised portrait of Jack's friend Neal Cassady.

When my father started bad-mouthing Jack, I defended him. I remember telling Dad that Jack's only sins were sins of omission and sins against himself.

But in my heart I was angry with Jack, too, for being who he was, which was not God's gift to women, and for many years my anger made it impossible for me to appreciate his work. When *The Subterraneans* was published in 1958 I found it full of echoes of my life. "How many times has he lived it?" I asked my journal. "Once was enough for me."

Jack was my first wild man and my first drunk. When I looked into his eyes I saw both his future and the eyes of all my future drunks. Jack aroused hostility in people—parents, bosses. At first I defended him to my authority figures, Dad and Hal and Dorris. But living with Jack, I found myself reluctantly coming to agree with the very people I started out defending him to. And this was awful, because it made me aware of a conflict in myself that I didn't want to face. The pain of my disappointment in Jack and the pain of rejecting him was compounded by the pain of rejecting the part of myself that felt most alive.

Some time in the early sixties we had a reunion. It was Thanksgiving—our time of year—and Jack took me to dinner at an Italian restaurant on Sheridan Square in the Village. I was recovering from hepatitis and Jack finished my wine for me. All the hurt and anger were gone and we were friends at last.

It was during this dinner that one of those wandering photographers who snap pictures of couples took the photograph that appears on the cover of this book. Something impelled me to track the man down a few days later and buy a print for my Kerouac scrapbook.

Jack and I were friends, but we were on very different paths. The fifties were his decade; the sixties were mine. I'd never made a very good beatnik. As I admitted to my journal, "In the end I am too pleasure loving and too spoiled by an indulgent papa to survive that artistic chaos."

But I did identify with the hippies who were the natural heirs of the Beats.

four LENNY

FROM BEAT TO HIP

Our normal waking consciousness, rational consciousness as we call it, is but one special type of consciousness, whilst all about it, parted from it by the filmiest of screens, there lie potential forms of consciousness entirely different. We may go through life without suspecting their existence; but apply the requisite stimulus, and at a touch they are there in all their completeness. No account of the universe in its totality can be final which leaves these other forms of consciousness quite disregarded.

—William James, *The Varieties of Religious Experience*

They's a lotta ole bull-crap go on in the world. . . . well, a man git high, he see right through all them tricks an' lies, an' all that ole bull-crap. He see right through there into the truth of it!

—Terry Southern, *Red-Dirt Marijuana*

I met Tommy in Washington Square Park on my lunch hour. I used to take the bus down Fifth Avenue and sit on the rim of the fountain where the folk singers would come on the weekends and draw a crowd. During the week there would be a few working girls like me and a few guys hanging around working on their tan. Tommy was one of those. We didn't exactly "date" since Tommy was just making it financially. Our first non-date came about because we both needed somebody you could poke with your elbow in the movies. But Tommy was a handsome, witty Irishman from Brooklyn who wanted to be a writer too and so of course we fell in love.

I remember lying in bed with Tommy and telling him about Kerouac. Actually, I think I must have told him about all my previous boyfriends. I think I thought this was what you were supposed to do, sort of like showing your passport with all the old stamps on it. When I had finished filling him in on my romantic past, Tommy turned to me and said, "Well, as for me, ma'am"—and here he broke into song in his beautiful Irish tenor: "I've never been in love before." Oh, Tommy.

By the time Jack Kerouac died I hadn't seen Tommy in years, but he made a condolence call. Tommy had class.

Jack wouldn't let me smoke dope; that was for the boys. He wanted me to stay sweet and innocent. I didn't take my first puff of marijuana until 1959, courtesy of a man named Monty whom I met through a redheaded actress who replaced me as Helen's roommate.

A dark, solid Jewish guy with heavy-lidded eyes, Monty was a devout pothead. For the life of me I can't remember how he paid the rent. I don't know if I ever knew. Ours was a limited, but totally satisfying, relationship.

Monty cared deeply about the quality of his grass, and was familiar with everything from "oregano" to "dynamite" and all the shades in between.

"Good, competent, working pot," he would announce respectfully after the first go-around. Like the wine buff who saves his Château Lafite for the fellow connoisseur, Monty did not lay his best Colombian on any bimbo who walked in the door. On the other hand, he enjoyed initiating a potential viper, so he must have gotten off watching me.

It was love at first toke, or almost. I'm sitting there in Monty's living room with Helen and Tommy and the redhead and whoever Helen was seeing at the time. The Modern Jazz Quartet is on the hi-fi with Milt Jackson on vibes. The red lightbulb in the only lamp that's lit casts an eerie glow.

Monty can't believe that I have reached the ripe old age of twenty-eight without ever smoking grass: "Let old Uncle Monty complete your education."

He is showing me how to hold the smoke in my lungs, talking in that pinched, gasping voice heads get when they don't want to waste any by exhaling. I'm following his instructions, the vibes are vibrating, and my gaze is fixed on this picture on the wall in front of me, a reproduction of Paul Klee's *Around the Fish*, when suddenly I notice that the picture has become three-dimensional. The objects in it are moving in rhythm to the vibes which are now inside my head and I am somewhere around the ceiling looking down at the scene in the room. In spite of the music there is a kind of portentous white silence around everything.

Monty is looking at me and saying something and I know I've been off in space somewhere and Monty is just finishing the sentence he started when the picture started to move: "I guess you're wondering why I brought you all here tonight."

He chuckles and tells me I'm tripping and congratulates me on my maiden voyage. The odd surreal glow that the red light-bulb imparts to everything in the room combines with the fuzzy resonance of the vibes in *'Round About Midnight* to enhance the effect of the drug.

Jazz had never been my thing but that evening I heard and understood it for the first time. I got into it because I got inside the moment.

Smoking grass reminded me of the time Tommy got me onto the Cyclone in Coney Island. When that old monster of a roller coaster plunged down the first big drop I *knew* it was off the track and that I was going to die. But instead of my whole life passing in review it was, oddly enough, the names of all the English poets that trooped through my head: Milton, Shakespeare, Keats, Shelley—almost as if these old friends were about to welcome me to the Other Side. And then, bam! We were back on the track and I was alive, screaming with delight, and no time at all had passed, even though I had died and been reborn.

Similarly, at Monty's I had been out there in the black reaches of the universe and yet when I made it back into my body in a supreme effort to maintain communication with my friends no time had passed. No time, or such a tiny amount that it bore no relation to what I had experienced in the interim.

It was this blessed release from a lifetime of slavery to the clock—and to all the authorities who used it to rob me of my freedom—that explains why, on the 14th Street crosstown bus on the way to work the next day, tears of joy rolled down my face.

A door had been opened, and I saw everything from a different perspective, a longer view. It was as if I had contacted the child in me who believed in magic and who had always been able to fly through time and space, and suddenly death was no big deal. And this was no illusion: it was the straight scoop, it was the way things were. To be sure, the drug had done something to my central nervous system, it had distorted my perceptions, but in so doing it had helped me to see through so-called normal reality to The Truth: everything is alive, time is a human invention, we are immortal. Though drug-induced, the experience itself was authentic. I was a believer.

Like any convert, I wanted to share my revelation with others. Sitting on the bus I had this powerful urge to hand out joints to all my fellow passengers so they too could see beyond the veil of illusion. We were all in it together, and I loved every one of them.

Fortunately, I was not holding.

But that was only a matter of time. I never became a heavy smoker but I did like the option of having it around. The fact that it was illegal was both an inconvenience and a turn-on. Actually buying the stuff meant crossing a barrier, an act that made me an official member of an underground culture that had a language of its own. I had always loved learning new languages. An ounce wasn't an ounce, it was an "oh zee," and you didn't buy five dollars' worth, you bought a "nickel bag." Over the telephone you never referred to grass by any of its numerous affectionate nicknames because your phone was probably bugged and Big Brother's Narcotics Squad might be listening in.

Paranoia was a normal and necessary part of the experience of getting high and you learned to live with it and allow for it in assessing your own reactions to situations. Besides, paranoia was just the flip side of ESP, and as such, a valid organizing principle. As my viper friend Jeff used to say, "I like paranoia: it makes sense out of the universe." He smoked regularly at the office of Greenwich House, his publishing company, claiming it enabled him to see fleeting expressions on the faces of his partners and competitors and kept him abreast of what was really going on.

The ultimate paranoid fantasy, which always struck when I was actually stoned, was that the fuzz would smash down my door with an axe and confiscate my stash and the headline in the *New York Times* the next day would read "Rockefeller Executive's Daughter Arrested in Vice Raid." You always had one ear cocked, knowing that if the chips were down you might have to swallow the joint you were smoking whole and flush the rest of the stuff down the toilet.

Suppose, though, it turned out to be a false alarm? In that case, as Lenny Bruce knew, there was only one thing left to do: "SMOKE THE TOILET!"

Before there was Jesus Christ there was John the Baptist, and before there was Lenny Bruce, there was Lord Buckley.

That first night after the Modern Jazz Quartet, Monty put on the record player an LP called *Way Out Humor* which should actually be required listening for anyone who wants to understand— not just the fifties, but life itself. If I had had kids, I would have sat them down and made them listen to "The Naz," Buckley's hilarious and heartfelt tribute to Jesus Christ ("the coolest, grooviest, sweetest, wailingest, strongest, swingingest cat that ever stomped on this jumping green sphere! He was a carpenter kitty. . . .") much as my mother sat me down and made me memorize the Sermon on the Mount. And to "Willie the Shake" ("They gave him a nickel's worth of ink and five cents worth of paper, he sat down and wrote up such a breeze, that's all there was, Jack, there was no more!"). And to a little creative wig bubble called "God's Own Drunk" about a semi-mystical encounter with a bear.

Buckley opened our minds to "wild truth—things that happen that supersede and carry on beyond the parallel of your practiced credulity, and you may say that's lyin'. . . *but it may be the truth!*"

Helen and I had deliberately cultivated hipster jargon, but here was a vocabulary and a vision that left our hip dictionary in the dust. The first time Monty played Lord Buckley for us I just assumed the man must be black. When Monty showed me the album cover with this mustachioed English-looking gent in a pith helmet, I could hardly believe my eyes.

Elvis Presley called Lord Buckley "the professor of Hipology," and although his jive monologues breathe an optimism that can seem antiquated today, his outrageous humor is undiminished by time. Bob Dylan, Robin Williams, Whoopi Goldberg, and yes—Lenny Bruce—have all acknowledged his influence on their work.

So now I was this big hipster, Miss Hip Smoke a Reefer of 1959. In the morning I would crawl to the office in shades with my hair in rollers and a bandana on top and give Hal a hard time if he tried to dictate a letter before I had my coffee and Danish. In the evening my friends would say, "Let's call up Helen Weaver and see if she has any of those dope sticks!" A double life. Dan Wakefield tells me I used to keep my stash in the back of my desk drawer at Farrar, Straus—because nobody would ever think to look for it there. How sensible!

In my bedroom on West 13th Street I had one of those twin beds with a trundle bed underneath that you could raise up and fasten to the top bed, creating a sort of temporary double bed. But the two beds tended to separate at the most inconvenient times. So after Tommy moved in I finally got myself a real double bed.

When my parents came for dinner I'd hide Tommy's clothes and shaving gear in the closet and pray they didn't see them. On one famous occasion my mother stared into my bedroom in amazement and announced, "I don't understand why Helen has to have such a LARGE BED!" She really didn't, and I didn't enlighten her. What could I say—"The better to get laid, Mom"?

Tommy was working for Railway Express. Before he got on the night shift we would both leave for work in the morning, but it was such a big deal for an unmarried couple to be living together that Tommy would usually wait a few minutes after I left so the neighbors wouldn't see us walking down the stairs together. There was a nosey (or lonely) woman on the second floor who used to shoot out her door and talk to me. One morning after a particularly good night Tommy and I said the hell with it, and walked down the stairs together. The nosey neighbor shot out of her door as usual, nodded in approval, and boomed, "Good! *Less furtive!*" She was a Villager!

By the time I turned twenty-nine I was bored with my job. I was afraid that if I didn't make a break before I was thirty I would spend the rest of my life writing rejection letters to nut cases in California who thought they could write. I quit my job and went to Europe.

I had reservations for three months and stayed a year and a half. In Florence I met an American painter who was living off the G.I. Bill and had a well-deserved reputation in the expatriate community as a hell raiser. Blond with blue eyes and a striking resemblance to Steve McQueen, Andy was a wit and a drunk who was always getting thrown out of Harry's Bar.

He had a friend named Bill who was even wilder than he was. Bill was a direct descendant of a famous New England writer and minister who once held his hand in the fire to punish himself for betraying a friend. The whole family was nuts. Bill's girlfriend and I used to conspire to keep Bill and Andy apart because when they got together all hell broke loose. They'd end up in the police station at dawn and Anna Maria and I would have to come and bail them out and there'd be a big headline about "*gli americani*" on the front page of the newspaper. It was Jack and Lucien all over again.

Naturally, I fell in love with Andy. I was drawn to his anger and bitterness, which I thought I could heal. Big mistake! But he taught me to live on nothing.

We hitchhiked through southern Italy to Brindisi and sailed fourth class for Greece, sneaking into first class in the middle of the night and getting caught with our literal pants down. In Greece we slept on the decks of boats with goats and chickens and Greek fishermen who had contests to see who could eat the biggest fish head. With his comical broken Italian Andy would charm the cook into giving us free leftovers. He was the archetypal con man.

In a year and a half our relationship went from a kind of

two-against-the-world romantic love affair to a nightmare of mutual contempt, drunken shouting matches, and physical abuse. We spent our last summer—and the rest of my money—in an international art colony on the beautiful island of Lesvos.

To keep from going crazy I wangled a job translating a book from French through the kind offices of Richard Howard back in New York. A pastiche of the theological writings of the Catholic poet Paul Claudel, the book was *Je Crois en Dieu*. And for the first time since I had given up church at the age of seventeen, I found to my surprise that that was true for me: I did believe in God after all.

I had to fly to Athens to buy a typewriter with a non-Greek alphabet and a French-English dictionary in case I got stuck. I sent lists of questions to my mother in Connecticut, such as the exact wording of quotations from the Douay (Catholic) edition of the Bible. She would look them up and send me back the answers.

But every morning when I woke up my first thought was, *I'm still here. I live with a man I don't love, who doesn't love me, who drinks, takes my money, and hits me. I could leave any time, but I don't. This is my choice.* My rationalization was that it cost me less to support Andy than it did to travel on my own, and I wasn't ready to leave Europe. But Europe was wearing thin.

After I mailed the last of my translation to Holt, Rinehart and Winston things got worse. I came down with hepatitis, turned yellow, and had to stop drinking. Andy took care of me for a while, then got bored and would go off and leave me for days without food. There were only three things on the island I could eat: quinces, carrots, and potatoes.

The only doctor in Molivos looked up *ikteros* (jaundice) in a medical dictionary that was published shortly after the discovery of penicillin. So that's what he prescribed, plus a daily enema. The old women in black who looked in on me recommended an alternative treatment. They knew of a man who could make a little hole in my forehead, and the disease would go out through the hole. When I looked skeptical, they assured me it wouldn't hurt at all. My doctor thought this was a good idea.

I told my troubles to Petra, the beautiful gray cat with green eyes we had adopted in the spring. She had become my best friend. She would sit on my chest as I lay in bed and we would stare into each other's eyes.

There came a point when, in addition to hepatitis, I had asthma, hives all over my body, and hemorrhoids. I would get up in the middle of the night and stagger down to the kitchen—it was a separate stone building with one tiny window—and heat up water in the kerosene stove: steam for my lungs, compresses for my hives, and a sitz bath for my butt. Sitting alone in the dark stone dungeon I pictured my father coming out of the sky in a helicopter to scoop me up and take me home. I was afraid. But I knew that I had got myself into this mess and that somehow I would get myself out of it. I vowed that if and when I ever got home I would get professional help.

The women in black who looked in on me every day would pound on the wall of my room and yell, *"Forbo!"* They were telling me I was young and strong and would get well.

With the help of friends I managed to get on a boat. I was so intimidated by Andy that I pretended I was only going to New York for a few weeks to sell some of his paintings. I left all my possessions behind as hostages, taking nothing but my typewriter and my cat.

In Athens I had a hilarious time trying to get the right papers for Petra. It seems no one had ever tried to take a cat out of Greece before. "They don't have cats in America?" At the American Embassy they said she had to have a shot. I finally located a vet, who received me in bed with his leg in traction. He asked me what kind of a shot I wanted. I shrugged. "Vanilla!" In the end, he simply signed Petra's passport, which indicated that she had tested negative for hoof-and-mouth disease.

It was a rough crossing on the *Olympia*: ropes everywhere, and even the crew was seasick. I was so weak from that weird diet that I knew I had to eat, so I did. To keep from throwing up I stood on deck reading, holding onto the mast with one hand and a paperback copy of Edith Wharton's *The Age of Innocence* with the other. Petra had to ride in a cage on the top deck with two poodles and a parakeet. Twice a day I visited her to let her know

I was on the same ship. She complained bitterly, but we made it. I landed in New York harbor in November 1962, the only one on deck to see the Statue of Liberty, with nothing to declare but Petra and my Olivetti portable. I weighed so little they could have mailed me home in an airmail envelope.

I spent several months recuperating in my parents' home in Connecticut. I wrote a poem "To a Cat Who Also Escaped by a Hair." As soon as I was strong enough to move back to my Village apartment, I started looking for a shrink.

Helen pooh-poohed my description of my experience in Greece as a "brush with death." I was exaggerating, as usual, but I knew what I had been through. I had hit bottom and I was ready to change. I had chosen a man who was sick, thinking I could make him well. Instead, I had gotten sick myself. I had picked someone I thought was wild and free, who would not smother me as my parents had, and I had ended up in a kind of prison, praying for Daddy to come and rescue me. I had been drawn like iron filings to a magnet to someone who couldn't love me. Somewhere inside, I knew now, I didn't believe I deserved to be loved. That's what had to change.

I dreamed that I was being followed by a man in a winding sheet whose body was partially decayed, a man who had escaped from a tomb, who was half dead and half alive, who would not let me go. I told the dream to Helen.

"Why would I be so frightened of a man who is half dead and half alive?"

"Because he wouldn't have much respect for life."

She got that right.

I took my dreams and my hope to Willard Gaylin, M.D., in the upper seventies, just off Fifth Avenue. He was the first shrink I ever had who listened and who actually answered me. (In 1962, still the heyday of "non-directive" Freudian therapy, that was rare.) Most important of all, he laughed at my jokes. He was awake!

Dr. Gaylin was a breath of fresh air after Dr. Levin, the *New Yorker* cartoon analyst I saw when I was living with Kerouac. I should have known he was made out of paper. But back then I wasn't ready to change. A paper analyst would do.

Doctor Goo Goo, as I had nicknamed him—I'm not sure why, except that I was coughing up all this baby stuff and maybe it made the whole process less terrifying—was a live one. The man had a mind. Neither of us knew it then, but he was a writer. He's written at least a dozen books, including one called *On Being and Becoming Human*. He should know.

The only time I ever saw him rattled was when I came to my session equipped with my Brownie camera and flash attachment. Before you could say Jack Robinson I was down on the floor, focusing. Now I had Doctor Goo Goo for all time: the nice serious face with the interesting cheekbones, the dark eyes with the heavy circumflex eyebrows, the deep smile creases. A kind of Puckish, elfin quality in spite of his height, the tall gangling body folded into his armchair like a stork, yet with a wall-to-wall honesty and dignity that were positively Lincolnesque.

Now that I'd been to Europe, had spent two whole summers on beaches, had been to hell and back, and had translated a book from French to English, I was not about to put on nylon stockings and high heels and go work in an office from nine to five. Forget it!

Those last two years at Farrar, Straus when I was so bored I made poor Hal's life a living hell, I had racked my brain for a way I could make a living at home. I had actually talked him into letting me co-translate one of our French books, Joseph Kessel's *Les Mains du miracle*, on my vacation in Fire Island. Those two weeks living in a friend's cabin in the Pines with my typewriter and my French dictionary—that little taste of the freelance life— ruined me forever for nine to five.

So now I had two books to my credit, and Dick Howard became my mentor. He farmed out some of his translating jobs to me and in overseeing and improving my work, he taught me my craft. Eventually he turned the books he didn't have time for over to me, so I had a new career.

It was hard work, tedious and solitary, and the books I got at first were heavy, technical stuff. But I could set my own schedule and work in my own space, and that made all the difference. Besides, I wreaked a subtle revenge for the dryness of the texts I had to work my way through like an ant crawling across the Sahara. In those pre-computer, pre–word processing days, I had to put the whole book through the typewriter two or three times before it was fit to turn in.

The translator's goal is to be invisible, to step aside and let the author's voice come through. So just for spite, I got in the habit of planting the title of a rock 'n' roll song in every book I translated, no matter what the subject. It was my secret signature, a way of undermining the anonymity of my craft, of integrating the two lives I was living in one body.

Once again I am tempted to believe in "destiny," for it seems that everything conspired to prepare me for the profession of translator. Even back in high school, French came so easily to me it was almost as if I were remembering it.

In a way, I was. After our family moved east from Madison in 1932 we spent the summer in Paris. As Mother pushed my baby buggy through the parks of Saint-Cloud the French ladies would coo at me and call me *cher petit chou* (dear little cabbage). I learned to walk on a croquet court near the *pension* where my parents were staying. The accents of that tongue were familiar to me and were associated with happiness, innocence, and success.

And then there was the lucky break that as an adolescent, two out of my three best friends spoke perfect French. Having a second language was very useful for passing notes in Study Hall about boys we had crushes on when maintaining secrecy was essential.

Finally, there was the double good fortune first, of having four years of French with Charles L. Reid Jr., who was far and away the best teacher of my entire academic life, and second, of meeting up with Richard Howard as soon as I got to the city, and having him take me under his formidable wing.

And of course there was my lifelong desire to be a writer.

Even as a child, I desperately wanted to write, but I had nothing to say—a dilemma that continued to plague me for years. I was in love with paper, pencils, and pens, and used to collect these tiny manila pads that cost a penny in the school store at Greenacres Elementary School. On these pads I would make row after row of meaningless but energetic scribbles. I stacked the scribbled-on pads carefully and secured them with rubber bands; they were my Manuscript.

So what if I had nothing to say? So what if I couldn't make up stories? At least I would go through the motions of writing until such time as I found my subject and my voice.

Like my seven-year-old self who used to scribble on those little penny pads, as a translator I could produce an actual manuscript without ever having to sit and stare at a blank page. It was still a few years before I started to fill the pages of my notebooks with my own ideas.

FREE SPEECH

The real geniuses of the comic are not those who make us laugh hardest, but those who reveal some unknown realm of the comic.

—Milan Kundera

It was the spring of 1963. John Kennedy was in the White House. Marilyn Monroe had died the summer before. Andy and I had been drinking retsina with our friends in a café in Molivos and having a heated argument about the new third edition of Webster's Unabridged Dictionary (which none of us had laid eyes on) when we got the news. We had toasted the American goddess with Greek wine.

Back in the U.S., the thousand days were running out. A comic named Vaughn Meader had made a record called *The First Family* satirizing JFK to perfection. The record had sold millions of copies and Meader had a follow-up album already in the can. Mort Sahl's shirtsleeves style of political commentary was popular with the college crowd. But the new favorite of the intellectual underground, whose shocking honesty and bizarre imagination earned him the epithet "sick," was the outrageous, the iconoclastic, the irrepressible Lenny Bruce.

Lenny was hot. Fantasy Records in Berkeley had just come out with *The Sick Humor of Lenny Bruce* and *I Am Not a Nut: Elect Me!* Helen had met Lenny one of the times she was working at MCA, dug him, took home his records, and played them for me. We had a new hero.

My introduction to Lenny Bruce was probably a bit titled "Non Skeddo Flies Again":

I talk about John Graham, he blew up a plane with forty people and his mother. And for this, the state sent him to the gas chamber—proving, actually, that—the American people are losing their sense of humor! If you just think about it, anybody who blows up a plane with forty people can't be all bad. Ridiculous! They tried to get a lawyer, they couldn't get Otto Kruger. . . .

There it was, that nervous, nasal, New York Jewish voice with its rapid-fire delivery, by turns staccato and pensive, the voice that had so many different voices hidden within it, ranging all the way from the sardonic edge and bite of the cool, seen-it-all hipster to the disarming innocence and vulnerability of a kid at the movies.

The album cover of *The Sick Humor of Lenny Bruce* showed a rather unimpressive little guy with a quizzical expression on his face lying on a tablecloth, having a one-man picnic in a graveyard. The photo has a kind of sickly greenish cast. Not a hint that the man himself, though not tall, was as dark and handsome as a sheik in a nineteen-forties grade B adventure movie.

Movies! Lenny was as obsessed with them as Helen and I were. Otto Kruger was a famous character actor from Lenny's childhood. When the back end of the plane blows off, the man who agrees to help the captain and the copilot cover their butts ("Are *we* gonna get yelled at!") whistles the theme from *The High and the Mighty*. The old railroad man who is asked to jump out of the plane to lighten the load is accused of doing Gene Lockhart bits. And so on.

There's a lot of anger in this bit. Besides the murderous rage of John Graham, the pilot and copilot hate their jobs (the copilot admits to having a fear of heights), the stewardess, and the customers ("Let's dump 'em!"), especially children ("He ruined the walls with the crayon!"). The only potential nice guy, the passenger who knows about planes and says he will help anyone who's in trouble, is really jive. He makes jokes about redecorating the doomed plane and only agrees to help because he fancies himself in the role of a movie hero.

An essential ingredient of Lenny Bruce's humor is the perception of all events through the metaphor of show business. The theme from *The High and the Mighty* and other references to the entertainment world create distance from the horror of the actual event and the cynical cold-bloodedness of the farce Lenny is spinning around it. Like the violations of the laws of nature that occur in violent cartoons—the defiance of gravity, the impossible survivals of annihilated characters—which break any illusion of reality and serve to remind us that "it's only a movie, " Lenny's repeated references to Show Biz help to dull any moral revulsion we might feel at the cruelty of what is going on.

This may not work for everyone. It worked for Helen and me. We both had plenty of anger at our parents and at authority figures in general. We hated nine-to-five jobs, bourgeois morality, the phone company, and most politicians (JFK was the exception; he had style). We were "alienated." Lenny was one of us, he was speaking to us, in that intimate, offhand tone that let us behind the scenes, as if we were all insiders digging reality from the unique perspective of Show Biz.

When I listened to "Non Skeddo Flies Again" thirty years later I remember feeling shocked, for the first time, at the bitterness and cruelty of its humor. In fact, I didn't find it funny at all—and that was before September 11th. Blowing up planes used to be funny because it was so bizarre and unthinkable. Now it hits us too close to home.

But in the sixties, when I still smoked dope, I loved that bit. When I had lift-off—that moment when you realize that your feet are no longer on the ground and your wristwatch has become irrelevant—I would solemnly announce to all assembled, "The back end of the plane just blew off! Are *we* gonna get yelled at! Listen, it's *our* word against theirs. . . ."

"Non Skeddo Flies Again" is permeated with drug-related imagery. The ultimate drug is death, and that is the stash concealed in Mrs. Graham's pocketbook in the form of a time bomb. John Graham's haste to get her on board parallels the haste of the addict looking for a place to fix. The captain and the copilot are intoxicated on the alcohol they consumed at the airport bar. I don't know how aware we were that Lenny himself was addicted to narcotics. I think he told Helen he was on something a doctor had prescribed to help him through withdrawal.

In any case, his use of mind-altering substances gave him a unique perspective on the human condition and served to heighten the sense that all life was an illusion and a performance, that religion, politics, and sex were all aspects of Show Biz, that every event was an act, a bit. In the great bit "Religions, Incorporated," a Holy Roller at a Mad Avenue–type board meeting gets a call from the pope: "Hello Johnnie, what's shakin', baby? The puff of white smoke? Knocked me out!" He tells him he can get him the Sullivan show on the nineteenth, advises him to "wear the big ring" and signs off with "No, sweetie, nobody knows you're Jewish!"

I could no longer drink alcohol—my little run-in with hepatitis had left me with some residual liver damage; but my viper friend Jeff, who had also had hepatitis (he called us "trans-hepatites") informed me that it was OK to smoke grass. I would roll a few joints and take my Lenny Bruce records and schlep over to Helen's new pad on West 10th Street. We would sit on her couch in a room with one red light on and I would smoke dope and she would drink Rheingold beer and we would play the records.

When we got hungry we would transfer our bodies to the little round table for hamburger patties, baked potatoes with sour cream, and hearts of lettuce with Russian dressing and play the records again. It was a religious ritual, complete with priest, believers, atmospheric lighting, incense, and the ingestion of sacraments, and there was very little talking in church.

When our boyfriends Bobby and Neil joined us—they were both aspiring actors—they were expected to listen with the same devout attention, and they did. They both considered themselves the coolest of the cool and the hippest of the hip and rarely showed enthusiasm over anything but pure Colombian, Mallomars, and other women's bodies. But Lenny was the boss, Lenny was the chairman of the board (forget Sinatra!), Lenny was—as Neil so aptly put it, "the best man in the world."

Yes, Lenny was one of us. He saw through all the bullshit that was going down, from sexual prudery and the middle-class aversion to dirt and dirty words, to the true obscenity of racism, poverty, religious bigotry, nationalism, and war:

There's a kid who's stuck in a well and the headlines scream for six days, "CHILD TRAPPED IN WELL—NATION AWAITS IN VIGIL." In the meanwhile, you can go in any cosmopolitan city and still see in the Classified, "Orientals may buy here, Negroes may buy here," and one schmuck gets caught in a well and everybody stays up for a week!

The civil rights movement was blowing in the wind, having been launched with the passing of the first anti-segregation legislation, Brown v. Board of Education, back in 1954. Lyndon Johnson would sign the Civil Rights Act into law in 1964. But segregation and discrimination were rampant and Lenny was merciless in exposing the hypocrisy and racial stereotyping of so-called liberals. From "How to Relax Your Colored Friends at a Party":

That Joe Louis, helluva fighter! There'll never be another Joe Louis! . . . That Bo Jangles, Christ, could he tapdance! . . . You people have a natural sense of rhythm, born right in you, I guess, hunh?

And in "Father Flotski's Triumph," the black prisoner on Death Row announces:

Soon I gwine up to Hebin on de big ribberboat. Den wen I gets up dere I gwineta gets me a lotta fried chicken and wateymelon. Yassuh, boss, you see, you don't mind dyin', boss, if you got a natural sense of rhythm, yak, yak, yak!

This was funny, but it also made both of us uncomfortably aware of the deep-down racial prejudice in ourselves. Helen told me how embarrassed she was when after a date with someone she referred to as "a Negro gentleman" she caught herself telling him at the door, "I'm very nice to have met you." She cringed and slapped her brow: "Oh, man. . . ."

Helen and I spent so many hours listening to those records that eventually we knew Lenny's bits by heart and found ourselves quoting snatches of them out of context. The uninitiated would look at us blankly but if we were talking to another Lenny Bruce fan there would be that instant recognition, like a jokester's convention where the comics only have to call out numbers to get a laugh. It's hard for me to imagine a time when I didn't know Lenny Bruce's best bits so well that bits of them—bits of bits—are part of the language I speak, as if they were idioms that everyone knows, when actually they constitute a private language, an old hipster idiom spoken by a few of my best friends.

There's a bit called "Marriage, Divorce and Motels" on the album *Lenny Bruce: American* where Lenny imagines the after-sex pillow talk of a couple who have gotten back together after a separation:

Man: "Listen, Vera, when we broke up—did you make it with a lot of guys? I made it with a lot of chicks, you're entitled to make it with a lot of guys. I'd just like to know for the hell of it."

Vera: "I didn't make it with anybody."

The man keeps on bugging his old lady to tell him who she made it with, and she keeps refusing to spill the beans. Lenny finally breaks into their dialogue to insist:

"Don't cop out, never tell 'em, deny it—if they've got PICTURES, deny it!"

Just this last Thanksgiving somebody at the table quoted the immortal line "If they've got *pictures*, deny it!" and when Miriam and Michael and I all broke up but no one else did, the others knew right away: "Must be Lenny Bruce."

From the album entitled *I Am Not a Nut: Elect Me!* which came out the year Nixon ran for president against JFK, Helen and I loved the bit about the phone company:

I really don't dig the phone company anyway. It's a monopoly! If you get too hot with the phone company, you'll end up with the Dixie cup and the thread!

In the classic bit "Father Flotski's Triumph," a spoof of B movies about prison riots, Lenny enacts all the parts to perfection. Father Flotski, who is modeled on the Irish character actor Barry Fitzgerald, tells Dutch, the convict who is leading the riot:

You know there's an old story that once a boy goes the bad road the good road is hard to follow. When the good road is hard to follow the bad road opens when the good road closes. . . .

Much of Lenny Bruce's material was too hot for television back in the sixties. In a bit about an impasse he reached with the producers of the Steve Allen show he comments:

I don't make any bones about the fact that sometimes I'm irreverent, and sometimes I allow myself—this is a rationalization—the same poetic license as Tennessee Williams or Shakespeare. . . . In other words, I'll never use four letter words for shock value for a laugh, but if it fits the character then I wanna swing with it and say it.

And some of his best bits are about language itself. A bit titled "To Is a Preposition, Come Is a Verb" is a kind of Allen Ginsberg–like Zen meditation on the way we talk in bed.

But like much of Lenny's humor, his ideas on censorship

are deadly serious. Take this disquisition on the toilet, or rather on the *word* toilet—or rather, on the entire subject of so-called scatological language:

I want to help you if you have a dirty word problem. There are none, and I'll spell it out logically to you.

Here is a toilet. Specifically—that's all we're concerned with, specifics—if I can tell you a dirty toilet joke, we must have a dirty toilet. . . . If we take this toilet and boil it and it is clean, I can never tell you specifically a dirty toilet joke about this toilet. . . .

Obscenity is a human manifestation. This toilet has no central nervous system, no level of consciousness. It is not aware, it is a dumb toilet. It cannot be obscene, it's impossible. If it could be obscene, it could be cranky. It could be a communist toilet, a traitorous toilet. It can do none of these things. This is a dopey toilet, Jim. So nobody can ever offend you by telling you a dirty toilet story.

Now, all of us have had a bad early toilet training. That's why we are hung up with it. All of us at the same time got two zingers: one for the police department and one for the toilet: "All right, he made a caca, call a policeman!" And we all got the policeman, policeman, policeman, and we got a few psychotic parents who took and rubbed it in our face, and those people for the most if you search it out, are censors.

They hate toilets with a passion, man, you realize if you got that ranked around with a toilet you'll hate it and anyone who refers to it. It is dirty and uncomfortable to you.

Lenny's language—his use of "dirty words" in both the sexual and the scatological sense—didn't bother me at all. Sometimes I think I fell in love with Lenny Bruce because my father wouldn't let me say "fuck" at the dinner table.

I first encountered the word one day in the fifth grade, but nobody would tell me what it meant. But I liked the sound of it. It had a certain undeniable impact.

As soon as I got home from school I went to my father's study, pulled the big dictionary onto my lap, and turned to the F's. But in Webster's Unabridged, Second Edition, "fuck" was nowhere to be found. The word wasn't in the dictionary! Right away, I knew I was onto something.

I looked again, just to make sure. But no, there was nothing between "fuciphagous" (eating seaweed) and "fucoid" (pertaining to or resembling algae of the family Fucaceae) where "fuck" should have been. Not a trace, seam, or ripple to show where it might have disappeared into that sea of words. Were there other words that weren't in the dictionary, and if so, how was I going to learn them?

We were a family of readers, for whom words were important. It was not unusual for the conversation at the dinner table to develop into hairsplitting arguments about the exact meaning, spelling, or derivation of words: arguments which would be resolved when someone—usually my mother—would go and get the dictionary.

At dinner that night my parents, my brother, and I sat sipping Campbell's Cream of Tomato Soup. I waited for a gap in my father's monologue on his day at the Rockefeller Foundation. When it came I turned to him and said in as casual a voice as I could muster, "Daddy, what does 'fuck' mean?"

Suddenly, there was soup everywhere. My father was choking, sputtering, dabbing at his mouth with his linen napkin. When he could finally speak he put down his napkin and said sternly, "Young lady, you are not to use that word in this house!"

"But what does it *mean*, Daddy?"

"The subject is closed."

Wow—that was power! If my father, the scientist and grammarian, refused to define it, "fuck" must be the dirtiest word in the universe.

Like the Hebrew word for God, *fuck* was so powerful, it couldn't be said out loud. In the end I decided that whatever *fuck* meant, I liked it. So *fuck* was a swear word, was it? Great, I'd use it to swear.

According to the immutable law whereby anything forbidden

automatically becomes irresistible, the word I wasn't allowed to say became my favorite word. It became my mantra, which I chanted under my breath when I needed to let off steam.

Whenever I had to do something I didn't want to do, like help Mother with the dishes on Dody's night off, a job I hated with every fiber of my being, I would repeat the magic word like a litany. *Fuck! Fuck! Fuck!* I would mutter to myself as I hurled knives, forks, and spoons into the drawer of the mahogany sideboard, punctuating each metallic clink with the ritual and oh-so-satisfying explosive syllable.

Early in life, I discovered the consolations of profanity.

Add to that that Mother said Jews were off-limits, and anyone can see that my falling for Lenny Bruce, twenty-odd years later, was written in the stars.

Helen and I used to go up to Times Square and eat raw clams on the half shell at an Irish bar called McGinnis's. Then we'd go next door and play Fascination, an addictive arcade game where you

slide wooden discs along a numbered board in hopes of winning enough money to pay for a few more rounds. When we got tired of that we'd go to the place where you could record your voice on a little 45 rpm record you could actually play on your turntable at home. There was a place where you could have any crazy headline printed on a bogus newspaper called The Daily Tribune. I had one printed up with the headline "Bruce Meets Weaver: Governor Alarmed."

Everybody who was alive on Friday, November 22, 1963, remembers where they were at noon that day. I was on my way to Helen's for lunch. I had stopped at the corner deli down the street from her building to pick up a sandwich when the news came on the radio. I remember that when I heard that the president had been shot in the head, the word that immediately came into my mind was "grazed." The bullet had *grazed* his temple, I told myself, that's what it had to be.

Helen and I loved Kennedy, mostly because he was young and good-looking and wrote his own speeches (or so we believed), and because for the first time in our lives people like Pablo Casals were invited to the White House. Helen and Jill and Nancy and I sat in front of the TV all afternoon, stunned and weeping. I remember that they couldn't finish their lunches—and I couldn't stop eating. I ate everyone else's lunch. I understand the Germans have a word for it—*Kummerspeck*, grief hunger. Grief affects people in different ways.

Eight days after the assassination Lenny Bruce had a gig at the Village Theater on Second Avenue in the East Village. (Later it became the Fillmore East of rock 'n' roll fame.) Helen and I had tickets to go with Neil and Bobby. We all knew Lenny would have to say something about what had happened and we wondered how he could possibly find humor in it. We almost went with a chip on our shoulder, daring him to make us laugh.

What we didn't know was that Lenny, the great satirist, loved Kennedy as much as we did. He walked out on the stage and went up to the mike and shook his head sadly, in disbelief. For a few moments, he said nothing at all. Then he looked at the audience, shook his head again, and said, "Man. . . . is Vaughn Meader *fucked*? Whew!" And we roared. Like a lot of Lenny's bits, it was an Inside Show Biz joke and it really was funny and God knows we needed to laugh.

By this time Lenny had been arrested in Philadelphia, San Francisco, Los Angeles, Chicago, and Miami on narcotics and/ or obscenity charges, and he was physically ill—a pulmonary embolism brought on by a careless accident while shooting up. Al Goldman, who later wrote the definitive biography of Lenny Bruce, was in the audience that night along with Leonard Bernstein, Bob Dylan, and a raft of other heavyweights. Goldman saw a "sadly diminished" Lenny Bruce. But we thought he was great, and I remember a long and dazzling improvisation he did on a particularly pretentious, sequin-spangled curtain.

On December 6 *Time* magazine published a photograph of the presidential motorcade taken just after Kennedy was shot. The photo showed Jackie Kennedy crawling out of the car and the caption said that she was "going for help." Lenny hated the hypocrisy of that: holding up some kind of Christlike ideal of self-sacrifice that makes people feel guilty and turns them off of religion because it is impossible for anyone but a saint. Jackie, Lenny insisted, was not a saint, but a terrified human being, and she was "hauling ass to save her ass:"

Why this is a dirty picture to me, and offensive, is because it sets up a lie: that she was going to get help. . . . That's a lie they keep telling people, to keep living up to bullshit that never did exist. Because the people who believe that bullshit are foremen of the juries that put you away.

It was probably this kind of honesty, more than the words he used to express it, that got Lenny in trouble with the law. He had another bit where Christ and Moses return to earth and go through East Harlem, where they see people living twenty-five to a room. They are shocked that Cardinal Spellman's ring is so expensive, it could support all the people they have seen.

At that time the Roman Catholic church under Cardinal Francis Spellman held enormous political power. New York's District Attorney, Frank Hogan, was a puritanical Catholic with a passion for ferreting out anything that smacked of pornography. Back in the forties, he had indicted Edmund Wilson's *Memoirs of Hecate County* for obscenity. As for Assistant District Attorney Richard Kuh, who specialized in obscenity cases, he had what can only be described as a personal vendetta against Lenny and was determined to see him in prison.

When Lenny opened at the Café Au Go Go on Bleecker Street in Greenwich Village in April 1964 everything was in place for an arrest that was designed to insure conviction.

Helen and I learned of Lenny's arrest through Allen Ginsberg. Allen hated censorship in any form; he was always bailing out poets who got busted on narcotics charges, had even set up a

Committee on Poetry with funds for this purpose. He wanted to help Lenny but didn't have the time. He knew that Helen and I were big fans, so he called Helen and told her that she and I had to write a petition defending Lenny's right of free speech and get as many signatures as possible. Jack's drinking buddy Lucien Carr was night editor at United Press International; maybe he could help us get it in the papers.

I couldn't get anywhere with the petition until Helen showed me her rough draft. Then I was off to the races. The final version read like this:

We, the undersigned, are agreed that the recent arrests of night club entertainer Lenny Bruce by the New York police department on charges of indecent performance constitute a violation of civil liberties as guaranteed by the First and Fourteenth Amendments to the United States Constitution.

Lenny Bruce is a popular and controversial performer in the field of social satire in the tradition of Swift, Rabelais, and Twain. Although Bruce makes use of the vernacular in his night club performances, he does so within the context of his satirical intent and not to arouse the prurient interests of his listeners. It is up to the audience to determine what is offensive to them; it is not a function of the police department of New York or any other city to decide what adult private citizens may or may not hear.

Whether we regard Bruce as a moral spokesman or simply as an entertainer, we believe he should be allowed to perform free from censorship or harassment.

Now that we had the language of the petition our real work began. We divided up the job. Helen went after the Show Biz types and I focused on the literary and academic lights. It was my first taste of anything resembling political activism and I have to admit I really enjoyed it. I say "admit," because in the end I don't think it helped Lenny that much. Goldman says he disliked many of the liberal intellectuals who came to his defense. But I met some amazing people. I remember having a long telephone conversation with Lillian Hellman, who had her own history of fighting for liberal causes. She could not have been friendlier or more helpful. Maybe I reminded her of her younger days.

In the search for people to sign the petition my right arm was Dan Wakefield. I had met Dan in the fifties, around the time he published his ground-breaking study of Spanish Harlem, *Island in the City.* A staff contributor for the *Nation,* Dan had been one of the few people who encouraged me to make the break from nine-to-five to the freelance life. (My father was afraid I would end up on the Bowery.) Dan said that even when you don't know how you're going to make the rent, "Something *always* happens." He knew every liberal in New York (before "liberal" became a dirty word) and sent me long lists of names, addresses, and phone numbers in letters addressed to "Fighting Helen" and signed "Fighting Dan, "a form of address we use to this day.

Helen's big coup was Elizabeth Taylor and Richard Burton, who had left their respective mates when they met on the set of *Cleopatra*; mine was Reinhold Niebuhr, dean emeritus of the Union Theological Seminary. In all we amassed close to a hundred signatures, including Woody Allen, David Amram, James Baldwin, Saul Bellow, the Burtons, Gregory Corso, Malcolm Cowley, Bob Dylan, Jules Feiffer, Lawrence Ferlinghetti, Allen Ginsberg, Albert Goldman, Robert Gottlieb, Elizabeth Hardwick, Lillian Hellman, Nat Hentoff, John Hollander, Richard Howard, Kenneth Koch, Robert Lowell, Norman Mailer, Arthur Miller, Henry Miller, Jonathan Miller, Paul Newman, Reinhold Niebuhr, Frank O'Hara, Norman Podhoretz, Susan Sontag, Terry Southern, William Styron, Lionel Trilling, Louis Untermeyer, John Updike, Gore Vidal, and Dan Wakefield.

Allen tried to talk Kerouac into signing the petition but Jack had no use for Lenny, mostly because of his attacks on religion: "I hate him! He hates everything! He hates life!"

I spent hours on the telephone every day tracking people down and conferring with Helen, Allen, and Dan. We were under pressure to get the news release to UPI and the story in the papers before Lenny's trial. I'd arrive at Dr. Goo Goo's in a state of nervous exhaustion and fling myself down on the couch. He'd say, "How are you?"amiably, and I'd groan, "A human rag!"

I always relaxed the minute I hit that couch, though; it had been warmed up for me by the man whose appointment was right before mine.

I would pass him in the waiting room, a short man in a rumpled suit with a mop of tousled gray hair falling over his deep dark-rimmed eyes which, on those rare occasions when we made eye contact, would glare at me from a pair of slightly pouchy sockets. Here was someone not to be trifled with, or flirted with at random. The man was actually rather attractive—he looked a little like Leonard Bernstein, only shorter—but he looked so angry most of the time that I assumed he was a privacy freak, and ashamed to be seen there. In those days there was still a slight stigma attached to seeing a psychoanalyst.

Yet he who was so cold to me when our ships passed in the waiting room had so much heat in that bantam frame that as soon as I lay down on the couch I felt the warmth of the body that had just left it, and never failed to remark, "Ooh, that warm man was here again!" And Dr. Goo Goo would chuckle appreciatively.

One day I happened to get a good look at this guy and by God, he really *did* look like Leonard Bernstein. I came in and confronted Dr. Goo Goo point blank.

"Was that Leonard Bernstein who just left?" But Dr. Goo Goo politely declined to answer, explaining that he had a professional responsibility to protect the privacy of his patients. I couldn't get an answer out of him. He just gave his Sphinxlike smile and sat with folded hands observing me in his alert, good-natured way.

"Well anyway, he can't be Leonard Bernstein; he's too short," I concluded.

"People always look taller when they're on a podium," Dr. Goo Goo remarked innocently.

Screw professional confidentiality! He wanted me to know that his patient was the *real* Leonard Bernstein, no mere lookalike. So it was none other than the famous conductor himself who warmed up the hot seat for me twice a week. And sure enough, years later I came across a biography of Bernstein and there in the index was Gaylin, Willard, M.D.

If I'd known that I could have handed him a copy of the petition and saved myself postage. He didn't sign.

But everybody else did, and at UPI Lucien took our press release, headed "Arts, Educational Leaders Protest Use of New York Obscenity Law in Harassment of Controversial Social Satirist Lenny Bruce," and made sure it went out over the wire three days before the scheduled trial date of June 16.

The Sunday papers all ran the story. The *New York Times* gave it a long piece headed "100 Fight Arrest of Lenny Bruce: Arts Leaders Protest, Citing Violation of Free Speech;" the *Herald Tribune's* article, "Rallying to Defense of Lenny Bruce," ran Lenny's picture and printed the entire list of signatories; and the *Post* checked in with "Burtons Join Plea for Lenny Bruce."

It was the best we could have hoped for. Now we could relax; the rest was up to Lenny and his lawyers, Ephraim London and Martin Garbus. The trial opened in New York Criminal Court before a panel of three judges (not the jury Lenny was hoping for) on June 16, but it had to be recessed until June 30th because he was hospitalized for pleurisy.

For me it meant getting back to work on the book I was supposed to be translating, a particularly tedious sociological tome which shall remain nameless.

One afternoon that June I was sitting at my desk almost falling asleep over my typewriter when the phone rang and a familiar voice in my ear said, "Hi! This is Lenny Bruce."

WEBSTER'S UNABRIDGED

Fuck is a dirty word, but it comes out clean.

—Lenny Bruce

Immediately, I was wide awake. "You're putting me on."

"No, this is me. I just talked to Allen, he gave me your number. He told me about all the work you did for me, and I want to thank you. That was really nice of you, and I'm grateful."

"Well, I had to do it, Lenny, I had no choice. I'm a big fan of yours—I guess you figured that out—and I can't stand what they're doing to you. Anyway, I didn't do it alone. I had a lot of help. You remember Helen Elliott?"

"The chick who works for MCA?"

"Right. She met you once. She actually wrote the first draft of the petition. We had a meeting with Allen but we all got stoned. So Helen knocked out something and showed it to me and was going to give it to Allen but it wasn't right so I changed it all around and threw in that stuff about Swift, Rabelais, and Twain. I sent it to the intellectuals, and she went for the Show Biz types. Actually, we had a ball. Everybody was so enthusiastic. You have a lot of fans! It's been a trip."

"So I was wondering . . . are you busy now? Could I come over and visit?"

"Are you kidding? I'd love to see you."

"What's your address?"

"325 West 13th Street, it's between a Catholic school and the Salvation Army, you can't miss it."

"Solid. I'll be there in twenty minutes."

It was more like half an hour. I needed it. I raced around, doing the dishes, tidying up the place, probably put on eye makeup, teased my hair, rolled a joint, put some Miles Davis on the record player.

Suddenly the buzzer rang, and then he was at my door, wearing a raincoat and a pair of bleached blue jeans.

His aura struck me almost like a physical blow when he walked in. It was a strange aura, almost repellent: very sexual, but like both sexes at once, like half man half woman. He reminded me of Di Angelo, my lesbian lover, that slightly sinister quality she had. It was as if this small, compact body contained secrets shameful to reveal, as if contact with this person would take me to the edge of my known universe of respectability and reason and over the edge and beyond into some world undreamed of in Scarsdale. Then I looked at his face and saw that he was an old friend of mine and the strange aura dispersed, or I entered it. I agreed to enter it. I wanted him to be in my house. I accepted all of it for an afternoon, and the strangeness fell away.

I offered him a drink, or a joint. He refused the drink, had maybe a toke to keep me company. All he wanted was a glass of water.

He was very sweet and sleepy-eyed, no bullshit, no star manner, just like a tired guy who was getting his ass kicked. He had this ironic humor, this laugh out of the side of his mouth, but he was so vulnerable, so defenseless, like a little boy. I wanted to comfort him.

We sat on the couch and were easy together. He told me about his busts, his lawyers, his troubles. He seemed relaxed. I ran and got the newspaper front page I had printed up in Times Square: "Bruce Meets Weaver: Governor Alarmed," and he dug it.

There was no barrier to our touching and being close. The strangeness was all gone. It was as if we had been lovers before, but hadn't been together for a while. There was nothing sudden. I knew him so well. I spoke his language, he lived inside my head and his words were in my mouth, on my tongue, had been there for so long he was already a part of me. He didn't have to show his passport or pass customs. I knew where he was coming from.

Besides, he was so solid. He was packed into those jeans! He had a pair of thighs that wouldn't quit, and these beautiful sad Jewish Sheik of Araby eyes. There was simply no question. All those hours Helen and I had spent listening to his voice on the records: that was our foreplay. And his gig at the Village Theater back in November: that was our first date. (And if that sounds like I got it backwards—hey, it was the sixties.)

Lenny Bruce had so much mental and sexual energy that I didn't even notice that he was sick. Lying in bed with him that afternoon after making love, I had never seen a body like that. Sick though he was, he was strong. Inside of all his pain and sickness and drugs there was also this tremendously strong spirit, just wailing. But the skin on the outside of the body was like a road map of all the places he'd been, all the trips he'd taken. It was a well traveled body. I had never seen a body so covered with scars, signs, and symbols, so written on by life.

On his left bicep was the tattoo of the American eagle he had had etched into his skin in the Merchant Marine (the subject of his "Jewish Seagull" bit). Then there were the long and scary scar from his recent operation; an old appendix scar; and on his right arm, some awful-looking scars from what I assumed were methedrine injections. I wouldn't have known heroin tracks if they had hit me over the head; later I learned that's what they were. His body was like a worn-out map of a life on the road. In the high state of consciousness I was in with Lenny Bruce lying in my bed, this dark body beside me covered with writing seemed like a map of the American unconscious, the American psyche of the sixties.

My bedroom doubled as an office, and while we lay in bed talking, Lenny looked over at my desk and pinned my copy of Webster's Unabridged Dictionary, Second Edition—the book Helen and I referred to affectionately as The Big Dick.

I hated the new, revised, updated and supposedly improved third edition. Whereas the great second edition had examples taken from Shakespeare, Milton, and Sir Philip Sidney, the third edition quoted—actually, some of the same people who had signed our petition, who were good writers, no doubt, but something very precious had been lost.

My copy of the old second edition had belonged to my father. Being a scientist and a believer in progress, he had bought the third edition while I was in Greece and sent the second "outdated" edition to an old friend in Florida. When I found out what he had done I put up such a fuss that he actually got his friend to send it back, and gave it to me.

Lenny Bruce never got past the tenth grade and may not have been much of a reader but he loved words—and anyone who loves words, loves dictionaries. When he saw that I had Webster's Unabridged on my desk he grabbed the book, and sitting cross-legged at the foot of my bed with the huge volume open before him he taught me The Dictionary Game.

He'd close his eyes and turn the pages at random and with his eyes still closed, stick his right index finger somewhere on the page. Then announcing, "I'll own you tomorrow!" to the still invisible word he had selected, he'd peer at the page and read the definition out loud, shaking his head wonderingly at the style of the definition, and improvising bits that came to mind.

As I responded with howls, this led to other bits. Lenny leaped to his feet and standing in front of the open bathroom door with the toilet and the claw-foot tub visible behind his naked body, he proceeded to give me a preview of some new bits he was working on.

Not to be outdone, I told him a story of my own. I explained that I had trouble breathing through my nose because of my chronic hay fever, and this had been going on since the age of five. Like him, as a child I was a lonely radio nut and I used to listen to all these gangster shows where people were always getting bound and gagged. Being a mouth breather, I knew that if that ever happened to me, I would die. I had a terrible fear of being bound and gagged and I rehearsed scenes where I'd tell the crooks that if they did this they'd be responsible for murder.

When I got older and had boyfriends I sometimes had trouble getting my breath while kissing. I imagined what it would be like to be asphyxiated while making love. I told him how I used to fantasize about being condemned to death by kissing, and I imitated a judge passing sentence: "You shall be taken from this place and kissed on the mouth until you are dead, and the Lord have mercy on your soul."

I told all this to Lenny, and when I got to the part where the judge pronounces the sentence he did a double take and screamed, "That's FUNNY!" like one comic to another at the Carnegie Deli. He stared at me, truly amazed that this little shiksa chick he'd just balled who wasn't even hip enough to come was saying something so crazy he might have made it up himself, was actually making him, Lenny Bruce, laugh.

Talk about a dream come true! For me, making Lenny Bruce laugh was better than an orgasm. It *was* an orgasm.

Well, all good things come to an end, and sooner or later Lenny had to leave.

I had steeled myself for this moment. We'd had a great time, but I knew as sure as I knew my own name that this was a one-time thing, that, as I told myself, "nobody owns Lenny Bruce." This knowledge stopped my ordinarily unstoppable fantasy machine in its tracks. I certainly didn't expect him to phone or send flowers. But somehow at the very last minute as I stood in the doorway of my apartment and watched him head for the stairs I had a moment of temporary insanity and out of my mouth came the words, "Are you going home now?"

At which he grinned and shot back, "No, schmuck, I have to fuck three more people!"

And we both cracked up as he disappeared down the stairs.

The next day I walked into Dr. Goo Goo's office feeling vulnerable and nervous. After all, he was an authority figure, a father figure, and in my real father's eyes I had not only been promiscuous, I had given myself to someone inappropriate, someone notorious for foul language and drugs, someone my mother would have taken one look at and instantly classified as a "thug."

So I started out jauntily covering my nervousness, "Guess who I went to bed with last night?"

And Dr. Goo Goo, who was nobody's fool, said, "Lenny Bruce?"

"How did you know?"

"Just a guess. . . ."

And in the pregnant silence that followed in which the little girl from Scarsdale expected her father to say, "Get out of my office, you dirty slut, and never darken my door again!" Dr. Goo Goo inquired casually, "How was it?"

From that "How was it?" I date the beginning of the end of my frigidity. Not "You're bad!" or "Get out!" but "How was it for you?" He really wanted to know, and I told him, and the keystone that supported the entire edifice of my parents' guilt-ridden morality was removed. From that "How was it?" to my first orgasm in the summer of 1965, it was only a matter of time.

"It was wonderful, because we talked afterward. . . ."

THE REAL OBSCENITY

I feel terrible about Bruce. We drove him into poverty and bankruptcy and then murdered him. We all knew what we were doing. We used the law to kill him.

—Vincent Cuccia, Assistant District Attorney,
New York State

Lenny Bruce's trial began on June 16, 1964. In Room 535 of the Criminal Courts Building at 100 Centre Street the onlookers were divided into two camps. Lenny Bruce's supporters sat on the left and his opponents on the right. On our side I saw some of the people who had signed the petition (Jules Feiffer, Richard Gilman, Al Goldman, and Nat Hentoff) and some who hadn't (a young and handsome Philip Roth, for one). I came every day, always dressed in white—I wanted to look sweet and innocent and as much like Scarsdale as possible—and sat on the left with Allen.

One day Assistant D.A. Richard Kuh came up to me and asked me who I was. Allen put his arm around me and told him, "She's a friend of mine!" That shut him up.

One person who didn't show up for the trial was Reinhold Niebuhr. The elderly theologian, who had recently suffered a stroke, had never seen Bruce perform and had signed the petition on the advice of friends. When Kuh saw Niebuhr's name in the *New York Times* as one of the signers of the petition he feared that the endorsement of such a distinguished authority could jeopardize his case. He immediately called Niebuhr on the phone at his home in Stockbridge, Massachusetts, and urged him to reconsider his support of Bruce. There's no way of knowing whether Kuh actually threatened to subpoena the sick old man as a witness if he did not remove his name from the petition, but some believe he did.

The trial itself is a bit of a blur in my mind. I do remember how clever Kuh was in undermining the credibility of all those normally articulate expert witnesses for the defense. I remember how he referred to the petition as "the manifesto," as if we were a bunch of communists. And who could forget that when the prosecution was insisting that Lenny had made a masturbatory gesture, Lenny's lawyer Ephraim London became so rattled that he referred to his client as "Mr. Crotch"? I remember how moved I was when columnist Dorothy Kilgallen, a devout Catholic, looked at presiding Judge Murtagh and said simply, "They're just words, judge."

And I remember that one afternoon after that day's session was over, Lenny asked me to come home with him.

He was staying at the Marlton, the same seedy hotel on West Eighth Street where Kerouac had holed up for a week after I threw him out and before Joyce took him in.

Lenny was taping his trial—he had had his briefcase fitted out with a built-in tape recorder—and as soon as we got in a cab for the ride north to the Village he opened it up and started playing back that day's session. He was outraged that the three judges were allowing the court clerk to read from a transcript of the tape the police had made of his performance at the Au Go Go—a transcript that was, moreover, riddled with errors.

"He's doing my act, and he's bombing!"

Making his own tapes was his way of fighting back and also his way of checking up on his counsel and studying the finer points of the law. He had become totally obsessed with the law and had actually become quite knowledgeable about statutes and precedents. He sat there in the cab hunched over and muttering to himself as he listened, shaking his head, reliving the day.

The cab let us out on Fifth Avenue. As we walked west on Eighth Street a guy passed us, pinned this strange figure in his powder-blue jeans suit and boots and briefcase looking for all the world like an Arab smuggler and said, "Hi, Lenny!" And Lenny, without breaking stride or missing a beat, nodded at this cat he'd never seen before and acknowledged him with an instant "What's happenin', baby?" and walked on, leaving the guy reeling with benediction in his wake. I remember thinking how generous he was to acknowledge a fan in the midst of all his troubles.

Lenny's room on the second floor of the Marlton was an unbelievable mess: law books, legal briefs, and spools of trial tapes littered the floor and every surface, including the bed. There were two or three men there, gofers or hangers-on, and when Lenny wasn't playing and replaying the tape he was talking with them or on the phone.

Lenny had hired Ephraim London because he wanted a big name but they had never been simpatico. By now Lenny was convinced that London wasn't even trying to win his case since he assumed the conviction would be overturned on appeal. Hence Lenny's eventual decision to represent himself, and his obsessive study of the law.

Susan Sontag says somewhere that contrary to popular belief, madness is not romantic and interesting, but repetitive and boring. At this point in his life Lenny Bruce was well on his way to madness. For no good reason he was being deprived not only of his right to free speech, but of his very livelihood. It was enough to drive anybody mad.

It was a very sad spectacle. And for me, sitting in that room where I might as well have been invisible, it was also boring. After an hour or so during which I sat there like an abandoned groupie, I told Lenny I had to go. Remembering that I was there, he shooed the men out of the room and we had a few minutes to ourselves, but it was a far cry from our time together in my apartment. There was no time for The Dictionary Game, and Lenny had no new bits to show me. The few gigs he was able to get in those days consisted largely of a running commentary on his persecution at the hands of the law, and although that was a farce, it wasn't funny. He had started telling his audiences, "I'm not a comedian. And I'm not sick. The world is sick and I'm the doctor. I don't have an act. I just talk. I'm just Lenny Bruce."

Richard Kuh did talk Reinhold Niebuhr into withdrawing his

support and even got him to put it in writing. In the last days of the trial Kuh tried unsuccessfully to get Niebuhr's letter admitted into evidence.

Even though it was too late to do any good, I wrote Niebuhr myself:

July 30, 1964

Dear Dr. Niebuhr:

As a member of the committee that sent you the Lenny Bruce petition, I want to apologize for any unpleasantness and invasion of your privacy occasioned by your sponsorship of that document. I know that both the Times *and District Attorney Kuh have called you about the matter, and I imagine there have been other annoyances as well. From what little of your letter to Mr. Kuh the prosecutor was permitted to read in court, I gathered that you had been led to regret ever having involved yourself in the Bruce affair.*

At the risk of sounding self-righteous, I would like to express my profound conviction that your initial impulse in adding your name to the list of signatories—even if prompted by the counsel of friends familiar with Mr. Bruce's work rather than first-hand experience with it—was pure and just, and provided the necessary note of gravity for an effort to combat, in one vital area, those forces of rigidity and reaction which are in such terrifying ascendency in America today. I think that if you could have watched one day's proceedings at the Criminal Court House here you would inevitably have been reminded of other trials that have taken place over the past two thousand years, other trials in which the community, using a legal process to stifle its sense of guilt, has rejected men who have the courage to see and speak the truth.

Now that these hearings are over, I hope that the trouble and embarrassment you may have been caused are also at an end. Mr. Bruce's troubles, however, may only have begun, depending on what verdict the judges reach when they have studied the counselors' briefs; and for this reason, I respectfully

*request that you consider carefully any understandable
temptation to withdraw your name from the document in
question. Unless we hear from you, Dr. Niebuhr, we will
continue to regard it as heading the list of those who believe it is
not the function of the police to determine what language adult
citizens may hear, or what materials an artist is permitted to use.*

> *Sincerely yours,*
> *Helen Weaver*

Poor Dr. Niebuhr! On July 31 I received a telegram from him stating that he had only secondhand knowledge of Mr. Bruce's art and insisting that his name not be restored to the petition, as it would be "a breach of faith with the D.A." And a few days later I got a postcard with a similar message, typed out by his shaky old hand.

In the last days of his trial Lenny had pleaded with Judge Murtagh: "Your honor, I so want your respect. Don't finish me off in show business!"

But that's exactly what they did. The six-week theater of the absurd at the Criminal Court Building ended with Lenny Bruce being convicted, by a two-to-one vote, of giving an obscene performance at the Café Au Go Go. Café owners Howard and Ella Solomon were also found guilty of allowing this indecency to take place on their premises.

Lenny was sentenced on December 22, 1964—the seventieth anniversary of the day Alfred Dreyfus, a Jewish officer in the French army, was falsely convicted of treason.

The trial left Lenny a bankrupt and broken man, unable to work in the most important city in show business and virtually unemployable elsewhere, since few nightclub owners would take the risk of hiring him.

In Lenny Bruce's obscenity trial, the trial itself was the only real obscenity.

On August 3, 1966, Lenny Bruce died of a morphine overdose in the bathroom of his Hollywood home.

On February 19, 1968, the conviction of the Solomons was reversed in a two-to-one decision which, though not formally applicable to *People v. Bruce,* constituted a kind of posthumous moral victory for Lenny. Frank Hogan appealed the reversal and on January 7, 1970, the Solomons (and by implication, Lenny) were vindicated again, this time six to one.

And in the ultimate irony, on the day before Christmas Eve, 2003, thirty-nine years after Lenny Bruce was convicted of obscenity for using dirty words in a nightclub act, Governor George Pataki pardoned the now legendary comic. The first posthumous pardon in New York history, Pataki called it "a declaration of New York's commitment to upholding the First Amendment."

The cartoonist Jules Feiffer, who had testified on Lenny's behalf as an expert witness on satire, said, "Lenny [Bruce] was sentenced to jail for what you see nightly on HBO and the Comedy Channel, except he was better." Ronald K. L. Collins and David M. Skover, authors of *The Trials of Lenny Bruce,* were active in the effort to gain the pardon, as were comics Robin Williams and the Smothers Brothers. Tom Smothers said, "So many of us today owe so much to Lenny Bruce." The Rosa Parks of comedians, he paved the way for almost every comic who came after him.

Helen and I mourned Lenny. He gave us a language for our rage and alienation and despair that did not rule out innocence and joy and a set of values through which, like the shades we used to wear at night, we could stand to view the world. He offered us membership in the one group we wouldn't be embarrassed to belong to: the royal order of outsiders. He was our hipster priest, our teacher, and our friend.

I realize that I have called Lenny and his devotees both "outsiders" and "insiders," and I think both terms are accurate. Bruce fans constitute an inner circle of outsiders, if you will: an "in" group that is beyond the pale, on the lunatic fringe, and pushing the envelope. The insiders live on the edge; they are outsiders who get inside jokes.

In the liberation movements of the sixties Lenny was on the front lines. When Steve McQueen said "bullshit!" for the first time in a Hollywood movie (*Bullitt*, 1968) Lenny's spirit was alive and well.

Five years after Lenny's death, writer and jazz critic Nat Hentoff wrote in the *Village Voice*: "Like the Ancient Mariner, I shall, until I die, tell the story every few years of how my friend, a most gentle man and a terribly innocent man, was destroyed. And I shall tell of Frank Hogan, John Murtagh, and Richard Kuh."

I think Jack Kerouac was wrong about Lenny. Lenny Bruce did love life; he just loved truth—and his right to tell it—more than his own survival. Mainstream America wasn't ready for some of the truths he exposed—it still isn't—but at least Lenny found his voice, and he had the satisfaction of knowing that there were some who heard him: few artists can ask for more.

When I heard about Pataki's posthumous pardon I thought I could hear Lenny chuckling from wherever he is, but not, as some of his friends believed, with a great deal of bitterness. I think he would have been amused, rather than bitter, that it only took thirty-nine years.

Lenny Bruce believed in the American legal system. He said, "I respect the law, and it will eventually vindicate me."

five CHANGES

ENDINGS

*If you drop a rose in the Hudson River at its mysterious
source in the Adirondacks, think of all the places it journeys
by as it goes out to sea forever—think of that wonderful
Hudson Valley.*

—Jack Kerouac, *On the Road*

After Lenny's trial I worked with Allen for a while on the legalization of marijuana.

Allen was my new hero. This was the Allen of the sixties,
with full beard and Indian kurtah: his hippie priest period. He had
started chanting OM to the accompaniment of his harmonium, an
Indian drone instrument, at peace protests, poetry readings, and
other public gatherings.

I'm not sure when he started actually singing in public, but I
do remember that Helen and I winced at his first attempts because
he was really awful: loud and not necessarily on key. But Allen
kept right on doing it and eventually, like every other art he turned
his hand to, he mastered it. He became not just a fine singer but an
inspired composer, setting the poems of his beloved Blake to music
and composing some unforgettable songs of his own.

I accompanied Allen to meetings of LeMar, an organization
to legalize marijuana that Ed Sanders, Randy Wicker, and he
founded in the sixties, and did a little secretarial work, but my
heart wasn't in it. Not that I didn't believe in the decriminalization
of hallucinogens—I still do, but without a major event like Lenny's
trial to galvanize me into action, I quickly ran out of steam. I

suspect my real reason for signing on was so I could spend more time with Allen. But as usual, I got distracted.

In 1965 I came as close to getting married again as I ever got in this lifetime. That affair turned into a lifelong friendship instead, but not before it put up a milestone in my life. Isaac and I always remember August 5 because that was the day it finally happened: at age thirty-four, in the middle of the sixties, I had my own personal sexual revolution.

Everything conspired to help me break through several generations of repression. First, there was Dr. Goo Goo, the father figure who let me know I was entitled. Then there was Isaac, the Jewish Cary Grant, who was both experienced and patient. And finally, there was my neighbor.

Stefanie's apartment was right above mine—in fact, her bedroom was right above mine—and she was a screamer. She was famous in our building; she told me that one man stopped her in the hall and asked her if she would give him lessons. Well, she gave me lessons without knowing it.

Listening to her didn't bother me at all. In fact, I started unconsciously imitating her when I was with Isaac. Not screaming exactly, but focusing on my breathing, and letting each breath be a groan. And—it worked! Breathing—or maybe the power of imitation, or maybe the combination—turned out to be the key that turned the lock of my frostbound sexuality. Imitation can be powerful, and the line between honest imitation and "faking it" is merely a matter of intention: you can fool yourself, you know.

Even Leonard Bernstein helped.

I used to vibrate on Dr. Goo Goo's couch like I don't know what: like some kind of whirling dervish, my whole body shaking like somebody suffering from hypothermia when they start to warm up. The kundalini waking up, no doubt, and if it hadn't been for Leonard Bernstein's body heat and the little bit of relaxation it imparted, I think I would have landed on the floor.

I remember that I had been dreaming about falling backwards and my father catching me, like some New Age exercise in trust. I kept hearing the words, "Daddy will catch you if you fall," telling me it was safe to let go. And then, the night of August 4,

I actually dreamed I was in my parents' bed in Scarsdale having sex with my father. It wasn't weird because I was my mother. Talk about Freud!

I also dreamed, or imagined, that I was a sea anemone, with my back rooted to the ocean floor and my legs myriad tendrils waving this way and that in the watery air. Or a baby, also on its back, having its bottom tended to by a loving hand. And all this innocent pleasure was my due. At the age of thirty-four, I finally felt entitled.

It was around the time I became orgasmic that I became a believer. It was a grand opening on every level: spiritual, intellectual, and emotional as well as physical. I found I had faith—not in God, necessarily, but in the power of faith itself. I felt as if I had somehow broken free from the limits of the rational materialist world view. I let go of some of my need to control. I no longer needed to grab and grasp at whatever I thought I wanted. Orgasmic—and with the proof of it a certain light in my eyes, and the disappearance of a certain cynical curl of the lip that showed up on my old 1961 passport—I found that I could simply be still and let things come to me. For the first time in my life, I felt magnetic.

Helen didn't like the change in me. She didn't like my new look: teased hair, eye makeup, pale lipstick, poor boy sweaters, miniskirts and boots. She told me I looked like a whore: exactly what her mother had told her as a teenager. She did a hundred and eighty degrees from the permissive mother she had been to me in the fifties.

Once again, I felt my life cracking open. Helen and I started drifting apart.

In the spring of 1969 I slept with a sculptor who looked like a cross between Bob Dylan and Rudolf Nureyev and got the clap; it was the only thing he ever gave me, I might add. A doctor in the Village prescribed massive doses of oral penicillin that completely defoliated my digestive tract. The result was a case of bleeding colitis that lasted four months—and P.S., it didn't cure the clap.

I became so weak that I had to go and stay with my parents in New Milford, Connecticut. I didn't tell them I had the clap.

By the end of July I was well enough to go back to the city. I had started meditating while I was in New Milford, and now I was ready to make some changes in my "lifestyle." I took up yoga. I started eating brown rice and other healthy food. And much to the horror of my scientist father, I took up astrology.

I had a reading with Zoltan Mason, a Hungarian astrologer whose office was on Lexington Avenue near Bloomingdale's. He told me that my name would be a household word. He also told me that I would fall in love with him. These things did not happen. But he told me other things he had no business knowing that were right on the money. I signed up for his class.

By August I wanted to go to the Woodstock Festival, but I couldn't find anyone my age who was willing to go with me. My new best friend Marcia Newfield reminded me that I'd been sick all summer and was still convalescing. Rain was predicted, and she said I'd probably get an asthma attack from lying on the ground. She was probably right but I was disappointed. I had a hunch it was going to be a historic occasion.

Nineteen sixty-nine was quite a year:

In July we landed on the moon.

In August, the Woodstock Festival did indeed make history in the Catskills ("The New York State Thruway is *closed*, man!").

And on the morning of October 21, Jack Kerouac died of an abdominal hemorrhage in St. Petersburg, Florida. He was forty-seven years old. Allen called to tell me that our friend was gone and to invite me to his funeral at St. Jean Baptiste Church in Lowell.

I didn't go.

Back in 1966 when Frank O'Hara was run over by a beach buggy on Fire Island and died, I had gone to his service in East Hampton, and it was a horror show. I didn't do funerals. I don't think Helen went, either. But unlike me, Helen did mourn for Jack.

I said that Helen and I mourned for Lenny when he died, but I have to confess that in my case that was not quite true. The truth is, I didn't really mourn for either Lenny or Jack. The deaths of those two young men didn't touch me, even though I had loved them both. I didn't understand what I had lost.

I told myself that both Jack and Lenny had courted death. They had both been "self-destructive." They were now "at peace." I really believed that. Maybe I was rationalizing my own callow indifference. Maybe I was right.

In the last years of his life Jack was horribly lonely and he would call his old friends on the telephone in the middle of the night. More often than not I didn't want to listen to sad crazy drunken Jack. I would tell him to call back tomorrow, which we both knew he would never do.

My last sight of him was a disastrous TV appearance on William F. Buckley's *Firing Line*, just a year before he died. Jack was set up: he wasn't told that other guests would be there to challenge his ideas. He had prepared a statement on the Beat Generation which he was given no opportunity to present. Jack wasn't a debater who could defend his life and ideas in public before a hostile audience. Hopelessly drunk, he rambled on about hoodlums, commies, and hippies jumping on the Beat bandwagon.

His response to an impossible situation was not without comic élan: At one point he jumped up, put on journalist James Wechsler's hat, and on a surrealist impulse that almost saved the scene, started singing "Flat Foot Floogie with a Floy Floy."

I found his humiliation unbearable. I excused myself from his passion, from the stations of his cross. When he died I was glad that his suffering was over and his soul was free, that he no longer had to live in the shadow of his death. With my newfound belief in astrology, reincarnation, and so on, I now also believed in the possibility of communication with the dead. In some strange way I felt closer to Jack after he died.

That fall I took a job as an editor at a small publishing house in the Village called Greenwich House. This may sound like a nine-to-five job, but it wasn't. It was only three days a week; I could make my own hours; and my boss, Jeff, was the same gent who got stoned every day at work and didn't mind if his employees did the same.

I remember doing yoga during my lunch hour when Jeff happened to drop by my office with the treasurer. He took one look at me standing on my head and asked Jeff, "Is she doing that on our time?"

Jeff smiled benignly and announced, "In yoga, there is no time!"

Shortly after Jack's death Allen told me that his agent, Sterling Lord, had a number of unpublished Kerouac manuscripts, including his masterpiece *Visions of Cody*. I immediately fired off a letter to Sterling Lord asking to see the manuscript. I had to wait for months pending the settlement of Jack's estate, but in April, 1970, Mr. Lord finally sent me the book. I asked Allen if he would be willing to write an introduction. He said, "With tears."

Then I read it—or tried to—and while I found some of it quite brilliant, the transcripts of taped conversations with the Neal Cassady character went on forever, and at 550 pages, I felt it cried out for cutting. Allen himself had originally found it "incomprehensible" but had since changed his mind. I asked Allen whether he thought it would be possible to publish an edited version and whether the two of us could work on it together.

But Sterling Lord told me he could never get the Kerouac estate to agree to an abridged version of the book. After *On the Road* was published Jack had a clause put in all his contracts with publishers saying that not a single comma could be changed. I discussed it with Jeff and since I was not enthusiastic about the book in its present form, he said, "I think we should let it go." So that's what happened.

Visions of Cody was published three years later with an introduction by Allen Ginsberg. It is now widely considered Kerouac's most important book after *On the Road*.

When I lived in New York City I used to bitch and complain about . . . living in New York City. But if anybody who was not a New Yorker criticized my city, woe unto them. But by the early seventies, things started to change.

When I first moved to the Village I could walk all the way across town from Chan's apartment on Sullivan Street to my apartment on West 13th Street at any hour of the day or night and the worst that happened to me was a harmless exhibitionist opening his raincoat and giving me a show. Well, I did get followed home once by a man who seemed up to no good but I managed to get through the door in time.

But after I moved to my last Village apartment, a one-flight walkup on West 10th Street, things like that started to happen more often. A guy tried to grab my camera right off my shoulder a block from my apartment. I cursed a blue streak at him and he fled.

On the subway on the way down town to collect my unemployment check after Greenwich House went bankrupt, a man who was the only other passenger in the car jacked off behind his newspaper while I pretended not to notice. Near Sheridan Square I saw a big bloodstain on the sidewalk. Another time in the subway a man punched me in the breast. I started taking cabs home instead of riding the subway. It got so I was afraid to walk to the corner deli after dark for a quart of milk. New York was getting scary.

I remember reading somewhere that the way to survive in the city and avoid being mugged or molested was to look as if you were crazy yourself. Carry a two-by-four over your shoulder and rant and rave about communist plots and fascist bastards, and people would give you a wide berth. I don't know if I was trying to look crazy or actually getting there, but I started kicking garbage. There was a lot of garbage on the street, especially in front of the big apartment building on the corner of my block, in various kinds of packaging. I became a connoisseur of the best garbage to kick. The big cans were too hard, they hurt your foot. Plastic bags were too soft, not enough impact to be satisfying. Cartons were perfect, they offered just the right amount of resistance.

When I told my friends half-jokingly about my new form of therapy they looked a little alarmed.

I began dreaming about the woods, wild animals, and sleeping on the ground.

My friend John Button said, "When civilizations are young, they value their cities. When they become decadent, they value nature." Was America becoming decadent?

Then I met Cynthia Chase (now Poten), who took me

camping, first in the Everglades and then in the Adirondacks. One perfect day in August, 1971, we climbed Mount Marcy. On the way we paid our respects to the headwaters of the Hudson River, to which the Native Americans had given the poetic name Lake Tear of the Clouds. When we got to the top of the mountain we smoked a joint and I had an epiphany.

I looked down and I saw my path, and it led out of the city.

Some Village friends took me to Woodstock on a day trip. Driving through, I thought it looked like a typical art colony. I was unimpressed.

And then they let me out of the car on the corner of Mill Hill Road and Tinker Street, right across from the tiny village green. I don't know what we'd been smoking but the minute my feet hit the pavement I got high.

Right in front of me was a sign that read, in a funky New Age Celtic calligraphy: "Occult and Spiritual Books Upstairs: Also, Incense, Oils, Tarot Cards, I Ching Coins, Astrology Tools, and Miscellaneous Metaphysicals." I walked upstairs.

Back in the city I had nobody to talk to about my new thing, astrology. Some of my intellectual friends put me down for taking it seriously. John Hollander told me I was turning my back on my heritage. Dick Howard was equally dismissive. Bob Gottlieb, who became vice president of Simon & Schuster when he was barely out of his teens, was skeptical, but loved hearing that he had "Jupiter exalted in the tenth house." Dan Wakefield and Allen Ginsberg were open to it. But nobody knew anything about it. My friend Marcia asked me to teach it to her so I'd have somebody to talk to, and had encouraged me to take Zoltan Mason's class.

In the city the only place I could buy astrology books was a store called Weiser's. Sometimes I'd go there just to soak up the vibes. But here in Woodstock, I was suddenly surrounded by people who believed in astrology. I felt like I was in a foreign country, but one where I spoke the language.

Cynthia had some sort of consulting job with a bank where

she only had to show up every couple of weeks. We started looking for a house in the country, not too far from Manhattan. We looked and looked, and were getting nowhere. Then one weekend we were in New Jersey and I looked around and it was flat. I told Cynthia: "We want the mountains."

We subscribed to *Woodstock Times*. Eventually we found a little house in West Shokan right across the road from the Ashokan Reservoir, just a few miles from Woodstock. The road we lived on was bordered on the reservoir side with the tallest pine trees I had ever laid eyes on. I remember being overwhelmed by those trees. I was like a starving man in front of a big meal. I could only look at one tree at a time.

At first we went back and forth between the city and the country. Then I sublet my apartment.

In May 1972, I moved to Woodstock.

Now that I lived in the country I had to have a car and I had to learn to drive—at the ripe old age of forty-one. My father bought me a white 1972 Volkswagen Super Beetle. I named her Sadie.

The first time I took the road test up in the town of Catskill, I failed. I showed up with a hippie driver with very long hair who was still in his teens and a sticker of some kind on my rear window. Long hair wasn't against the law but the sticker was so I started off on the wrong foot. The kiss of death was when I drove down the middle of a narrow street which I assumed to be one-way. It was a trick street. I knew I'd blown it, but I did a perfect parallel park just to uphold the family honor.

Not long after I failed the road test, while visiting friends in the Village, I ran into Helen Elliott on the street.

Helen and I were on the outs again. She, who was the main character of my New York story, the person who had made it worth telling, was getting strange, too. Or maybe it was me who was changing. I remember that when she decided to have a baby and raise it as a single mother, I thought it was a terrible idea. I felt sorry for the kid.

Helen and I had a stilted conversation in which I told her I had learned to drive, but had failed the road test. I said my friends had all told me not to worry, you never pass it the first time. And she said in that nasty, sugary voice she sometimes got, as if she were talking to a particularly dense four-year-old, "Your friends are just being nice to you, Helen."

And that did it. I had friends who supported me. I had had it with her bitchy, undermining ways. I didn't speak to her for years.

MY CLAIM TO FAME

I am the man who has best charted his inmost self.

—Antonin Artaud

Allen was always telling me I had to read Artaud, the French writer
and actor who invented the Theater of Cruelty and was one of the
great prophets of the modern sensibility. Allen admired Artaud for
his intimate knowledge of opiates and for his relentless, anxiety-
ridden, hallucinatory exploration of what is sometimes referred
to as "inner space." Susan Sontag called him "one of the great,
daring mapmakers of consciousness *in extremis.*"

When Farrar, Straus asked me to translate some of Artaud's
writings for an anthology Sontag was putting together, I didn't
hesitate to agree. Susan had always been a hero of mine and the
opportunity to work with her was very appealing. My Greenwich
House job had ended when they filed for Chapter Eleven and
Marcia and I had rented a house on Fire Island for the summer, so
the timing was good.

My original contract was for a little over a hundred pages
of material that had never been translated from the French. I
was given some existing English translations to look over to see
whether they were usable or needed reworking. I found them to
be not only tone-deaf but inaccurate and we decided to scrap them
and let me begin again from scratch. The only exception to their
poor quality was John Ashbery's translation of the important
correspondence between Artaud and Jacques Rivière of the

Nouvelle Revue Française, the sensitive editor who took the time to encourage the anguished and isolated young writer.

Susan kept finding more and more things to include, the job kept expanding, and pretty soon I began to smell a National Book Award. Although Ashbery's translation of the Rivière correspondence was faultless I began picturing my name on the title page as the sole translator. I offered to re-translate the Rivière correspondence for free, and my offer was accepted. And whereas I originally felt that Ashbery, already a leading poet of the so-called New York school, should translate the poetry, I decided to tackle it myself.

My first contract specified 30,000 words; a second one had to be drawn up for 85,000 words. By spring 1971 the book had swelled to 175,000 words with more coming. I decided to ask for a third contract, this time with a small royalty. With the help of Bob Gottlieb, the wunderkind of Simon & Schuster (by now editor in chief of Knopf), I drafted a letter to Roger Straus:

When I took on this project, I little realized either the volume of material that lay before me or the quality of the effort that would be required. Although some of the text consists of letters and articles written in a fairly straightforward prose, a great deal of it adopts a surrealistic or incantatory style which might as well be poetry. . . . In other words, what started out as a 135-page translation plus an editing job has gradually swelled into a 700-page volume, a sustained creative effort, a magnum opus which will, by the time it is completed, have received my primary energies and attentions for the better part of a year.

I told Roger that at the rate I was being paid for the job and given the time I was putting in on it, I was making a little less than a New York cab driver made before a recent rate hike. I went on to argue that literary translation was an art, that translators were shockingly underpaid for their work, and that in the case of an important and difficult author, particularly one who was dead, the translator should be entitled to a modest share of the royalties.

I urged Farrar, Straus to take the lead in reforming the present inequities.

I ended with a not-so-veiled threat to withhold delivery of the second half of the manuscript pending the promise of a new contract.

Well, Roger went ballistic. He called me on the phone and said, among other things, that he "could hear [my] balls clanking together." He claimed that his hands were tied, that the French publisher Gallimard would never agree to a translator's royalty. With Gottlieb's help I stuck to my guns and in the end the contract department was able to work out a new cost breakdown that included a one and a half percent royalty for me—and a better deal for Susan as well.

The bad news was that the contract was drawn up in such a way that the book would have to have been a best seller for me to start earning royalties, and unfortunately that was not the case. I never saw a cent beyond my standard translator's fee. But I did make my point and in the long run there were compensations that turned out to be more important than money.

In the short run there was the immense pleasure of working with Susan Sontag. I would send long lists of questions to her in Paris and would receive back long lists of answers, together with letters that warmed my heart: "Sharing this impossible, endless labor on Artaud with you has created a secret bond between us that I hope we'll be able to express some day." And after four pages of answers to my queries, "Dearest Helen, I'm grateful for all the work you've done. I, as well as St. Jerome (the patron saint of translators), bless you."

In October, 1972 my editor wrote me that Susan's forty-page introduction, which took her two years to complete, would be published in the *New Yorker* in April, 1973, and our book "immediately after." Ha! "Our book" was not published until 1976.

We were plagued by delays of various kinds, some endemic to a project of this magnitude (our copy editor, Carmen Gonzalez, was an angel of patience and precision), others more personal in nature. My original editor, who shall be nameless because although his work was excellent he either had a mental block about the Artaud or was simply overworked, sat on the book for the better part of two years. In the end it had to be pulled out from under him and given to Bob Giroux, now a partner, who shepherded it through to conclusion.

Susan and I almost always agreed on matters of style, but there were some amusing exceptions. In Artaud's *Letter to the Legislator of the Law on Narcotics* in which he argues for the legalization of the substances he needed to alleviate his pain (and which Lenny Bruce would have loved) there's a passage that goes "Anguish that drives men mad, anguish that drives men to suicide," etc.

Every time Susan, staunch women's libber that she was, got her hands on that page she would cross out "men" and write in "people," thus not only violating the music of the phrase, but forcing on Artaud a political consciousness alien to his own. Every time I got the manuscript back I would change "people" back to "men."

In the six and a half years it took to produce the book certain pages came to resemble war-torn Europe in the forties, or indeed, the battlefield of Artaud's own inner landscape. My translator's contract granted me "last look:" an opportunity to review any editorial changes before the manuscript went to the printer. My editors at Farrar, Straus honored our agreement, so on that and other fine points I had the last word.

Antonin Artaud: Selected Writings was finally published in the fall of 1976. The critics took the book seriously, a first for Artaud, and praised Sontag's work, especially her dazzlingly brilliant introduction. And to my delight the translation was well received. Roger Shattuck in the *New York Review of Books* wrote that "Artaud's voice is clearly audible, even in the texts that tremble on the threshold between poetry and prose;" and John Flutas in the *New Republic* wrote, "Helen Weaver's English flows as if Artaud, like Beckett, simultaneously made his own translations." It doesn't get any better than that.

In March 1977 Bob Giroux called to tell me that I had been nominated for the National Book Award in translation, along with Ch'en Li-Li, Robert Fagles, Gregory Rabassa, and Charles S. Singleton. The award went to Li-Li for *Master Tung's Western Chamber Romance*, a Chinese classic. I was actually relieved that I would not have to go to the city and make a speech.

I sent a copy of the book to Charles Reid, my high school French teacher. I would have sent one to Richard Howard as well, but I knew that Artaud was not his cup of tea.

The more interesting my translating assignments became—the more closely the process resembled the creative act of writing—the more I longed to be writing my own words rather than rendering the words of others while remaining myself invisible. In my desire to be a writer I had always felt limited by my inability to make up stories: to write fiction. But writing nonfiction presupposes expertise in some field: you have to know something about something, or at least think you do. Being immersed for all that time in Artaud, whose most compelling subject was his own mind, showed me that one need only be an expert on one's self: that ultimately, one could write about anything at all; that it could be, like *Seinfeld*, a show about nothing.

In any case, translating Artaud healed the split between my translating life and my "real" life. I didn't have to bury a rock title in this book. Artaud rocked, and rocked my life onto another level.

And after that, Allen always introduced me as "the woman who translated Artaud."

In the summer of 1978 Gerald Nicosia was doing research for a biography of Kerouac and interviewed me at my home in Woodstock.

I had resisted at first because I knew that eventually I would be writing a book of my own about Jack, but Gerry was persistent. Eventually I agreed to see him provided he sign a statement giving me full editorial control over any passages in his book that might result from the interview. He agreed.

He had also interviewed Helen Elliott, and the errors and distortions in the manuscript he sent me were no doubt attributable to her lapses of memory and to our current estrangement. I came off as a wealthy girl from Scarsdale who was horrified at the sight of the ragged poets who landed on her doorstep but who tried to trap Jack into a conventional marriage, and who threw him out because her analyst told her to. Arrrrrrrgh. . . .

Gerry honored our agreement. I revised the pages he sent me, and he made every one of my changes.

The same week I tweaked Gerry's version of my time with Jack a book of my own was about to go to press. Well, not altogether my own: McGraw-Hill had hired me to translate from the French a dictionary of astrology by a "practicing astrologer" who, it turned out, needed a lot more practice. His book was a veritable mine of misinformation, by which I do not mean that it was full of astrology. Whatever you may think of it, astrology is a coherent system that is not inherently inimical to science; it is simply based on a hypothesis that most scientists reject *a priori* as unworthy of examination. This gentleman was ignorant not only of astrology but of elementary astronomy. He lived in a universe, *par exemple,* where it was possible for Mercury to be opposite the sun. It can't happen here!

I convinced my editor at McGraw to let me revise and expand the book. I hired a Woodstock astrologer friend named Allan Edmands and enlisted the aid of several distinguished astrologers in America and England. In the end Allan and I basically rewrote the book, throwing out most of the original text, adding hundreds of new articles, and tripling it in size, with no reward other than the gratitude of the astrological community and the satisfaction of a job well done.

All the royalties went to this Frenchman (who, oddly enough, also wrote a book about Artaud). McGraw-Hill did zero promotion and New American Library sold twenty thousand copies of a paperback edition and then let it go out of print. I offered to buy the copies they had left in their warehouse but my offer was refused and the remaining copies were shredded. The project was a heartbreaker from start to finish. The *Larousse Encyclopedia of Astrology* is now generally regarded by astrologers as an out-of-print classic.

Needless to say, my father the scientist was horrified when I began the serious study of astrology in 1969. For years we couldn't talk about the subject at all.

Then, two years before he died, I began interviewing him on tape. I knew that I was going to lose him, and I wanted to hear his stories. Stories I had tuned out because I used to resent his monologues at the dinner table, I now wanted to know.

I began by bringing him various objects he had collected in his travels around the world: a set of temple carvings from Kyoto, a nineteenth-century wooden stirrup from Mexico, a pre-Columbian wine vessel in the shape of an otter, his shell collection exquisitely arranged in a rosewood cabinet from Hong Kong, a set of Egyptian prayer vials that were a gift from the mayor of Jerusalem. And he would start to talk.

Eventually, he began asking me about astrology and listening to my answers and—wonder of wonders!—at the end of his life, my father opened his mind to the astrological hypothesis, became excited about it, and wanted us to write a book together, to be called *The Dimensions of Personality*. But it was too late, he was too tired, and when Knopf asked me to translate *L'Homme devant la mort*, Philippe Ariès' magisterial study of death in the Christian West, Dad urged me to take that job instead.

Warren Weaver died on November 24, 1978, the day before Thanksgiving. A few years later I dedicated my work on the *Larousse Encyclopedia* to him.

In 1983 two important books about Jack Kerouac were published: Nicosia's critical biography *Memory Babe* and Joyce Johnson's *Minor Characters*, a memoir by the former Joyce Glassman, my ancient rival for Jack's affections.

I read Joyce's book with mingled envy and awe. She had learned her craft and wrote with grace, wit, and an ironic edge that accorded very well with the skepticism of the age.

I was ashamed that I had dismissed her as a dumb blonde. I found that any bitterness I had felt toward her was long gone. I didn't even mind that she caricatured me as a long-legged bitch from the Midwest who "made people dance with me" to my Elvis

Presley records. In her place I would have done the same, and anyway, she changed my name (and the other Helen's) to Virginia.

I read *Minor Characters* out loud to my eighty-nine-year-old mother, who drank in every word as if it were the juiciest soap opera since *Days of Our Lives*. I was now living in New Milford, where I had moved to take care of her. I wrote a rave review of the book for the *Woodstock Times* and sent a copy of my review to Joyce at Dial Press, where she was now an editor.

My review ended with, "I'd like to hand Joyce a bouquet of roses. And I'd like to think that after all these years, she'd be willing to take them from me."

I was Ruth Heaper in *Desolation Angels*, Virginia in *Minor Characters*, and myself in *Memory Babe*. When was I going to tell my own story in my own voice?

A VISIT TO A POET

Be kind to the universe of Self that
  trembles and shudders and thrills
  in XX Century,
that opens its eyes and belly and breast
  chained with flesh to feel
  the myriad flowers of bliss
  that I Am to Thee—

—Allen Ginsberg, *Who Be Kind To*

In the summer of 1985 I took my Woodstock friend Miriam Berg to meet Allen Ginsberg in his apartment in the East Village.

Standing on East 12th Street in front of his building I remembered Allen's instructions and directed a lusty shout up to the fourth floor. Almost immediately Allen appeared naked at the window and threw down a black sock with the key in it. We entered a tenement hall with broken mosaic tile on the floor in the shape of a six-pointed star and a dirty marble staircase.

Four flights up a door opened at the end of the hall and an old coot, bearded like the Ancient Mariner, appeared and ushered us in. He had long greasy gray hair tied back in a ponytail, a big hump on his back, bare swollen feet, open sores on his arms and legs, owlish glasses, and a gray beard and moustache. Through bad teeth he introduced himself as Harry Smith. He said that Allen was taking a shower. He told us to sit in the kitchen and have tea.

Allen yelled from the shower to please put a cup of bleach in the washing machine, that the bleach was in a bottle at the foot of the machine, that he'd be right out. I found the bleach bottle and a ceramic mug and added bleach to the agitating shirts in the old top-loading washer. It was booming loudly in the tenement kitchen, making it difficult to talk, especially to Harry Smith who mumbled throwaway lines like "What mortals these fools be!" out of the side of his mouth.

Harry asked us if we wanted coffee. We declined. He told us he drank hot water with lemon and honey. I remembered reading an article that said that Allen drank hot water with lemon in the morning. Harry pointed to a mug in front of him and commented, "That was warm once."

I got up and found a pot, put it on the stove, and tried various burners, accidentally pulling off a burner knob. Harry Smith exploded that he had fixed that knob and I'd ruined it, but somehow his irascibility was tongue-in-cheek; there was the hint of a twinkle in his eye. I ignored his ranting and proceeded to make hot lemon and honey for all. Under duress, Harry allowed me to add hot water to his tepid cup. I admired a beautiful mug with a multicolored oriental design. After I picked it up Harry said, "No one is allowed to touch that cup! It's Allen's cup and a Chinese doctor gave it to him." (Later Allen said this was nonsense.)

Harry stated that white sugar was bad for you, honey was OK. Harry smoked Salems and punctuated his conversation with phrases from Gilbert and Sullivan operettas such as "A paradox a paradox a most ingenious paradox."

Allen came in with wet hair, wearing a white shirt and pants. He shook hands with Miriam, remembered meeting her at Omega, the holistic center in Rhinebeck. Her madrigal group, Woodstock Renaissance, had been studying with an ensemble called The Western Wind the same week Allen gave a poetry workshop. I stood up and Allen and I hugged and kissed. Allen said, "Long time no see."

Allen opened the lid of the washing machine and took out a shirt. The machine hadn't extracted all the water. I helped Allen wring shirts out in the sink.

Bob Rosenthal, Allen's secretary, a nice-looking young man in a black short-sleeved T-shirt and jeans, arrived, carrying an enormous load of mail: two ten-inch stacks, a typical day's mail.

He took the mail into Allen's study in the back of the flat, a hot messy room with closed windows which I recognized from an article in the *New York Times Magazine*. Bob's job, for which Allen paid him a thousand dollars a month, was to answer the phone and take care of the mail so Allen wouldn't be inundated. Allen shuddered at the amount of mail.

Bob Rosenthal did something to the washing machine and it spun out the clothes. Allen found some wire hangers and I helped him hang up blue shirts on a bar in the hallway so he would have clean shirts for the Ezra Pound Conference in Maine the next day.

Bob Rosenthal walked through this scene with a low-key quiet dedication, calmly tolerating disorder and Allen's friends. Allen introduced us to Bob, who was polite but absorbed in his work, and he reintroduced us to Harry Smith. He said Harry was a filmmaker and record producer, that he had lived for twelve years in the Chelsea Hotel.

Allen found a tiny microphone set up on the kitchen table. It had looked like a cigarette lighter to me. Harry had been recording all the sounds in the room. He claimed that today he was just testing the microphone. Allen said that Harry Smith drove him crazy recording everything that went on but that his tapes of street noises were great *musique concrète*.

Harry asked Miriam what she did. She said, "Singer." What kind? "Renaissance." Miriam and I sang a verse of "Noel Sing We Now All and Some" and Allen said, "Exquisite."

I had a list of things to ask Allen. Was the rosette in his buttonhole in the picture on the back of his book jacket really the American Academy of Arts and Letters? It was! What time was Peter Orlovsky born? "No idea." Where was he born? "Around the corner." I wrote "NYC" in my notebook. I gave Allen a gift certificate for a shiatsu massage with my friend Steve. I tucked it into the frame of a big photograph of Tolstoy on the mantle.

Allen said his new thing was photography. Two photographer friends, Robert Frank and Berenice Abbott, were helping him learn the craft. He had two cameras, a Rolleiflex and a little Olympus. He took a lot of pictures of Miriam and me. He had trouble with the mechanics, forgot to focus, said "One two three!"

before he pressed the shutter. He showed us a box of 8 x 10s and three boxes of 11x17s, pictures from 1953 to the present: some great old pictures of Jack Kerouac in 1953 looking like a god, Neal Cassady, Gregory Corso, William Burroughs, San Francisco friends. Many of these were very good, some were great. Allen knew how to compose and when to shoot and of course he had always known incredible people. One of Julian Beck, the actor and director, in a hospital bed looking almost dead but radiant (he recovered and was in remission) was miraculous.

Allen got a phone call from Bob Dylan, who wanted him to go to Russia with him to meet with Yevtushenko. Allen hadn't heard from Dylan in a long time, half wondered if it was a plot.

His next call was from a sound equipment store on Union Square. Allen had left his MasterCard there and he had to go over and retrieve it.

Harry complained that Allen didn't cook for him. He said, "Your suggestion that I put my foot in the refrigerator and stir is impractical." Allen asked if I would make Harry some Farina. I agreed. As I cooked, Harry dictated a shopping list which included caviar, sour cream, yogurt, paper towels, and Farina (the box was almost empty). Harry played a record of an opera singer from the 1920s for Miriam, told her she couldn't leave until it was over.

After much shuffling around and more demands from Harry, we left with Allen. Just before we went Harry told us that he didn't really like Allen, but he was the only one who would take him in. I believed him, but I also believed that he did like Allen. How could anyone not like Allen?

On the way down the stairs Allen said that he and Harry got on each other's nerves, that he thought he had hit him once in exasperation, but that he would only be there for ten more days and then some other people, an artist couple with a home in the country, would be taking him in.

Ten days of Harry sounded like an eternity to me.

As long as I had known Allen there had always been someone like Harry Smith, someone who was Not Quite Right, as my mother would say, whom Allen was giving shelter to, lurking around the place. It was almost as if Allen, whose mother died in an insane asylum, had to have someone a little marginal around to feel at home.

We decided to have lunch in a Hungarian restaurant around the corner. Allen became more relaxed and expansive outside of his apartment. He ordered cheese blintzes with sour cream and applesauce, Miriam had homemade mushroom barley soup, I ordered borscht. We all had big glasses of freshly squeezed orange juice. Allen borrowed newspapers off a nearby table and read about a hijacking. He said he used to be obsessed with the news, read the *New York Times* from cover to cover every day.

Allen asked us both about our love lives and what we did for money and listened attentively to our answers.

I told him I was in a celibate phase but had wonderful dreams: "I make it with Mozart in period costume!"

He asked me why I never remarried.

"I guess I've gotten too fussy. No one marriageable has crossed my path. I've had a series of bizarre affairs. I guess I'm not really a householder." He nodded.

Miriam said she was married. Allen looked at her incredulously. (Miriam is a big beautiful woman who at that time weighed about three hundred pounds.)

Allen said, "You're *married*? You have a *husband*?"

Miriam said, "Yes, I'm married, and I have a husband."

Allen said, "He likes big women?"

Miriam said, "Yes."

Allen said, "There's somebody for everybody!"

I noticed that this was a terrible thing to say and I suffered for my friend, but nobody called Allen's attention to it and the lunch went on.

In spite of this trouble spot it was a lovely lunch. A friend of Allen's from his building walked by and Allen asked him to join us, introduced everyone. I could hear people at the table behind me muttering "Allen Ginsberg . . . Beat poet. . . ."

After lunch, we shared a cab over to Union Square so Allen could pick up his credit card. Allen sat up front with the driver to make room for Miriam and they carefully worked out the route, discussing one-way streets for maximum efficiency. When we dropped Allen off he said goodbye to Miriam. I gave him my hand and he kissed it. He looked in the window at us from the street corner and said, "Toodle-oo!"

After we drove away Miriam said, "He's a nice guy." This, in spite of the fact that he had offended her. Later she said that his fat-phobic remark seemed out of character for him, but I said "No, he has blind spots and prejudices like everybody else."

I thought—I still think—that Allen's unconsciously cruel remark was really a reflection of the way he felt about his own body: that so often when we say hurtful things we are really talking about ourselves. I meant to say something to Allen, or write him a letter about it, because I didn't think he would deliberately hurt anybody. But I never did. Too bad, because I think he would have thanked me for it.

THE CITY OF SPINDLES

The town is Galloway. The Merrimac River, broad and placid, flows down to it from the New Hampshire hills, broken at the falls to make frothy havoc on the rocks, foaming on over ancient stone towards a place where the river suddenly swings about in a wide and peaceful basin, moving on now around the flank of the town, on to places known as Lawrence and Haverhill, through a wooded valley, and on to the sea at Plum Island, where the river enters an infinity of waters and is gone. Somewhere far north of Galloway, in headwaters close to Canada, the river is continually fed and made to brim out of endless sources and unfathomable springs.

—Jack Kerouac, *The Town and the City*

In the summer of 1986 I was seeing a man who was into what he called Earth Mysteries: ancient megalithic structures that were still standing all over twentieth-century America. New England was particularly rich in these anomalies. Enrique had taken me to see stone chambers and dolmens in Putnam County and we had spent the night of the summer solstice at Mystery Hill, a place known as "America's Stonehenge" in North Salem, New Hampshire. Enrique knew of a Druids Mound in Lowell, Massachusetts, so on the way home we stopped to see that and also to visit Kerouac's grave.

Gerald Nicosia describes Lowell, with its empty mill buildings and ninety bars for a hundred thousand people, as "the most horrible place in the world," a town that never really emerged from the Great Depression of the nineteen-thirties. And in her

1973 biography of Kerouac Ann Charters describes Lowell as "poor, dirty, and rundown" and "not a town that's easy to feel sentimental about." They both wrote as if it was some kind of a miracle that a great writer could come out of such an awful place. So I was not prepared to discover that Lowell is beautiful.

My first view, out the window of Enrique's car, took my breath away: red brick factory buildings with tall smokestacks across a series of bridges that gave a European feeling, hilly streets with Victorian San Francisco houses that made me realize how Jack must have loved and felt right at home in that town. Later I learned that the Industrial Revolution began in Lowell; those red brick factories were the oldest ones in America.

Edson Cemetery is similar to some of the great French cemeteries which are also parks. Instead of the usual expanse of greensward with military rows of gravestones and here and there a tree, Edson is broken up by a series of avenues which are in turn intersected by a series of lanes, creating many small areas full of trees and flowers, all beautifully kept but not too formal.

Jack's family is on Seventh Avenue, and his stone is flush with the earth. Even the grass was taller than it was, with a modest profusion of flowers all around. A sheaf of half a dozen red roses had been cut and placed there that day. The stone itself is simple granite with the words "Ti Jean / John L. Kerouac / March 12, 1922–October 21, 1969 / He honored life." And below that, "Stella his wife / November 11, 1918—". (In 1966 Jack had married Stella Sampas, a Greek nurse whom he had known since his high school days in Lowell.)

On the left side was carved an emblem of the Holy Ghost as a dove descending with the host in its mouth. The peace and cared-for-ness, the disciplined abundance of those flowers, all contrasted so vividly with the quality of his life.

There was a guitar pick on the grave. I've been back many times since, and there are always offerings: empty wine bottles or beer cans, rolled joints or roaches, I Ching coins, peace buttons, candle wax, poems, flowers: you name it. Once even a typewriter, I understand. Jack's in-laws, the Sampases, have to come and clean off his grave on a regular basis.

What with its crazy quilt design, many one-way streets, lack of street signs—only one-quarter of Lowell's streets have signs—and the tendency of the natives to steal the few there are, Lowell is a difficult town for visitors to drive in. It took Enrique and me forever to find our way out of Lowell. We kept missing the turn for the Lowell Connector and going back and forth over the same roads. It probably didn't help that both the driver and the navigator were stoned. Enrique kept sticking his head out the window of his car and shouting, "Jack, we can't get out of Lowell!"

Jack, we decided, was the Lowell Connector.

Francis Cabot Lowell, the pioneer American cotton manufacturer for whom the town was named, was related to the poets Amy Lowell and James Russell Lowell and to Percival Lowell, the astronomer who predicted the orbit of Pluto, and was an ancestor of the poet Robert Lowell as well.

In *A Week on the Concord and Merrimack Rivers* Thoreau called Lowell "the city of spindles and Manchester of America, which sends its cotton cloth round the globe." After Manchester, England, Lowell had the largest collection of cotton mills in the world. The Industrial Revolution moved south because union labor was too expensive and Lowell was too poor to rebuild. Now most of the town has been designated a national park, so it's frozen in time. The whole town is a memorial to a vanished America, with a heavy overlay of French Catholicism: Holy Ghost Park, Jeanne d'Arc Credit Union, St. Joseph's Hospital. Many churches and yes, many bars—Jack's dichotomy in stone.

When I first visited Lowell the only public memorial to its most famous, or infamous, native son, was the gravestone in Edson Cemetery. Allen said it was an international disgrace that there was no monument to Jack in his own home town. The conservative element in Lowell saw him as a drunken bum who happened to be a writer and who had been periodically dragged home from bars by his Greek in-laws.

In January, 1986 the Lowell Historic Preservation Commission voted to establish the Jack Kerouac Commemorative and in

October the Lowell City Council voted seven to one to locate the Commemorative at the Eastern Canal Plaza, a parcel of land off Bridge Street near the Massachusetts Mills. The one dissenting vote was cast by a harsh critic and the ensuing controversy became national news. Norman Podhoretz led the attack with a syndicated column objecting to a memorial to a man whose writings, along with those of Allen Ginsberg, had helped to spawn the counterculture of the 1960s and had "played a part in ruining a great many young people who were influenced by their distaste for normal life and common decency." But the *Boston Globe* and the *Washington Post* praised Lowell's action, to which a former critic of Jack's, John Updike, had lent his support.

The Jack Kerouac Commemorative was created by sculptor Ben Woitena and dedicated on June 25, 1988. Paul Marion, Cultural Affairs Director of the Lowell Historic Preservation Commission, who led the campaign for the commemorative, wrote that this monument "breaks new ground in the way we publicly recognize the achievements of American writers."

Passages from ten of Kerouac's books are inscribed on eight columns of polished granite that are arranged in a kind of Christian-Buddhist mandala that forms a cross within a circle. The columns with passages from his Lowell books—*The Town and the City, Maggie Cassidy, Doctor Sax, Visions of Gerard, Lonesome Traveler* and *Vanity of Duluoz*—and from *On the Road* are on the perimeter of the paved plaza, while those from the more esoteric or spiritual books, *Mexico City Blues, Book of Dreams,* and *The Scripture of the Golden Eternity,* are in the center of the space.

Marion writes:

The literature is presented in the open air, sand-blasted into the reddish brown granite. . . . For an artist who so loved the American landscape, it is appropriate that the Kerouac Commemorative is of the American earth. The granite was quarried in South Dakota; the stones were cut in Minnesota; West Virginian graphic designers worked on the text; the sculptor is a Texan who studied art in southern California.

I visited the Jack Kerouac Commemorative in 1989 and I, who had not shed a tear when Jack died twenty years before, was moved by Lowell's recognition of its native son. Standing in front of the granite slab on which the opening lines of *On the Road* are engraved, my tears finally came.

I moved on to the column with the first paragraph of *The Town and the City*. I remembered first reading those lines lying in bed in my room on West 11th Street after Jack had gone down south for Christmas and thinking to myself, *By God, he can write!* I remembered all the contempt that had been poured on Jack's writing, how Truman Capote had sneered, "It's not writing—it's *typing!*" And I thought, *Nobody has engraved his words on stone.*

I went back to Lowell many times. I took photographs of the house on Lupine Road where Jack was born; the Stations of the Cross with its horrific bas-relief sculptures that had terrified him as a child; the Lowell Library where he used to rush on Saturdays for "avidities of reading;" Ste. Jeanne d'Arc, scene of his first communion and of a later vision; St. Jean Baptiste, the church where his service was held; and many of the houses where his peripatetic family had lived.

Lowell reminded me of my own childhood. It was the houses: the beautiful innocent Victorian houses like the ones Edward Hopper and John Button painted and loved. The poured concrete steps of the Sherman-Berry house where I stayed were exactly like the steps of my grandmother's house in Madison.

Falling in love with Lowell, I fell in love with Jack all over again. I realized that I had been angry at Jack for years: for disappointing me, for not being the answer to my prayers, for failing to deliver on my version of the American dream.

Now, for the first time since he died, I wanted to read his books, all the ones I had never bothered to read, and to reread the ones I'd read with the jaundiced eye of the disappointed lover.

When I read *The Town and the City* for the first time and recognized Jack's talent, I was still in love with him and still under the spell of our mutual dream, our mutual illusion of love ever after and logs on the fire. By the time I read *On the Road* I had lost that dream. I was bitter and angry. I couldn't hear the poetry.

I knew that Jack's correspondence with Neal Cassady was the catalyst for Jack's finding his voice. So Neal was important, but I couldn't warm up to Dean Moriarty, the Neal character in the book, who raced around stealing cars and juggling women—a male chauvinist if there ever was one. I wasn't a feminist yet, but I couldn't see past the sexism to the music of Jack's words.

In my journal, I held *On the Road* up against other books, well-made novels with characters that developed instead of being stuck in amber, trapped in the endless repetition of their "self-made suicidal cage of rage, their false dream of freedom."

What are you rebelling against? the chick had asked Marlon Brando in *The Wild One.*

What've you got? he famously replied.

Their rebellion was my rebellion, but I wasn't allowed to join it.

I couldn't forgive the "lack of discipline" in his writing because I couldn't forgive the "lack of discipline" in his life. I couldn't forgive him for being late for dinner, for not taking care of me. For taking care of his mother and his writing, but not me.

But now I was able to read those books without ambivalence. Having finally forgiven Jack, I was free to listen to his voice.

Jack always said that his books were poems, but I never really believed him. I remember the exact moment when I discovered that it was true.

I was visiting my niece Annie and her boyfriend Nate up in Vermont. I had brought my tapes of Lord Buckley to play for them, as part of their education. In between Buckley bits Nate played his records of John Coltrane. A big poster of him was on the wall.

I was talking about Kerouac and how he uses words I didn't know and also makes up words and lately I'd started looking them up. Words like *prognathic* (jutting-jawed) and *hincty*: that last one wasn't in Webster's Unabridged, and I wondered if he made it up.

So Nate got his Oxford English Dictionary down from the top of the bookshelf. Even with a magnifying glass the type was too small for me, so Annie read the definition out loud. It said "hincty" was American slang and meant conceited, snobbish, stuck up, and it quoted (among others), J. Kerouac, *On Road* (*sic*), "Wetting their eyebrows with hincty fingertip." The OED said it was on page 86 but we looked in Nate's paperback copy of *On the Road* and we couldn't find it.

Just in case we missed it I read page 86 out loud while John Coltrane blew. That page fell in the middle of the story about the little Mexican girl, with a great description of the streets of Hollywood.

And that was when it happened. For the first time in my life, I heard the music of Kerouac's words. For the first time in my life, I *got* it. And I remembered hearing somewhere that people who don't think Kerouac is a great writer should try reading him aloud.

I learned recently that when Henry James used to visit Edith Wharton at The Mount in Lenox, Massachusetts, she got Henry James to like Walt Whitman by reading him out loud. Henry James, who didn't like anything or anybody! That's the secret, that's the test of poetry. And that's the reason *On the Road* has sold over three million copies. *On the Road* is a poem.

At Oberlin my favorite professor, Andrew Bongiorno, had told us that *Vanity Fair* was a poem. I never really understood that, but I believed it. Now I saw what he meant. "Great prose is poetry," Yuri, the Gregory Corso character, says in *The Subterraneans*.

But it was when I first read *Doctor Sax* that the scales fell from my eyes:

It was in Centralville I was born, in Pawtucketville saw Doctor Sax. Across the wide basin to the hill—on Lupine Road, March 1922, at five o'clock in the afternoon of a red-all-over suppertime, as drowsily beers were tapped in Moody and Lakeville saloons and the river rushed with her cargoes of ice over reddened slick rocks, and on the shore the reeds swayed among mattresses and cast-off boots of Time, and lazily pieces of snow dropped plunk from bagging branches of black thorny oily pine in their thaw, and beneath the wet snows of the hillside receiving the sun's lost rays the melts of winter mixed with roars of Merrimac—I was born.

Doctor Sax is an evocation of Jack's childhood and early adolescence in Lowell, a blend of memory and dreams, and his imaginary friend Doctor Sax is a blend of The Shadow (from the nineteen-thirties radio program of the same name), Dr. Faustus, W. C. Fields, and a local hawk-nosed pool shark whom Jack admired as a boy.

Like all of Kerouac's writing, and like his life, this childhood fantasy is haunted by the presence of death. "Death hovers over my pencil," he wrote in *The Vanity of Duluoz*. His brother Gerard died when Jack was four years old, and when he was twelve he and his mother saw a man carrying a watermelon drop dead of a heart attack as they were walking across the Moody Street Bridge, an event he recreates in *Doctor Sax*.

Doctor Sax is a dark book, and Doctor Sax is a shade, a denizen of darkness, dumps, mists, fogs, and moonlight. In a very real sense, darkness was Kerouac's element as well. The composer and performance artist David Amram tells how once he and Jack were walking on MacDougal Street in the Village and Amram suggested that they cross the road so they could walk "on the sunny side of the street." But Jack refused to cross over because, as he told David, "a writer must be a shadow."

The bright light of television and the glare of media attention were not for him. In a way he was our collective shadow, in the Jungian sense. He articulated and embodied America's dark side, he exposed our national denial of death, and that is one reason we rejected him.

But *Doctor Sax* is not all darkness and death. When I reread it recently it occurred to me that the heart and soul of the book, and the most important character in it, is not Doctor Sax or even the narrator, Jackie Duluoz, but the Merrimack River, and the river represents life. At the Stations of the Cross, "Everything there was to remind of Death, and nothing in praise of life—except the roar of the humpbacked Merrimac passing over rocks in formations and arms of foam. . . ."

And the roar of the humpbacked "Merrimac" (Jack always leaves off the final "k," maybe because it looks more French without it) is ever-present, sounding in Jack's ear and providing the *basso continuo* and the vital energy of the book, and the Great Flood of March 1936 is the book's climactic center. *Doctor Sax* is not so much a novel as an ode to a river, and Sax is its river god, its tutelary spirit and *genius loci:*

Deep in myself I'm mindful of the action of the river, in words that sneak slowly like the river, and sometimes flood, the wild Merrimac is in her lark of Spring lally-da'ing down the pale of mordant shores with a load of humidus aquabus aquatum the size of which was one brown rushing sea.

So the book is really neither all darkness nor all light but rather *chiaroscuro*, like the conundrum of Kerouac himself who all his life alternated between the gloomy credo at the end of *On the Road*—"I wrote the book because we're all gonna die"—and the equally strong belief that "life is holy and every moment is precious."

Doctor Sax is a work of tremendous energy, invention, mystery, emotional power, cinematic drama, humor, mythology, and philosophy; a work of personal confession and a fable of mythic grandeur; an epic poem of preadolescent fear, glee, and wonder: a classic.

Mozart even makes a cameo appearance as Amadeus Baroque.

What gives the book its real power and keeps it from flying away into pure fantasy is the constant rich detailed evocation of Jack's actual childhood in Lowell, a miraculous achievement in itself after an interim of nineteen years.

Like Proust, Kerouac is all about memory and time:

A shudder of joy ran through me—when I read of Proust's teacup—all those saucers in a crumb—all of History by thumb— all of a city in a tasty crumb—I got all my boyhood in vanilla winter waves around the kitchen stove.

If Lowell brought me back to Jack, it was *Doctor Sax* that brought me to my knees before the rushing river of his words.

IT'S ALL A DREAM

I intended to pray . . . as my only activity, pray for all living creatures; I saw it was the only decent activity left in the world.

— Jack Kerouac, *The Dharma Bums*

I fought the Dharma, and the Dharma won.

— Allen Ginsberg, *Do the Meditation Rock*

I began work on this book on Good Friday in 1990.

On Holy Saturday I went down to the New Milford Library to see what I could find out about Jack Kerouac in this picturesque little New England town whose green, with its World War II tank and bandstand, had once appeared on the cover of the *Saturday Evening Post*.

I learned that eighteen of Jack's books were still in print, many in recent editions. And how many of those eighteen were in the New Milford Library? None. Not one! Not even *On the Road*! Oh, they had *On the Road in an RV*, *On the Road with Charles Kuralt*, *On the Road with John James Audubon*—even *On the Road with the Rolling Stones*—but no *On the Road* with Sal Paradise and Dean Moriarty. I observed in my journal, "This is one uptight, conservative, Bible-thumping, boring ass town."

In May that year I told Allen I had finally started writing my memoir of Jack. I said I didn't know why it had taken me thirty-four years. Allen said, "Ripeness is all."

Four years later, his message was simpler: "Hurry." Allen was a sick man, which did not keep him from flying all over the world

188 • THE AWAKENER

giving readings and interviews, teaching, speaking, encouraging poets and fighting for the cause of free speech wherever he could. As early as 1986 he told me, "I'm steering my course between the Scylla of hypoglycemia and the Charybdis of kidney stones and gout, which are mutually exclusive."

In the spring of 1990 I went to Lowell to work with the Kerouac archives at the University there. At Mogan Cultural Center, which houses the University's library, I saw Jack's rucksack and typewriter inside a glass display case. I was kneeling before this shrine and making a list of everything that was in his rucksack when some school children came through on a tour. I must have looked like a statue because their teacher said, "We thought you were part of the display."

I said, "I am!"

Gerald Nicosia had given me permission to listen to tapes of the interviews he had done for his biography of Jack and to make copies of the transcripts he had made. Standing at the copy machine with headphones on I heard Helen Elliott's voice for the first time in years. I could hear the ice in her glass tinkling on the tape. I remembered that Nicosia had told me she kept him up all night talking and drinking.

I learned that when Jack called her up in the middle of the night she did not brush him off as I had done. For her it was a point of honor never to hang up on Jack Kerouac. I was glad that one of the Helens was available when he was so lonely in the last years of his life.

Someone had made a tape of Jack reading from *Doctor Sax* and *Old Angel Midnight* with the bluest of Sinatra's albums, *In the Wee Small Hours*, playing in the background. Jack would break off from time to time to sing along with Frank, harmonizing on "I Get Along Without You Very Well," occasionally singing alone with the orchestra. When he sang "Look at you: if you had a sense of humor, you would laugh to beat the band," he sounded so much like Frank it was almost impossible to tell the difference.

I stood there with the headphones on, xeroxing and weeping.

In November Dan Wakefield asked me to come to the city so he could interview me for his book *New York in the Fifties*. The Peacock, our favorite coffeehouse, was still there on Greenwich Avenue, so that's where we met.

We talked about Jack. I told Dan I had completely underestimated him as a writer and he said that he had, too. Back in 1958 he had written a snide put-down of a performance of Jack's at the Village Vanguard for the *Nation*. But when *Desolation Angels* was published in 1965, Dan reviewed the book for the *Atlantic Monthly* in what amounted to a public apology:

Probably no other American writer . . . has been subjected to such a barrage of ridicule, venom, and cute-social-acumen as Kerouac. For years now he has been battered by aloof social and literary observers, including myself, who have never failed to make satirical mileage out of his connection with the no longer fashionable Beat brigade. . . . The book is very sad and sometimes funny, sparing of neither the hero-narrator nor his fellow travelers, and it provides a far better feeling of the awful forlornness of modern Bohemian life than could possibly have been conveyed by any of us condescending outsiders.

I told Dan I had gone through a similar process and that I had no idea how good a writer Jack was until I read *Doctor Sax*. Reading it made me feel ashamed for my multiple rejections of him as a man and as a writer. I felt that we all owed him an apology. I said that I was writing my own book about him, at least in part, as an act of atonement.

Dan had just interviewed Allen Ginsberg a few days before. He and Allen had talked about the mystery of time, and about growing older. Allen had recently taken his aunt to dinner on her eighty-fifth birthday. Allen had asked his aunt what she had learned by now, what life was all about, and she had said, "Life is a dream. It's all a dream."

As Dan and I walked around the Village we commented on all the changes that had occurred: the Howard Johnson's on the corner of Eighth Street and Sixth Avenue where Joyce Glassman met Jack Kerouac replaced by a bookstore; the Loew's Sheridan

Theater where I stole the H for Helen's and my door torn down to make room for a maritime building.

I said, "You know, when I see the Village now, with all the new buildings instead of the places we knew and these kids walking around as if it was *their* Village, I have the feeling that what we see now is just a stage set, a facade, and the real Village, our Village, is still there underneath, just like it used to be. The facade takes in the new generation, but it doesn't fool a pair of old-timers like you and me."

And I told him, "We have to write our books, because we're survivors."

In the fall of 1991 Dan gave me a gift subscription to *Tricycle: The Buddhist Review*, a new magazine whose premiere issue arrived with a big picture of the Dalai Lama on the cover. Dan had written a book review for that issue and they had given him a free subscription for a friend. Dan chose me because I had recently told him that I'd become a Buddhist.

Say what?

Well, I'd tried everything else.

Raised as a Christian and forced to attend Sunday School and church—two whole hours of organized religion—I had renounced all that as soon as I got to college and out from under my mother's control. I celebrated my newfound freedom by putting a sign on my door with the words that appear over the entrance to the underworld in Dante's *Inferno:* "*Lasciate ogni speranza, voi che entrate*" (Abandon all hope, ye who enter here). For years I thought of myself as an atheist.

But even as a child I had loved the Christian hymns I sang in the choir and I was always fascinated by the practice of communion. And then living in Greece something about the light there had turned me into a believer.

When I first moved to Woodstock in the seventies I had another stab at Christianity. At the Church of Christ on the Mount, a tiny miniature cathedral in the woods presided over by "hippie priest" Father Francis, a friend of Bob Dylan, there was no confession, no offering collected, no dress code, anyone could take communion, and Sunday morning services started at a compassionate eleven a.m. My kind of church! The denomination was Old Catholic—the western branch of the Eastern Orthodox rite, which split off from Rome in the nineteenth century over the issue of papal infallibility. So far, so good.

But although I had a great time singing in a choir made up of Buddhists, Hindus, Jews, students of Native American spirituality, agnostics, and even a few Christians, there were parts of the liturgy I simply couldn't go along with. I hated all those *mea culpas*, all that guilty breast-beating, and I had to cross my fingers during the Nicene Creed where it says that Jesus Christ is the *only* son of God. I didn't believe that for a minute.

W. H. Auden said the two hardest things to hold onto were the Christian Trinity and the galley proofs of a book. I agree, and I've always found that particular trinity a wee bit unbalanced. Let's face it: the Christian trinity as it has come down to us in the West consists of two men and a bird: a glaring lack of female energy. I understand that in the East the Holy Ghost is Hagia Sophia, the goddess of holy wisdom. That makes a lot more sense to me.

I revere the teachings of Jesus as expressed in the Sermon on the Mount. But I don't believe in original sin, and I don't think Jesus did, either. I think it was St. Augustine who came up with that one four centuries later. I particularly dislike the doctrine of redemption, which Paul borrowed from the pagan mystery cults and which is all too reminiscent of the barbaric practice of animal sacrifice. I don't want anyone paying for my sins. I hope to learn from my mistakes. I believe that when I die, I'll be my own judge and jury. Amen.

After giving up on Christianity, at least in its organized, churchgoing form, I'd sampled a whole smorgasbord of what Lenny called nonscheduled theologies, of which there was no lack in Woodstock. I'd fallen for gurus only to get up and walk away because I couldn't tolerate their lack of tolerance for other religions or the holier-than-thou attitudes of their followers.

I had studied Native American spirituality, attended Medicine Wheel gatherings, built a medicine wheel and a sweat lodge in my mother's woods. After that it was feminine spirituality, goddess worship, and witchcraft. I had always been drawn to traditions that honored the Earth. Some of the most profound spiritual experiences of my life had taken place outdoors, in nature.

When Andy and I were living on the island of Cos that first summer, something happened that permanently altered my perception of reality. I call it my Ant Illumination.

Every day we would pick up lunch for a few drachmas and have a picnic at our favorite spot on the beach, within swimming distance of Turkey. And every day, the ants would collect our crumbs and haul them back to a nearby anthill.

Sometimes we would smoke a joint and become absorbed in watching the activities of the ants. We would drop stones on the ant hill, blocking the entrance, and watch in stoned fascination as the ants scurried around, creating another entrance in seconds.

One day, after one of our bombings, we noticed an ant that had been wounded. Another ant was struggling to drag the wounded ant back to the hill, but she wasn't strong enough. The helper ant went back to the hill, disappeared for a moment, and re-emerged with a third ant. Together they returned to the wounded ant, and one on either end, as if holding a litter, they carefully dragged their comrade back to the hill.

They might as well have had little red crosses on their caps.

There were no more bombings after that.

After the Ant Illumination, I began to practice kindness to insects. To this day, I escort bugs outside in jars, provide rafts for drowning ones, coexist peacefully with spiders.

In a letter to his friend John Clellon Holmes Jack once wrote that when the aliens finally landed on planet Earth, they would be shocked to see the way humans treat their animal brothers and sisters, "down to the very worms yay."

One thing I did like about Jack's Buddhism was its respect for all sentient beings.

But I didn't like what Allen called his "gloomy harping on the First Noble Truth" of the Buddha, that life is suffering. Buddhism gave him a metaphysics that explained and justified his own intuitive sense of impermanence and loss. Even in his first book, *The Town and the City*, there is a sadness underlying everything and a sense that "nothing is real."

When I was twenty-five and in love with Jack I didn't want to hear that life is suffering and that it was a sin to bring children into the world. I didn't believe that the solid world around me was an illusion. I thought that Jack was using this borrowed philosophy to justify his irresponsible behavior. When I tried to talk about our problems he would just say, "Everything is fine, don't worry, it's all a *dream*!" I thought that was a load of crap. So at that time Buddhism—at least Jack's version of Buddhism—was my enemy.

But as I aged, and especially after my father died, I began to accept the idea of life as tragic. Even the idea that the physical world is an illusion began to sound less strange, especially in the light of quantum physics. At age sixty Jack's mantra that "nothing is real, it's all a dream" began to make perfect sense to me. In fact, it sounded like a pretty accurate description of the universe.

Around the time I started going to Lowell, I finally got around to reading a little book my Woodstock friends had been telling me about for years: *The Miracle of Mindfulness* by the Vietnamese Buddhist monk Thich Nhat Hanh. As soon as I got to page three, where he talks about "washing the dishes in order to wash the dishes," I was hooked. I felt as if I had come home.

Through this poet and Zen master who was exiled from Vietnam for his peace activities and nominated for the Nobel Peace Prize by Martin Luther King Jr., I was gradually drawn to the Dharma. In 1991 I went on a silent retreat with Thich Nhat Hanh at Omega, a spiritual learning center in Rhinebeck, New York. On the last day I took the Buddhist vows known as The Five Precepts.

A few years later, at the Padmasambhava Buddhist Center in West Palm Beach, Florida, I fell in love with two Tibetan monks, Khenpo Palden Sherab Rinpoche and his younger brother Khenpo Tsewang Dongyal Rinpoche, who had escaped from Tibet, and renewed my Buddhist vows. I even got a Buddhist name, Padma Kadron, which I was told meant "Lotus who maintains the light of beneficial action."

Allen wrote me from Prague:

Delighted you took refuge and the teachers Khenpo Palden and brother are supposed to be excellent persons, and Nyingma [lineage] the creme de la creme tho all roads go nowhere so to speak. . . . All that Buddha bio. in Tricycle [the magazine published *Wake Up!*, Jack's life of the Buddha, in 1993] *was 1955 and before—Jack was preternaturally gifted in that understanding tho I wish he'd had an elder to learn from.*

Unfortunately, this lotus did not live up to her name. The excellent persons lived too far away. In my self-imposed isolation as caregiver to my mother in the eighties and early nineties, I failed to sustain my practice. The only thing that stuck was my profound respect for the Buddha's teachings, and my own watered-down version of meditation.

Alan Watts, the early popularizer of Buddhism in the West, once asked the great mythologist Joseph Campbell what his practice was. Campbell replied, "I underline." That pretty much sums it up for me. I am that contradiction in terms, a Buddhist without a teacher.

Probably I'm not a Buddhist at all, but a kind of spiritual dilettante. Buddhism appeals to me philosophically because it's tolerant of other religions and less warlike than most; does not demand unquestioning belief, but encourages doubt; is not at war with science; is life-centered rather than otherworldly; emphasizes compassion and awareness, and provides tools for developing these qualities. Unlike religions that focus on the life to come and give you a set of beliefs, Buddhism focuses on the present and gives you a practice.

But as I said, my own practice has never really taken hold, and in this I am a little like Jack.

Jack Kerouac is highly respected in Buddhist circles as an ancestor, as an important figure in the American Buddhist lineage. He introduced Allen Ginsberg to Buddhism, and through his writing he played a major role in introducing Buddhism to America. Almost singlehandedly, he disproved Kipling's myth that "East is

East and West is West and never the twain shall meet / Till Earth and Sky stand presently at God's great Judgment Seat."

But except for brief periods around the time he spent with Gary Snyder and wrote *The Dharma Bums*, and although in a very real sense his writing was and is a form of meditation, Kerouac did not have a practice of his own. He was too restless and in too much pain from his old football injuries and the chronic phlebitis in his legs for formal sitting. His daughter Jan, whom I met later at conferences, said, "Neither of us could keep our seat." And unlike Allen, who went on to become a student of the Tibetan master Chogyam Trungpa Rinpoche, Jack never connected with a living teacher.

In the fall of 1994 I was in Lowell for the seventh annual Lowell Celebrates Kerouac! Festival and attended a Symposium on Kerouac and Spirituality at Boott Cotton Mills Museum. Before the symposium I walked through the vast nineteenth-century weave room crowded with power looms and belts, the boom of the machines so deafening that they make you wear earplugs. Imagining women working there eight and ten hours a day in summer heat was mind-boggling. The museum made me realize that I hadn't even scratched the surface of this remarkable town.

Upstairs, the panel on Kerouac and Spirituality was chaired by the Reverend Stephen Edington of the Unitarian Universalist Church and consisted of poets Allen Ginsberg and Robert Creeley; Brian Foye, author of *Guide to Jack Kerouac's Lowell* and tireless worker for both the Kerouac Commemorative and the festival; literary scholar James Jones; and Buddhist scholar Manju Vajra.

Allen emphasized Kerouac's enormous accomplishment in laying the groundwork for Buddhism in America. He said that when Jack introduced him to Buddhism, "he chanted the refuge vows in a voice like Frank Sinatra." Allen read *Mexico City Blues* to his teacher, Chogyam Trungpa, who called it "a great manifestation of mind."

But all seemed to agree that of the two faiths Kerouac embraced, his Catholicism had the deepest roots; and it was the one he returned to in the end. Of the two strands of Buddhism that appealed to him, suffering and impermanence, suffering was the one closest to his vision. Allen pointed out that Kerouac saw suffering as permanent, like the Catholic hell; according to Buddhism, all hells and heavens are impermanent.

Manju Vajra described Kerouac as a man of great vision with little practical support, an exceedingly painful position to be in. Vajra said the Buddhist path consists of an intellectual understanding; an experience of the nature of reality; and a radical transformation through practice. Jack had both the understanding and the vision, and was able to communicate the nature of reality, but he lacked the practical support to bring about the transformation. He was one of a small band of pioneers who set out to map unknown territory of spiritual life, but he lacked the tools to explore it. "He saw the other side, but didn't have a solid enough raft to cross the stream."

In the sixties, the age of buttons, there was a button that read "Reality is a crutch." I quoted this button to Allen, who thought a moment and then replied, "It's not a good enough one."

The Buddhist idea that all is illusion wasn't a good enough crutch for Jack. Theoretically, if all is illusion, then suffering is illusion too, and shouldn't be a problem, but that syllogism didn't work for Kerouac. The Catholics got him early and death got him early and I think that on some deep level he believed that life was tragic—a belief that coexisted in him with the seemingly contrary and equally strongly held belief that "life is holy and every moment is precious."

In his early enthusiasm for Buddhism and his eloquent transmission of its teachings he showed us a path he couldn't take himself. The bridge doesn't get to the other side; it remains suspended, a bridge for others to pass over.

Manju Vajra's image of Jack as the doomed way-shower always reminds me of the verse in Dante's *Purgatorio* that my Oberlin teacher Andrew Bongiorno, himself a Roman Catholic, called the most touching image in *The Divine Comedy*. In Canto

XXII the poet Virgil is described as one carrying a lantern behind him and lighting a path for others, though not for himself:

> *Facesti come quei che va di notte,*
> *che porta il lume retro e se non giova,*
> *ma dopo se fa le persone dotte.*

> *Thou didst like one who goes by night,*
> *and carries the light behind him, and profits not himself,*
> *but maketh persons wise that follow him.*

The word "Buddha" is Sanskrit for "awakened." In his dedication to *Howl*, Allen Ginsberg described Jack Kerouac as the "new Buddha of American prose." Kerouac's life of the Buddha is entitled *Wake Up!* Whether Kerouac was fully awake or not himself, for many others he surely served as an awakener.

REUNION

The appearance of the Beatniks was that sigh trapped in the chest of American society.

—Yevgeny Yevtushenko

In the spring of 1994 NYU hosted a conference called "The Beat Generation: Legacy and Celebration." It was the fiftieth anniversary of the meeting of Kerouac, Ginsberg, and Burroughs, the triumvirate that planted the seeds of the Beat movement.

The program for the conference, which was co-chaired by Allen Ginsberg and Ann Charters, came to me in Connecticut along with a schedule of research papers, panel topics, poetry readings, films, and other events. The type on the film schedule was so small I had to use a magnifying glass to read it and the map of NYU was illegible even with the glass. I realized with a start: we beatniks are senior citizens!

Mother would be a hundred years old in September. I had been living with her for thirteen years. She was now totally bedridden and in an advanced state of dementia, but I was able to get coverage for her in time to attend the conference.

At the showing of *Pull My Daisy* the first night I saw someone who looked like Gregory Corso with long white hair tied back with a cord.

I never did care much for that movie, a very sexist affair with a few moments of utter brilliance. In it the men have names but the woman is The Wife. She represents bourgeois conformity, cleanliness, and punctuality while the poets, played by Allen and Gregory, represent creativity, freedom, and pleasure. The narration is provided by Jack, who made it up on the spur of the moment: "The Wife runs around fixing everything." This reminded me of the scene in *On the Road* where Dean Moriarty, having stayed up all night talking, drinking beer, and smoking butts with Sal Paradise and "the boys," decides that the thing to do is to have his girlfriend Marylou, who is asleep in bed, get up, make breakfast, and sweep the floor.

Jack's comments include one to the effect that Buddhism means you can do anything you want, which sounded all too familiar, and "By God, even The Woman feels good!" In this world women are the nay-sayers, party poopers, and wet blankets who clean up the messes the poets have made and get the children to school on time. But the cockroach cadenza ("Is everything holy? Is a cockroach holy?") was hilarious. Once again I was disarmed and forgave the boys for being boys.

In movie heaven Gregory Corso still looked like a Russian ballet dancer with mad cheekbones and flashing eyes.

NYU's campus is in the Village and the streets were full of people from early morning joggers to late night strollers. It was wonderful to be able to walk around at night in New York City without fear. I hadn't walked around the streets of Manhattan alone at night since the fifties, and I remembered how it felt to be young.

At the conference there were scholars from all over America and also from Spain, Belgium, Canada, and England, presenting research papers on every conceivable aspect of the Beats.

The first night there was a concert with David Amram and others called "Keeping the Flame Alive." When I walked into the auditorium I saw my former rival Joyce Johnson standing in the aisle and went up to her and said "Hi."

She said "Hi" but looked a little vague so I said, "Do you know who I am?"

She said, "Of course—you're Helen Weaver."

I said, "Are we speaking?" At this, she spontaneously hugged and kissed me.

That was worth a trip to the city!

Dan Wakefield was one of the acts that evening and at the

intermission he told me that for his contribution he had decided to read the part of *New York in the Fifties* about Jack and me. This made me a little nervous but I said, "Fine, as long as I don't have to get up on stage." Dan agreed.

Before he read the piece he acknowledged me graciously and I nodded and beamed. It was very odd sitting there and hearing my story being read out in front of hundreds of people. But I was grateful to Dan because I couldn't have done it myself and the next day, I was famous.

The next morning I bumped into Joyce in the elevator at Loeb Student Center. We sat together in the front row for the "Plenary Session on Women and the Beats" and commented on the papers that were read. I missed one of the papers when I had to make a phone call.

When I got back Joyce said, "I shot off my mouth."

I said, "I'm sorry I missed it."

She said she gets tired of hearing how oppressed women were in the Beat era. She had to speak up and say what was good about being with the Beats, the excitement of being in the middle of all that erotic and creative energy, that it had stimulated her own writing.

I asked if she was going to attend the official opening of the conference that afternoon. She grimaced and said she had to attend the graduation ceremony at Columbia where she teaches creative writing. There was no getting out of it.

I'd miss her. I had to pinch myself to believe it: Joyce and I were friends.

Thursday afternoon the conference proper began in Eisner and Lubin Auditorium. There were hundreds of people of all ages, old timers with white or gray hair, bohemians, hipsters, beatniks, hippies, poets, artists, musicians, filmmakers, survivors, middle-aged professionals, scholars, teachers, students, hip-looking young people, and masses of media—photographers both still and video, tape machines going constantly recording everything, and a whole section of chairs roped off for the press.

Ann Charters welcomed everyone and told about meeting Allen Ginsberg and Peter Orlovsky in Berkeley in 1955, when she attended the now-famous poetry reading at the Six Gallery where Allen first read *Howl*. Peter had been her blind date for the evening, and on the way home they had argued about whether Allen was as great a poet as Whitman: Peter yes, Ann no.

Charters reminded us that John Updike was one of the many established writers who initially put Kerouac down, parodying his style, but that in 1984, at the dedication ceremony for Kerouac Park in Lowell, Updike admitted that he had been wrong. He said, "Kerouac turned up the temperature in American letters, and it's never been turned down since."

John Tytell, a professor of English at the City University of New York in Queens, said that the meaning of the term Beat evolved over time. The original reference was to the exhaustion of the derelict, who has nothing to lose, is open, receptive. The sense of beatitude came later and was largely Kerouac's vision.

Allen Ginsberg traced the history of the movement. The breakthrough came with the publication of *Howl*, *On the Road*, and *Naked Lunch*. By 1959 the Beats were giving poetry readings at Chicago, Harvard, Columbia, and Yale.

A man in the audience, a teacher from some southern university, stood up and said that at his school his colleagues dismiss or are unaware of Kerouac. He said he felt like crying because here at last Kerouac was being given the respect and attention he deserved.

At a "Gala Poetry Reading" at Town Hall that night William Burroughs, now eighty, was unable to attend because as he told Ed Sanders, "my cats need me." But in his honor a phone electronically rigged to be heard throughout Town Hall was brought on stage and Ed Sanders placed a long distance call to Lawrence, Kansas. After a lifetime of experimentation with various drugs including heroin, Burroughs seemed to have all of his unusual marbles intact.

The high spot for me was Gregory Corso. Gregory looked exactly the same as he did thirty-seven years ago, plus a new white hairdo that made him look like a founding father, and a jovial Falstaffian belly. Gregory walked out on stage in a beat-up raincoat, took off the raincoat and threw it on the piano, and ambled over to the mike.

He began by reading a few short "shots" he had written that morning. He had forgotten to bring anything else and asked if anyone in the audience had a copy of one of his books. Several hands went up waving paperbacks. A book was handed on stage and Gregory thumbed through it, commenting on his work ("That ain't bad!") and asking for requests. Inevitably he had to read "Marriage," and it brought down the house.

After a few more poems Gregory said he'd better wind up because "These fuckers are union, we have to be out of here by eleven." He collected his raincoat from the piano, put it back on, and ambled off stage.

At an afternoon panel on "The Beat Generation and Censorship" the next day Barney Rosset, founder, publisher, and editor of Grove Press from 1951 to 1986, spoke of the Beat writers as a political movement. With the help of his counsel, Edward de Grazia, who was one of Lenny Bruce's lawyers back in the sixties and was also on the panel, Barney Rosset spearheaded the revolution for absolute freedom for sexually oriented expression in publishing. Rosset believed that the search for beauty was as important as the search for truth and that both were protected by the First Amendment. He published D. H. Lawrence's *Lady Chatterley's Lover*, Burroughs's *Naked Lunch*, and Henry Miller's *Tropic of Cancer*, among other controversial works, and reprinted Ginsberg's *Howl* in the *Evergreen Review*.

Allen Ginsberg said that he himself in *Howl*, Burroughs in *Naked Lunch*, and Kerouac from *On the Road* onward pursued "the candid exploration of our own minds." Allen said that the same censorship of the printed word that prevailed in the sixties persisted in the nineties on radio and TV. The voice of the poet was censored.

A young Czech man in the audience spoke movingly of life behind the Iron Curtain. He said that in the sixties some holes appeared in the Iron Curtain and through them came the Beatles, jeans, Coke, some poems of Allen Ginsberg, and *On the Road*. In 1965 Allen was crowned King of the May and then expelled from Prague. Allen Ginsberg became "a reliable litmus test of the political atmosphere. If one of his poems appeared, you knew things were getting better, there was a thaw. If no poems, it was frost."

The last panel Friday afternoon was "Women and the Beat Generation," with Joyce Johnson, Hettie Jones (ex-wife of black poet LeRoi Jones), Carolyn Cassady (Neal Cassady's widow, who also had an affair with Kerouac), and Jack's daughter, Jan Kerouac.

Chair Anne Waldman said male Beat writers have been accused of having a "boys' club mentality." Shades of political correctness on the panel ranged from Hettie Jones's cheerful, outspoken feminism: "I didn't sleep with all of them, but that might have been nice. Strong women need strong men, or at least noisy ones," to Carolyn Cassady's more traditional stance: "I was happy listening to them and filling their coffee cups. They always treated me with respect. My own conditioned attitudes were wrong." (But in her memoir *Off the Road: My Years with Cassady, Kerouac, and Ginsberg,* Cassady tells how she stopped playing the victim and gained control of the situation in a very "modern" way.)

Jan Kerouac read from an unpublished work by her mother, Joan Haverty, Jack's second wife who died of cancer in 1990. Haverty wrote of "an unspoken commitment to listen to everything Jack had to say with neither contribution nor criticism." (In 2000 Haverty's memoir was published as *Nobody's Wife*.)

Joyce Johnson remarked, "We took care of our male counterparts, they didn't take care of us. We would have been excess baggage on the road." But one felt no bitterness in Joyce. After all, these men, however revolutionary their ideas in some areas, were products of their time, and Joyce stressed that being with them was exciting and fun. Feminism came later. "Call us transitional," she suggested.

Someone, I forget who, reminded us that the Beats respected the few women they knew who managed to find the time and space to write, and to those in the past who anticipated their ideal of candor. Virginia Woolf, who pioneered the stream of consciousness novel along with James Joyce, was a hero to them.

At a "Beat Cabaret" that night, Ed Sanders stole the show and my heart with his stirring tribute to all left-wing undergrounds of the past, present and future, "Hymn to the Rebel Café." Ed, who was lead singer of The Fugs in the sixties, founded the Peace Eye Bookstore in the Village, and once put out a publication called *Fuck You: A Magazine of the Arts*, was starting to look more and more like a hippie Mark Twain. His old-fashioned troubadour style of alternating poetry and music suited me better than the more typically Beat amalgam of simultaneous poetry and jazz.

On my way to Temple In The Village, a macrobiotic restaurant on Third Street, the next day, I ran into Allen, who was headed for the same place, so I got to spend a few minutes with my old friend.

I told him I was working on my memoir of Jack again. He looked at me and said, "It's very important." His look, coming from his sixty-eight years to my sixty-three, said to me clearly, "We won't live forever."

In the break before the final panel I bumped into Joyce, who asked me if I had seen Helen Elliott. She had been there for the panel on women and the Beats the day before, and was also there today. Joyce said she looked terrible, "like an old woman." She had bad arthritis and her skin had a yellowish cast. She struck Joyce as an angry, bitter person. Helen asked Joyce why the panelists didn't talk about "all the competition among women."

I asked Joyce, "Did you tell her I was here?"

"Yes."

"How did she react?"

"She took it in."

I hadn't seen Helen in over twenty years: not since the time

I'd run into her on the street after I failed the driver's test. Some time after I moved to New Milford to take care of my mother she had called me there to tell me she had become an astrologer and to ask me what time I was born. I was eager to have her birth data too but after that exchange I brushed her off.

I told her—I can hardly believe I said this, but ex-wimps can be vicious—that I wanted as little to do with her as possible. She said in a choked voice, "Then let's get off the phone." I knew she would not have forgiven me for that.

So she was here. I girded up my loins, but though Helen and I were in the same room two days in a row and Joyce ran into her twice, I never saw her. True, it was a very big room, but the same lucky stars that had put me in the elevator with Joyce the first morning had also seen to it that I need not encounter the angry ghost of an enemy who might not have fired her last shot. As they say in Woodstock, it was not meant to be.

One day during lunch break I saw Gregory Corso sitting on a terrace surrounded by a circle of young people, mostly women. On my way back he was still there. I waited for a lull in the conversation and went over and stuck my face in his face.

"Hi, Gregory. I'm a ghost from the past."

He said, "You're not a ghost from the past, you're what's happening now." But he looked puzzled. He knew he knew me, but it had been thirty-seven years.

"We made it!" I announced—a big hint.

"Helen!" he said immediately.

"Helen *Weaver*," I qualified.

"Oh, I know—you were the sweetest one!"

"I thought you were mad at me for making you sit up in a chair all night writing poetry."

"Never, I was never mad at you."

"I felt guilty for being unfaithful to Jack."

"I made it with Jack's girlfriend before, that was in *The Subterraneans*."

"And it was heavy for Jack, because history was repeating itself."

"You wrote me a beautiful letter with wings on it."

"You didn't answer it!"

"I never answer letters!" Gregory said.

"So can I come and visit you some time?"

Here Gregory looked a little disconcerted. This whole conversation was being followed attentively by the circle of young admirers.

"Can I come and visit *you?*" he asked.

"Well, I live in Connecticut with my ninety-nine-year-old mother. . . ."

"Hmm . . . ninety-nine-year-old mother. . . ." Gregory was temporarily stymied. Nevertheless, we exchanged addresses and phone numbers and Gregory exclaimed over the wings on my card.

He introduced me to his son and two daughters, and I congratulated him on having reproduced, and looking exactly the same, plus the white wig.

At the final banquet that night I sat with Joyce. She introduced me to her son Danny: a nice round open face like his mother's, sort of a young Michael Wilder type. He was covering the conference for the *Village Voice*. He must have been at least thirty-one; it had been that many years since Joyce and I had seen each other.

Joyce and I recalled our last meeting. It was at Helen's apartment on West 10th Street, just a few days after Joyce's husband of only one year had been killed in a motorcycle accident. Helen had met Joyce on the street. Joyce said that when she told Helen about her husband's death Helen had said, "I know how you feel; Treff died."

I didn't tell Joyce that I understood how Helen felt about losing her dog. It was a dumb thing for Helen to say.

Jan Kerouac was at the next table, next to Gerald Nicosia. Joyce asked me if I would like to meet her, and I said I would.

At last I looked into those blue, blue eyes and saw up close the face so like her father's I almost wept. Jan was magnetic as a star, yet utterly approachable, like the young Kerouac, the Kerouac I knew. She turned to me with an expectant smile, turned on me those eyes that knocked you dead and that could hardly see—she was very ill with diabetes—and I stood there, just looking at her.

Even with her bad eyes she must have seen the tender look on my face because she said, "Do I look like my father?"

I laughed. "You've seen this look before. Yes, you look so much like him, it's uncanny."

"How does it make you feel?"she asked unexpectedly. I had drawn up a chair and was sitting next to her.

"It makes me love you." The words came out of my mouth on their own. I was afraid this might be too much for her but she said she didn't mind being loved. I felt as if I had known her all my life, as if she were my long lost sister—no, as if she were my child.

"It makes me sad, too, because I threw him out."

"He wasn't that easy to live with, was he?"

"No. I couldn't take the drinking. Joyce"—she was still beside me and we could smile about it now—"was a lot better at it than I was."

Joyce introduced me to Helen Elliott's son Luke, a tall, nice-looking young man with Helen's deep dark eyes and a ready smile. He recognized my name and extended a cordial hand.

At age twenty-six Luke was living with his mother in the same apartment on West 16th Street that she had been in since the seventies. He seemed embarrassed about that, but I said, "It's the economy." We agreed that rents in the city were terrible.

He was working in an insurance agency and going to school at night, a business course. I remembered that Helen's father sold insurance for Mutual of Omaha. He said he didn't want children. He hadn't read *On the Road* or any Kerouac, said he liked art and literature, especially Whitman, but that he wanted to make money. I said I had heard Helen was writing her memoirs. He said, "She needs to get motivated."

Luke asked if I wanted their phone number. I said I already had it, which was true. He said he was sure his mother would be glad to hear from me. I didn't try to set him straight. I left him with "Say hi to your mom," as if she were an ordinary mother, as if she didn't still haunt my dreams. Actually in my dreams I often had warm feelings toward her and she was the one who had not forgiven me for shutting her out of my life.

The evening had an eerie quality: Jack's daughter and Helen's son!

After I got home I called Bob Rosenthal, Allen's secretary, to make an appointment for an interview with Allen. I asked Bob if he'd been at the Beat conference at NYU. He laughed and said, "I'm not nostalgic about the Beat Generation. I live with it every day!"

I told him I was writing a memoir of Jack and that Allen had said I could come and interview him. Bob said the demands on Allen's time were incredible. He suggested I call back around the middle of June.

I never did. Mother's care was becoming very intense, and I got distracted, as usual. I never saw Allen again.

IMPERMANENCE

*They are all gone into the world of light! And I alone sit
ling'ring here. . . .*

—Henry Vaughan, *The Ascension Hymn*

My mother died on May 5, 1995. She was a hundred years old.

At a certain point in her nineties my intelligent, book-reading,
letter-writing mother started losing it mentally. I watched her go
through the stages of "senile dementia of the Alzheimer's type,"
the passages of loss.

First it was time: this woman who had always been the time
keeper of the family didn't know what day it was, then what year
it was, and finally what time of day. I'll never forget the day I
brought her lunch in to her in her hospital bed and she insisted she
had already had lunch and supper and it was time for bed.

I said, "Mother, it's noon, the sun is high in the sky! If you
were to walk to the front door [which she could no longer do] and
look up and see the sun directly overhead, would that convince
you?"

And she looked at me steely-eyed and said, "I don't know
that it would." We're talking stubborn!

Next to go was space: "I want to go home."

"You *are* home."

Or, "I want to go to Junction" (Junction City, Kansas, where
she was born).

I'd joke, "Just click your heels together three times and say
'There's no place like home.'"

Finally, it was people. Sometimes she knew me, sometimes

she didn't. She would forget that I was living with her. "Where did *you* come from?"

And I'd answer, "Out of your stomach!" And we'd giggle like schoolgirls at the ultimate mystery.

At first she fought against the dying of her mind and that was a bad period; this well-bred lady spewing out anger and venom from God knows what ancient source. But eventually she gave in, and then she became the child she had been before *her* mother, the formidable Grandma Hemenway, had tamed her passionate spirit. In her dementia, my mother actually became a lot nicer. Seldom demonstrative before, she became a hugger.

She even forgave me for disappointing her by not producing children, and I forgave her for her disappointment.

Maybe she became enlightened; maybe it was just some chemical change in her body. Who cares? For the first time in my life I had a mother who *showed* her love. Of course she had always loved me; that was a given. But now, when I walked into her room, her face lit up and she held out her arms to be hugged. I heard her tell the nurses, "She's the light of my life."

Mother died at her favorite time of the year. The dogwood, the lilacs, and the star magnolia were all in bloom, laying a balm on my heart and helping me to face the whirlwind of change created by her sudden absence.

As her executor I had to deal with taxes, banks, and lawyers, clear out the house with the help of my nieces, put it on the market, move back to Woodstock and find a house of my own.

My brother, whose health had been failing for several years, waited until I had sold Mother's house and was safely back in Woodstock, and then he died, too. My nieces were scattered in four different states. After fourteen years of living with Mother and her helpers, I was suddenly alone.

My only remaining link with the past was my dog Daisy. Shortly after I moved to New Milford I had adopted a female beagle mix at a local shelter, and Daisy had helped us all get through a difficult time by providing unfailing affection and comic relief. In the fourteen years I had been there nurses and aides had come and gone but Daisy had been a constant companion. Now she was my whole family, and she was getting old.

In the time I spent in Connecticut, outside of articles for *Litchfield County Times* and *Woodstock Times*, my ever-present journal, and a few false starts on this book, I had done very little writing. The lack of privacy was hard for this loner and constant interruptions were the order of the day. Time and again I had to put this book aside.

But now that I was in my own home at last and in my own long longed-for element of solitude, I found that I was once again caring for an elderly female. As Daisy's health failed I began writing the story of her life, and when she died, I self-published it as *The Daisy Sutra: Conversations with My Dog*. I sold my love letters from Jack to pay the printer up in Toronto. Jack had loved animals, so I knew that I had his blessing.

In April 1997, Allen Ginsberg was laid to rest.

Allen was born the day after Jack's brother Gerard died. Allen was Jack's true brother and the best friend he ever had. Allen died just a couple of months after my brother died, and he was my true brother, too. Still in shock from all my recent losses, I did not attend his service, but I grieved. And I marveled at the ease and the grace with which he was able to let go of his incredible life. Gregory Corso had called him on the phone at the hospital to say goodbye, and he said that Allen's last word to him was "Toodle-oo!"

I remembered meeting Allen one year at Omega Institute, and Allen's saying, "We should see each other more often." But we didn't, and now he was gone. That deep, generous presence that was always ready to help, that quiet, intelligent Jewish voice on the phone, always calm, never rushed, meditative, matter-of-fact, that poured forth information, wisdom, and humor, was stilled. *Woodstock Times* was full of tributes. Poet and performance artist Mikhail Horowitz wrote:

Allen Ginsberg, heir to the visionary poetics of Blake and

Whitman . . . has finally passed from fully embodied Voice into the afterlife of books and recordings. More than any single person, he was responsible for removing the NO TRESPASSING signs on Mount Parnassus, rescuing our national poetry from stuffiness, academic hermetica, and complicity with the military/industrial/surrealist complex. He spoke Truth to power. He opened the language to naked Eros, putting his "queer shoulder to the wheel" long before such sentiments were publicly expressed. He wed the personal to the political in poems notable for their ambitious reach, attention to minute particulars, and remarkable candor. His largesse, especially to his fellow poets, was legendary. . . . He leaves behind hundreds, maybe thousands, of poets who are his spiritual children, but no heir apparent. A poet of such embrace and expansiveness comes along once in a lifetime. I'm grateful it was during mine.

Amen.

The honor roll of dead friends and teachers kept growing. Gregory in 2001, Roger Straus and Susan Sontag in 2004. I kept dreaming about my unfinished manuscript, this huge pile of unbound pages that I kept lugging around, attempting to save from fire and flood, uncertain whether it was the story of my own life or the story of the remarkable people I had known.

I knew that time was passing and that I had to finish it before I, too, disappeared, but something was keeping me from doing it, something that felt different from mere garden-variety writer's block, though it certainly looked like that.

When Helen Elliott didn't show up at the banquet the last night of the Beat conference but sent her son instead, I suspected she did not want to encounter me, and I didn't blame her. I hadn't answered her last letter, and then there was that phone conversation in which we exchanged birth data and I let her know I wanted nothing to do with her.

After my mother died Helen sent me a condolence note. At the end she wrote, "I loved you, and am still sorry you made the choice you did." Again, I didn't respond.

But once I got back to work on this book I could no longer ignore her. I realized anew how important she was and what an impact she had had on my life. Without her, there would be no book. I was grateful to her, and at the same time the thought of writing about her made me very nervous.

Then there was the matter of the pictures Helen took of me and Jack and Allen and Gregory with my Brownie camera. They were just snapshots but they were evocative and I wanted to be able to use them in my book. So in May of 2003, in a spirit of shameless self-promotion, I drafted a permissions agreement and sent it to her with a letter offering to pay her for use of the photos.

Weeks went by with no response. Thinking maybe she had moved and my letter had not found her, I sent the whole thing again by certified mail so she'd have to sign for it. Sure enough, the little green card came back with the familiar signature.

Now that I knew her address was good, I sent her a copy of *The Daisy Sutra*, inscribed to her and Treff and Gudrun (a dachshund she got to keep Treff company in the last years of his life). I hoped that the book and the fact that I remembered the names of both of her dogs would help to make up for my years of silence.

More weeks went by, and I had just about given up hope of hearing from Helen. Then one day while checking my e-mail I was startled to see her name in my In Box.

Her answer, not surprisingly, was No: "32 years of deafening silence and an offer of $100 a picture (!!) do not a chasm close." And she signed off with "As Dan Wakefield used to say 'as ever, your humble servant,' Helen."

The e-mail address was actually that of her son Luke, who was not only more computer literate than she was but, as I later learned, had taken on the job of caregiver to his ailing mother.

I e-mailed her back:

*I completely understand. There has indeed been a chasm between us. I was hoping for a dialogue that might help to bridge it.
I'm sorry if you were insulted by my offer. If you have a price in mind for the photos, something that would the chasm close, please let me know. If not, I respect your wishes. Your pictures*

would have enhanced my book, but this is your decision to
make. I'm glad to know that you're alive and still full of piss and
vinegar.

Again, there was silence on her end. Then a friend of mine,
a Kerouac fan and collector who had bought a drawing of Jack's
that I had sold along with my letters, asked me for Helen's
address. He wanted to send her his copy of *Desolation Angels* to
be signed. So I e-mailed Helen again to see if it was OK to give
Joe Lee her address.

I got another e-mail from Helen, via Luke, thanking me for
the book, which she said she read the same day it arrived, and
agreeing to respond to Joe. I had ended my contract letter with
the wish that she and Luke were well "in these terrible times." She
advised me to watch Jon Stewart on the Comedy Channel and to
read Paul Krugman in the *New York Times.* She told me, "I am
awash with life-threatening ailments. I do a lot of deep breathing
and I get around in a wheel chair." She signed herself "AEYHS,
Helen."

I did start watching Jon Stewart. I could feel the ice between
Helen and me starting to thaw. I e-mailed her back:

Wonderful to hear from you. I'm so sorry though to hear that
you are "awash with life-threatening ailments." Growing older
is not for sissies. . . . I will give Joe your home and e-mail
addresses. He'll be delighted to hear from you, I know. . . . I
wish you well. The things I remember about you most clearly
are your beautiful singing voice and your great sense of humor.
(Moose Shit Pie—but good!) I have every letter you ever wrote
me, and even one you wrote my father. . . . AEYHS, The Other
Helen.

That was October. By March Helen was apologizing for *her*
silence and signing herself with love. Helen said that Joe was
"aces." That was her word for anything good: I hadn't heard
anybody say "aces" in years. I suspect her father was a poker
player.

When Lenny Bruce was pardoned on the day before Christmas Eve I e-mailed her that I hoped he was having a good laugh over this.

On March 12, Kerouac's eighty-second birthday, on a play date with my new dog Brindle and the two dogs of some visitors, I was knocked onto the frozen ground of my fenced-in yard by one of their greyhounds and sustained a compression fracture to the fourth and fifth lumbar vertebrae. I couldn't put on my socks and shoes.

I e-mailed Helen about my fall. She e-mailed me back:

Was so sorry to hear about your accident and your poor back! (You have, as someone pointed out to me, a very good basis for a law suit!) My spinal stenosis, two fused vertebrae at L4, is what has actually crippled me. Combined with X, Y and Z it makes one cry. I'll get back to you again about the pix. I had an idea but have to ask a lawyer. XXOO Helen

That was the last I heard about the pictures, but I didn't care. My friend was in pain. I was in pain, but I would get over it. She probably wouldn't. We had known each other for almost half a century. She was a piece of work, but I loved her anyway. Funny, I was never tempted to pick up the phone and call her, or if I was, I resisted the temptation. This reconciliation—by e-mail, of all things—felt delicate; I didn't want to make waves.

Maybe I was afraid that if I actually heard her voice I'd remember some of the mean things she'd said to me over the years and this whole delicate structure of forgiveness we were building in cyberspace would collapse. Or maybe it was just the opposite: maybe I didn't want to hear the pain in her voice, that beautiful voice grown old. Maybe a little of both. E-mail was safe. It was the perfect solution, just the right degree of intimacy: not too close but not far either and a whole lot better than nothing. A sort of disembodied reconciliation, as if we were both angels like Jack said and "safe in heaven dead."

In May I received a package from Helen in the mail. Inside was a big canvas handbag in a yellow, black, and white stripe, one of those bags with many compartments and a matching coin purse.

I was floored. A handbag, and a coin purse! It seemed ironic because when Helen and I lived together money was one of our issues.

I was also mystified about the timing of the gift, but now I think it was an early birthday present. Maybe Helen was confused about the date, or maybe she wanted to mail it early in case something happened to her. She had already been hospitalized once that year.

This time I sent her a "real" letter of thanks. And when Marlon Brando died I e-mailed her again. I knew how much she had loved him and how proud she was that he was from Omaha, too.

June and July went by without a word from Helen. In August, Joe asked me if I would help him get Lucien Carr to sign his copies of *On the Road* and *Visions of Cody*. I had interviewed Lucien in D.C. in 1990 but had long since lost his phone number and address. So I e-mailed Helen to see if she could help:

Are you there? Long time no hear. I do worry about you. I'm still here and hope you are, too. . . . Even if you don't know how to contact Lucien, I hope to hear from you. If it's too hard to write, maybe Lucien's namesake can help. Love, Helen

The next day I received an e-mail from Luke. Helen had died on August 29 at Cabrini Hospital, of congestive heart failure and a weakened respiratory system. He said that she did not go in pain, but that this last summer had been very painful for her, that she had suffered a great deal, "more than she wanted others to know." He said he got solace from the thought that she was now reunited with Jack, Lenny, Stan (Getz, a particular friend of hers), Allen, her sister Maddy, and especially her father, whom she had loved most of all. He said he was glad that she and I had had some contact in the last year of her life.

And I was glad too that the two Helens had found a way to communicate, and that she was now at peace.

Helen gave me so much! Living with her was not easy, but she had been a teacher for me. She had encouraged me to be sexual and had thus been an ally in my long struggle to overcome all the guilt and fear I'd been saddled with by my well-meaning parents and by the very air of the time.

She gave me Jack, Allen, and Lenny. She is the glue that holds my story together. And by dying, she gave me the freedom to tell it at last.

I did help Joe get his books signed by Lucien. I got Lucien's address from Allen's archivist, bibliographer, and biographer Bill Morgan, and wrote him a "real" letter.

I reminded him that I was the dame who punched out Kerouac in the middle of the night to the strains of *My Fair Lady*, thus earning from him the nickname "Slugger."

Lucien wrote me back and said he'd be happy to sign the books, but he wanted no direct contact with "the gent":

You could have him mail the books to you; you would send them on to me; I'd sign 'em and send 'em back to you, and you'd send them to him. That way I would not get involved with him, he'd get his books signed, and you would spend a lot of time at the Post Office.

I agreed to this plan. And since I knew Lucien was a dog lover I sent him a copy of *The Daisy Sutra* for good measure. He wrote back:

Dear Slugger:

Enjoyed your book. First half made me weepy. Second half beyond my stage of development. Perhaps later in life. After all, I'm only pushing 80.

The "second half" of my book is about animal communication and is a bit much for a skeptic to swallow. Lucien was more gracious than most.

My next communication with Lucien was about another

request for contact with him, this time from Helen's son. Luke wanted to talk to Lucien about his mother, but Lucien declined. He signed the letter with love.

A few weeks later, Lucien Carr was dead. I had suspected he was ill—his handwriting had become almost completely illegible—but I hadn't known that he was in the last stages of bone cancer. I felt so blessed to have had that affectionate communication with him at the end of his life.

It was Lucien Carr who had introduced Jack Kerouac, Allen Ginsberg, and William Burroughs at Columbia in 1944. The *New York Times* called him "a founder and muse—and one of the last survivors—of the Beat Generation of poets and writers" and "a literary lion who never roared." Wilborn Hampton's obituary went on:

If he had been more of a midwife to the Beats, Mr. Carr was an extremely vocal mentor to two generations of journalists who came up through the ranks at U.P.I. He was a great champion of brevity. "Why don't you just start with the second paragraph?" was his frequent advice to young reporters overly fond of their own prose.

This reminded me so much of my brother, the *New York Times* political reporter, who had once remarked of a piece I had written for *Woodstock Times* on the death of my father, "Nobody could accuse you of being terse." And who used to tell me, "Once you have your lead, you're halfway there."

These two seasoned newspapermen were both my brothers, and I'd try to keep their advice in mind as I sat down to write.

AN AMERICAN CLASSIC

Literature is a lamp of sacrifice, consuming itself to light the coming generations.

—Marcel Proust, *On Reading Ruskin*

I hit him. I tore out a chunk of his hair. I asked him to leave. When he rang my bell in the middle of the night, I didn't let him in. When he called me up in the middle of the night, I wasn't available. I didn't go to his funeral. I rejected his book.

If I had it to do all over again, I'd probably do the same. I am who I am, and he interfered with my sleep.

Of all my sins against Jack Kerouac there is only one I truly regret, and that is that I never appreciated him as a writer until well after his death. In this I am like many of the so-called literate members of my generation. In a way, my journey is a microcosm of America's.

I have saved many of the reviews of his books over the years and it's fascinating to watch the gradual change in tone from ridicule to respect, the changing image of Jack Kerouac from *enfant terrible* to American icon.

With few exceptions the early reviewers didn't bother to conceal their contempt for this drunken bum who fancied himself a writer. John Updike mocked Kerouac's style in a *New Yorker* parody called "On the Sidewalk." *Time* magazine called Jack "the latrine laureate" and *Maggie Cassidy* "just one undammed thing after another" and said that the book should be "stuffed, mounted, and sent to the Smithsonian Institution."

The malice stemmed not only from the eccentricities of Kerouac's style but also from the perceived immorality of the content. David Dempsey in the Sunday *New York Times* found *On the Road* "enormously readable and entertaining" but called the characters "sideshow freaks" and was clearly shocked by their behavior.

In "Know-Nothing Bohemians" Norman Podhoretz said that the Beats were having a corrupting influence on the youth of America, that their "anti-intellectualism" led to juvenile crime. He spoke of Kerouac's "poverty of resources" and "simple inability to express anything in words."

When Kerouac died in 1969 the *Times* obituary by Joseph Lelyveld correctly stated, "Mr. Kerouac's admirers regarded him as a major literary innovator and something of a religious seer, but this estimate of his achievement never gained wide acceptance among literary tastemakers." But Vivian Gornick in the *Village Voice* called *On the Road* "an American classic," and Lester Bangs in *Rolling Stone* remarked, "Jack was in so many ways a spiritual father of us all, as much as Lenny Bruce or Dylan or any of them."

By 1978 the shift had begun even in the *New York Times:*

Although Jack Kerouac has been dead for nearly a decade, neither the man nor his works have been adequately understood. The works suffered from the most malicious early reviewing ever accorded a major American novelist—reviews full of unsubstantiated conjecture about Kerouac's intelligence, his life style, his ambitions, his literary sense, his creative methods.

That was Richard Kostelanetz; and in 1983 in the *Times* Morris Dickstein wrote:

Though many critics took him for some kind of unlettered barbarian, he had been reading and writing avidly since childhood. . . . The reviews of all his books were killing, but he never stopped experimenting with form and language. . . . Far more attention should be paid to his endlessly inventive ways of

turning his life into writing, before drink dulled his prodigious
memory, his musical sense and his powers of concentration.

But the conservatives were not converted. When Lowell
chose to honor its native son with the Kerouac Commemorative,
George Will, writing in *Newsweek*, made the common error of
mistaking Kerouac for a radical, associating him with all that
was worst about the fifties that led to all that was worst about
the sixties—a view with which, ironically, Kerouac would have
largely agreed; he had no more use for the sixties than Will did.
George Will went on:

This native was not . . . truth be told, a man of large and lasting
accomplishments in the arts. . . . it is sweetly incongruous that
he should be memorialized in a park, a place of contemplation,
something strange to him. Better they should name a truck stop
after him.

At the Beat conference at New York University in 1994
we were just a bunch of white-haired bohemians, beatniks, and
hippies—all doctrinal differences merged in the general slog
toward eternity—and the academics who paid respectful attention
to Jack's work were preaching to the choir. But by then even in the
pages of the *New York Times* one could detect a sea change:

Neither the formal setting nor the academic trappings could
extinguish the Beats' vitality, ambition and sheer spunk. The
Beats wanted nothing less than to reimagine the world. Against
the materialism and conformity of post–World War II America,
they sought ecstatic transcendence and spontaneity. . . . The
Beats, for all their excesses and poor imitators, brought poetry
to its senses.

But it was the publication by Viking Press in 1995—
twenty-six years after his death—of two books, *The Portable*
Jack Kerouac and *Jack Kerouac: Selected Letters, 1940–1956*,
both edited by Ann Charters, that marked the turning point in

the critical reception of Jack's work. Columbia University scholar Ann Douglas wrote in the *New York Times Book Review*:

Kerouac's work represents the most extensive experiment in language and literary form undertaken by an American writer of his generation. On the Road *is only one of about a dozen major novels from his hand, all carefully designed to form a vast chronicle of American life in the mid-20th century.*

In contrast to Malcolm Cowley, an early admirer of Kerouac who nevertheless believed that he failed to create believable characters, Douglas wrote that "his novels offer brilliant portraits of his many friends." She concluded, "Jack Kerouac's road is worth traveling."

And at the end of a respectful and balanced review in the *New Yorker* Joyce Carol Oates observed:

The evidence of Jack Kerouac's oeuvre is that, for all its flaws, it, and he, deserved to be treated better by the censorious "literary" critics of his time. Kerouac was dismissed as a "beatnik" by many commentators who had not troubled to read his work, still less to read it with sympathy. The Portable Jack Kerouac *may well be seminal in a reevaluation of Kerouac's position in the literature of mid-twentieth-century America.*

She lists the most important works of Bowles, Salinger, Nabokov, Ginsberg, Mailer, Burroughs, and Updike, and concludes: "*On the Road* is a classic of the era to set beside these."

In 1998 both the *New Yorker* and the *Atlantic Monthly* published selections from Kerouac's unpublished journals with respectful introductions by historian Douglas Brinkley.

In the same year Morris Dickstein in a *New York Times* review of Ellis Amburn's *Subterranean Kerouac* comments that "the Beats seem to fascinate us more than ever. Perhaps this is because they were genuine writers, not simply media material." And about *On the Road*:

Greeted mostly by withering reviews when it first appeared, it changed many readers' lives and stimulated writers and performers as different as Norman Mailer, John Updike, Ken Kesey, Bob Dylan, Robert Stone, Thomas Pynchon, Hunter Thompson, Jack Nicholson, Nick Nolte, Jim Morrison and even the buttoned-up Tom Wolfe.

In 1999 Penguin Books announced the publication of "beautifully designed deluxe editions of 20 of the 20th century's most extraordinary novels" including *Heart of Darkness, The Grapes of Wrath, The Age of Innocence, The Adventures of Augie March,* and *Love in the Time of Cholera.* And coming soon: "Franz Kafka, Toni Morrison, James Joyce, Willa Cather, Jack Kerouac, Marcel Proust, D. H. Lawrence, and other masters of 20th century literature."

In 2001 the original 120-foot-long scroll on which Kerouac composed *On the Road* was auctioned at Christie's in New York City for $2.4 million, a world record for a literary manuscript. The buyer was Jim Irsay, owner of the Indianapolis Colts football team, who said he wanted to make sure it was kept in America.

In 2004 Walter Kirn wrote a review for the *New York Times Book Review* of *Windblown World: The Journals of Jack Kerouac, 1947–1954,* edited by Douglas Brinkley, that represents such a total reversal of the previous attitude toward Kerouac that I cannot resist quoting it at length. Poetically entitled "The Rush of What Is Said," it reads in part:

The entries tell a story of self-invention, perseverance and break-through that should help rescue Kerouac from the cultists and secure his admission to the mainstream hall of fame, where he deserves to rest. . . .

Kerouac was an indefatigable mapmaker, assembling city by city, state by state and river by river (the occult vitality of rivers was one of his abiding preoccupations) a spiritual atlas of postwar America. The traditional rap against Kerouac—that he was a sort of half-baked dopehead primitivist who prized sensation over sense—crumbles on a reading of his journals. . . .

What he wanted most, the journals reveal, was to dig down into the dark American earth as his heroes Twain and Whitman had and turn up his own rich shovelful of truth. His enemy in this labor, he believed, was the cowardice of aesthetic perfectionism. He trusted, finally, in his own energy, but it was an energy produced from the finest sources: great books, adventurous friends, high moral purpose and wide experience. "It's not the words that count," he wrote, "but the rush of what is said."

Much of the criticism that has been directed at Kerouac's work has treated his doctrine of spontaneity as a form of self-indulgence, whereas it was actually a particularly rigorous form of discipline. His aesthetic was related to Catholicism: in the confessional, it's a sin to hold anything back. Kerouac believed it was his duty to record his experience exactly as it happened or at least exactly as he honestly remembered it, exactly as it occurred to him in the act of remembering, which he attempted (often with the aid of drugs) to merge totally, with no intervening steps, in a kind of automatic writing, with the act of recording it on paper. Hence his aversion to editing (which was actually an acquired aversion: *On the Road* went through several drafts before he found his voice).

His insistence, reflected in his publishing contracts, that not so much as a comma be changed, was not the irritating whim of an eccentric and demanding personality, but the natural result of an article of faith.

I thought that clause was ridiculous at the time, but I now see that he was right. Punctuation is personal, it carries a voice. Commas are about breath. The rhythm of Jack's sentences carries that voice to this day.

His aesthetic was related to Buddhism as well: like the mandala at Kerouac Park that so beautifully integrates Christianity and Buddhism in its design, Kerouac's writing process integrates the Catholic practice of confession with the Buddhist practice of meditation. Although formal meditation did not take hold for him, his writing was intimately related to Buddhist practice in that it was a conscious exploration of the way the mind works. And every line he wrote was steeped in his constant sense of the impermanence of all things and his close attention to the fleeting present moment.

This accounts for some of the difficulty encountered by his early readers in understanding his work. It is best to approach Kerouac in the same way one approaches meditation: in an attitude of friendly openness to whatever arises. Reading Kerouac can actually be an excellent preparation for meditation, and conversely, meditating can help to develop the patience that is often required for a true appreciation and enjoyment of his unique gifts.

Kerouac's writing is about taking in everything that's happening even when nothing seems to be happening. It's not about plot or action; with a few exceptions, it's not even about character. It's about perception. It's about consciousness, and mortality, and compassion. It's a meditation on life.

Had Jack Kerouac been willing to work with an editor and to shape his work in a more conventional manner (as indeed he had done in *The Town and the City*), the results might have been interesting, even excellent, but they would not have been Kerouac. Kerouac's primary purpose was not to pursue literary excellence but to tell the truth about his experience as it impinged upon his mind and senses. Had he pursued literary excellence singlemindedly he might have achieved it, but he would have sacrificed a certain raw—and gentle—power.

No, we need Kerouac exactly as he is, rough and ready as the American West used to be, spontaneous as a kitten, unvarnished as a flower, in all of what Gilbert Millstein so felicitously calls his "informed innocence." We need him as an antidote to the naysaying life-denying minimalist chic humorless clever ironic rational materialism of the American literary establishment, of all literary establishments. We need him for a quality he never achieved in his life: balance.

Genius takes many forms. "The house of fiction," Henry James famously wrote, "has not one window but a million."

Just because Kerouac did not write the kind of novels that Austen or Flaubert or Tolstoy wrote doesn't mean his writing is, as Capote believed, merely "typing." He had extraordinary gifts and energy and a unique point of view—the gifts and view of a poet and philosopher, perhaps, more than a novelist, for he saw everything that happened through the lens of death—*sub specie aeternitatis*, from the viewpoint of eternity. Kerouac lived every moment as if it were his last, as if his whole life were passing in review at the moment of death. Unlike the rest of us, he remembered everything that ever happened to him. That was his burden, and his gift.

Each of us has within us something similar to the 120-foot scroll on which Kerouac typed an early version of *On the Road*. On this endless scroll is inscribed everything that ever happened to us. This endless scroll is the modern version of the little book that hangs from the sinner's neck on a little cord in medieval representations of the Last Judgment. All of us have it, but few are given the gift—or learn the art—of reading it. Proust did, and paved the way for the modern novel. He changed everything for every writer to follow him, including those who have never read him.

Like Proust, that other great French rememberer in whose footsteps he consciously walked, Kerouac thought of all of his books as one book that was nothing more than the story of his life. Like Proust, his goal was to produce a long philosophical novel in many installments whose subject was memory and time.

Kerouac may not have completed his "long novel explaining everything to everybody," but surely he was one of the great recorders of his time. Butting his head against the brick wall of eternity, he actually made it give. His words have been inscribed on granite and his ideas on the consciousness of the generation he named. To a remarkable degree, he did accomplish what he set out to do. Whether his goal of all-inclusiveness was a worthy one will always be subject to dispute. As long as there is art, there will be the Leaver Outers and the Putter Inners, and the dialogue between the two.

At the very least, I agree with Ann Charters that *On the Road* belongs on the same shelf with *The Scarlet Letter, Moby Dick, Huckleberry Finn,* and *Notes of a Native Son.*

In 1926, while she was struggling with *To the Lighthouse,* Virginia Woolf wrote in her diary:

I shall here write the first pages of the greatest book in the world. This is what the book would be that was made entirely solely and with integrity of one's thoughts. Suppose one could catch them before they became "works of art"? Catch them hot and sudden as they rise in the mind. . . . Of course one cannot; for the process of language is slow and deluding. One must stop to find a word. Then, there is the form of the sentence, soliciting one to fill it.

In a sense, Jack Kerouac did what Virginia Woolf decided was impossible.

On March 26, 2005, the house in Lowell where Jack Kerouac was born was designated a historic landmark. Also in 2005, by an act of the state legislature Jack's birthday, March 12, was officially made Kerouac Day throughout the Commonwealth of Massachusetts.

But the man whose book became the voice of a generation died a lonely drunkard's death, having achieved notoriety instead of the respect as a writer he longed for and deserved.

Kerouac is only one in a long line of artists who were reviled or ignored during their lifetime and canonized after their death.

Herman Melville, whose *Moby Dick* is the closest thing we have to an American epic, died in obscurity, feeling that his life was a failure.

Oscar Wilde, whose plays are a standard part of the dramatic repertoire and whose words are quoted every day, died alone in a Paris garret, his health broken by the jail sentence imposed by a homophobic society.

And Wolfgang Amadeus Mozart, whose 250th birthday was celebrated with concerts all over the world, died a pauper and was buried in the common grave.

There's a scene toward the end of *Amadeus*, a film that captures the spirit, if not the letter, of Mozart's life, where Mozart—drunk, sick, exhausted, near death—staggers home at dawn after a night of revelry with his tricorn askew and his wig unkempt while the good citizens of Vienna are hurrying to work. A strange beast in his own town, ragged and doomed, he's barely able to walk, to face his wife and his unfinished Requiem.

When I saw that scene, I thought of Jack, and Lenny, and all the geniuses who are seemingly condemned to lead disordered lives: to sacrifice health, comfort, and sanity in order to give the world that precious gift it honors only after it has buried them: their art.

But mostly, I thought of Jack.

And these days as I celebrate my seventy-fifth year on this planet I think of the things he said that I didn't want to hear at twenty-five: that "we're all gonna die" and that "nothing is real" and that "it's all a dream." And I think again that he was right.

And Allen's eighty-five year old aunt was right: life is a dream.

At the end of *On the Road* Jack said, "I wrote the book because we're all gonna die." And somewhere else he said that literature is "the tale that's told for no other reason but companionship."

Isn't that why we all write? To fly in the face of our mortality? To celebrate life and to honor the dead and to keep each other company before we join them?

As a writer who got started late in life, I am obsessed with the thought that among those dead—my dead—are some whose stories remain to be told, starting with my father.

Storytelling, like all our arts, has healing power. So whether you agree with those who believe we only live once, or whether you suspect there's more to it than that, we need to tell our stories.

Helen Elliott was one of the few people I've known who liked to talk about the weather. The weather was small talk: the default subject when conversation ground to a halt.

The weather isn't small talk any more.

As I finish this book the ice caps are melting, the polar bears are drowning, and global warming is real, no matter what the vested interests say. I'm glad my father isn't alive to see such disrespect for science in our land.

But whether our Earth becomes uninhabitable in a billion years or only a hundred, we need to tell our stories.

Even though Mozart and Shakespeare and all our art may one day be lost forever, nevertheless, we need to tell our stories—and to catch the stories of our elders—while we still have time.

FOR JACK

there was always something between us
your glass of red wine
my eyes full of tears

on the day you entered history
carrying a sack of manuscripts on your back
I watched you like someone
who has been watching a door for twenty years
sees it suddenly blow open
admit a breath of snow and stars
and then blow shut again
perhaps for a lifetime

I watched you lay your athlete's body down
across the railroad earth
to make a bridge for souls

I saw you give your manhood
so generations could wake up from a death
that only you could see with such sad clarity

I watched with tears
for you who blew into the dead winter
of my young womanhood
fresh from America
and filled me with a sound like children laughing
and loved my morning song
were not at peace

I saw it in your eyes
the road ahead of you led through the abyss
you bowed your head and went on through
no time for simple joy

it's all a dream, you said
by dying you proved yourself right

there's nothing between us now
as you pore over the endless scroll of life
and your cats sleep in the sun

the image fades into the light
faint brush strokes on the blinding page

six EPILOGUE

JACK'S VOICE

Yours the eyes that saw, the heart that felt, the voice that sang and cried; and as long as America shall live, though ye old Kerouac body hath died, yet shall you live.

—Gregory Corso, *Elegiac Feelings American*

As I get ready to send this book out into the world I understand the long overdue movie of *On the Road* is still spinning its wheels, having run out of gas for the umpteenth time.

I've seen most of the movies in which an actor plays the Jack Kerouac character, and none are successful. For Jack they always pick some young man who is short, dark, and handsome and who looks "sensitive" but who doesn't look or sound anything like Jack.

The only Hollywood actor who actually looks like Jack is Mel Gibson. He's not as handsome as Jack was but has very similar features and that same wild gleam in his eye, the same combination of wildness and sweetness—the athlete and the poet, Braveheart and Hamlet—and the same good-humored crinkles around the eyes. He, too, is one of those bantam-size men—they're both only five feet nine—that women want to take home and feed a hot meal.

There's a scene in *What Women Want* where Mel Gibson dances by himself in a sort of forties musical sequence, wearing his hat at a rakish Ol' Blue Eyes angle, where he looks so much like Jack, it's uncanny.

For years I had a picture of Mel Gibson on my refrigerator, not because I had a thing about him, but to remind myself that I'd better hurry up and finish this book before Mel got too old to play the young Jack.

Unfortunately, that's what's happened. Gibson is too old now, even if he wanted the role. He might object on moral grounds: his violent brand of Christianity is very different from Jack's Catholic-Buddhist blend, though each in his own way has been obsessed with the Stations of the Cross.

Then there's Jack's walk. He walked like a Frenchman, hands in pockets, head down on one side not taking up too much space—remember he told David Amram "a writer must be a shadow"?—neat, efficient, but loose, almost shuffling, humble but alert. I've seen old men in Lowell with this walk. Whoever plays Jack should go to Lowell and walk around.

But the big problem with the casting of Jack in the existing movies is not that the actors don't look like him or walk like him, but that they don't *sound* like him. The most important thing about Jack is his voice, that unique blend of Massachusetts vowels, French-Canadian intonations, jazz rhythms, and Sinatra croon: something like what you might get if Frankie had been born in Boston instead of Hoboken. But those actors don't even try for the Lowell accent.

There's another quality to his voice that is part and parcel of his ethnicity and his vision. There is a certain way of speaking English that all Native Americans have, regardless of tribe. Maybe it comes out of their common experience as outsiders who are close to the land: a tone of voice that is difficult to describe but instantly recognizable; a tone both innocent and knowing, unpretentious yet powerful. It is the voice of someone who has pledged allegiance to the truth, a voice full of sadness but devoid of irony. Life is too serious for irony. It's the voice of a nature lover and an old fashioned believer. Sun Bear, Medicine Story, Wallace Black Elk: they all had it, and Jack had it, too. The American plains are in it.

Jack may well have had Iroquois blood; he believed he did. At any rate, that ancient French and Indian quality has to be in there as well: the innocence of the American Indian, the purity, the love of truth.

Some years ago I heard that Johnny Depp bought Jack's raincoat from the Kerouac estate for $25,000 because he wanted to play Jack. When I first heard this I was dubious. Johnny Depp is a great actor but he doesn't look like Jack, and I couldn't imagine him playing a man who got a football scholarship to Columbia.

But then I watched *The Source*, which is my personal favorite of the documentaries about the Beats. In this film, footage of Kerouac, Ginsberg, and Burroughs is juxtaposed with shots of actors reading from their works: Johnny Depp reads Kerouac; Dennis Hopper, Burroughs; and John Turturro, Ginsberg.

I knew this, and yet the first time I watched this video, I was fooled. I was watching along and I recognized Jack's voice when lo and behold, to my amazement, Johnny Depp appeared on the screen. Johnny Depp read Jack's words with such devoted fidelity to the Kerouac timbre, accent, and rhythms that until his image appeared on the screen, I thought it was Jack. Unlike all the previous actors who have attempted to impersonate Jack on film, Johnny Depp actually studied his speech patterns and was able to nail that voice, which is unlike any other with the possible exception of Sinatra, whom Jack could imitate to a T.

The secret here is simple. Johnny Depp can "channel" Jack for the same reason Jack could sound so much like his idol Sinatra. Intelligence and talent are important, but the real secret, of course, is love. Love takes the time to pay close attention. Love listens. That's what's needed.

So I hope that whoever gets the part will take the time to study Jack's voice.

APPENDIX

THE TWO HELENS' DICTIONARY OF HIP

(This is as far as we got. . . .)

all that jazz

ball
beat
beat it to a pad with
a chick
blow
blow the joint
bug

cat
catch
chick
come on like
cool
crazy
cut

destroy
dig
down
drag

flip, flip your lid

get with it
go man
gone
goof
got it

had it
have a ball
hip
hot
hung up

I don't know what
it don't mean a
thing if it ain't got
that swing
it's a gas

just won't quit

like
loot

make it
make the scene

man
man like wow

new set of threads
nowhere

off the wall

pad
pick up on
put down

rock 'n' roll

score
snow
sounds
split

square
stoned
swinging

take your hands off
my material
the beat
the big beat
the end
the most
the whole bit
too much
tourist

way out
wiggy
with it
wow baby

AN ASTROLOGICAL APPENDIX

*My mother and Blanche are discussing astrology as they walk
under the stars.*

—Jack Kerouac, *Doctor Sax*

A word about the language of astrology, which was harder to
learn than French and will be foreign to many of my readers.

Out of respect for skeptics and as a courtesy to anyone un-
familiar with its terms, and except for the brief report on my
experience as editor of the *Larousse Encyclopedia of Astrology*
and my dialogue with my father, I have deliberately avoided
references to astrology in this book.

A policy of simple translation (as in the case of French)
would not have worked, since so many of the terms—planets,
signs, and houses, for example—are multivalent, i.e., they have
not one but a whole constellation of meanings, rendering a one-
to-one explanation impossible.

But I *am* an astrologer, and I'm fortunate enough to have
accurate birth data for Jack Kerouac, Allen Ginsberg, Helen
Elliott, and myself, all of whom were open to astrology. So for
those readers who do share our interest, I offer this introductory
glance at our charts.

I have tried to strike a balance between a style I might adopt
in speaking to astrologers and one that gets bogged down with too
much explanation of terms. For further information on any of the
terms used I recommend *Larousse*, which, though out of print, is
easily available from Amazon and other online booksellers.

In *Doctor Sax* Kerouac writes: "It was in Centralville I was born . . . on Lupine Road, March 1922, at five o'clock in the afternoon."

A birth time exactly on the hour is always regarded with suspicion by astrologers. The five p.m. birth time is accepted by Kerouac's earliest biographer, Ann Charters. It was also used by Carolyn Cassady, Jack's friend and lover and an amateur astrologer, whose interpretation of his chart appeared in an appendix in the first edition of Charters' book. The astrological reading was eliminated from later editions, perhaps to give greater credibility to the first scholarly biography of Kerouac to appear.

In his biography of Kerouac, *Memory Babe*, Gerald Nicosia gives the time of his birth as 5:30 p.m., and the 5:30 time was also given to me in correspondence in 1972 by Juanita Koprowski, who was doing research for a book on Jack.

It is worth noting that Kerouac had a prodigious memory and also that Kerouac's mother, the most likely source of birth data since this was a home delivery, respected astrology. It was astrology that Jack's mother and his cousin Blanche were discussing on that traumatic evening in Jack's childhood when the man carrying a watermelon dropped dead before their eyes on the Moody Street Bridge.

Back in the 1990s when I began work on this book, I hired Laurence Ely, an astrologer who specializes in rectification (a complicated process in which the astrologer works backward from major events in the person's life to arrive at an exact birth time), to rectify the time of Kerouac's birth. After extensive study of a long list of events in Jack's life for which times were available, he cast his vote in favor of the five p.m. time.

No matter which time we use, Jack Kerouac's chart is dominated by a Full Moon in Virgo opposite a Sun in Pisces lying across the Ascendant-Descendant axis (roughly, the horizon) and forming a Mutable Cross with a Gemini Midheaven (literally, the middle of the sky: the point where the upper meridian intersects the ecliptic) and Mars in Sagittarius at the I.C. (Imum Coeli, literally, the bottom of the sky: the point directly opposite the Midheaven).

In the language of astrology the mutable signs are characterized by changeability, adaptability, and service. The mutable quality has been compared to wave motion in physics, or to information. All of the mutable signs are connected in some way with communication. Taking them in order around the zodiac: Gemini with writing and speaking; Virgo with precision and detail; Sagittarius with publishing and preaching; and Pisces with poetry and dreams. When planets in all four of the mutable signs

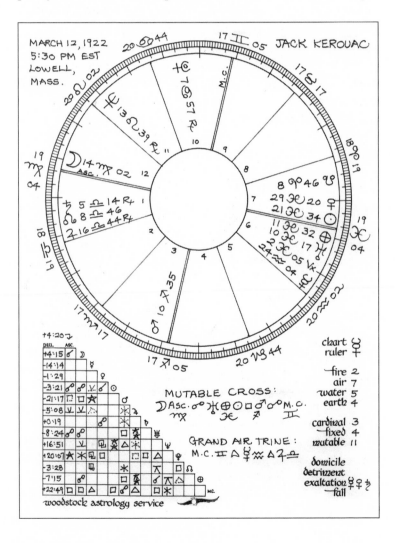

form a Grand Cross in the chart, the result is a major configuration that implies a life of service that is often devoted to some form of communication.

The Mutable Cross: the astrological term takes on new meaning when we consider Kerouac's Catholic upbringing, his tormented life, his belief that writing was his mission on Earth, and his lifelong obsession with death and impermanence.

In his groundbreaking 1973 work *Cosmic Influences on Human Behavior*, on the basis of massive statistical studies, the French statistician Michel Gauquelin reported significant correlations between vocation and horoscope. Ironically, Gauquelin had set out to disprove astrology and was somewhat embarrassed when his findings validated the astrological hypothesis. Ignoring the signs of the zodiac, Gauquelin focused his attention on the diurnal positions of Mars, Jupiter, Saturn, and the Moon in the charts of 25,000 European professionals.

He found that writers were most often born when the Moon was rising or culminating, i.e., arriving at the upper meridian of the birthplace. By using the biographies of writers he arrived at a tentative description of the lunar temperament. Some of the terms that kept cropping up: "originality, diversity, inventor of forms, bohemian, eternal nomad, improvisation, dreamy, imaginative, prolific, disorderly, moody, changeable, unstable, naive, lazy, poetic, juvenile, widely known, shy, adaptable." In short, the lunar temperament has a rather elusive, pliable, chameleon-like quality.

Not only does Jack Kerouac's chart with its Full Moon rising (i.e., on the Ascendant) accord with Gauquelin's findings on the charts of writers, but the terms Gauquelin found to be associated with the lunar temperament provide an eerily accurate description of his personality.

Gauquelin found that in the charts of 1,553 sports champions, the planet Mars was found to be rising or culminating "with a frequency whose probability of occurring by chance was one in a thousand."

In discussing the Mars temperament—which was typical of a champion athlete, and very different from the lunar temperament—

Gauquelin noted, "The variability of the lunar temperament can be a handicap for champions."

In astrology, planets on *all* the angles (Ascendant, Descendant, Midheaven, or I.C.) are regarded as powerful influences. With his Mars in Sagittarius at the I.C. and therefore opposing the Midheaven, Kerouac scored a winning touchdown as the star running back of the Lowell football team and won a football scholarship to Columbia. Had he not been primarily a lunar type personality, he might have gone on to fame as an athlete, but bad feelings between him and Columbia coach Lou Little caused the moody, erratic young athlete to walk off the field in disgust.

To Gauquelin's list of lunar traits astrologers would add extreme receptivity, and with the Moon rising in Virgo, a shy, private, discriminating nature, a need to serve, attention to detail. The birth is at dusk, and the Full Moon will be exact before the sun rises the next day, so there is all the tension and intensity of the approaching aspect, the building toward the maximum illumination and release of the Full Moon.

Now, to the poetic, dreamy, unstable quality of the Moon rising is added a Pisces Sun conjunct Venus in the extreme 29th degree of Pisces, the sign of her exaltation, as well as Uranus and the Part of Fortune also in Pisces—a stellium (cluster) in the sign of the poet, martyr, dreamer, mystic, musician—and alcoholic. Revolutionary, creative, nonconformist Uranus in the sign of Pisces suggests a kind of universal rebelliousness that was in the air during the roaring twenties of Jack's childhood, the Lost Generation to which the Beat Generation he fathered was later compared.

The Moon and the Ascendant are the most personal points on any birth chart, because they are the fastest moving. So with Uranus in Pisces opposing his Moon-Ascendant conjunction, this *zeitgeist* is channeled through Kerouac's chart in a very personal way.

The slower-moving outer planets Uranus, Neptune, and Pluto are related to trends that characterize an entire generation. Uranus in Pisces: Ginsberg's taking his clothes off at poetry readings and declaiming his wild prophetic *Howl* is an apt metaphor for this new poetry with its credo of utter nakedness and candor, its throwing off of academic timidity and classical forms, its insistence on using the language and rhythms of everyday speech. Beat poetry was inspired by the improvisational style of jazz and bebop and the hip black drug culture and Times Square scene that seemed so much more alive and "with it" than the white middle-class world these boys were expected to join. The Uranian revolution that was the Beat Generation prefigured the social movements of the sixties and the expansion of consciousness that opened the way for Eastern ideas in the West and helped to usher in the constellation of values loosely termed New Age.

The Uranus in Pisces generation created a revolution in poetry, the so-called San Francisco Renaissance of which Jack Kerouac and Allen Ginsberg (ironically, both easterners) were the flag bearers. Ginsberg's Pisces Moon, Mars, and Uranus all lie over Kerouac's Uranus/Fortune, Sun, and Venus like spokes of a wheel in three close conjunctions whose mathematical precision suggests that these men were destined to do this work together—one of the most startling examples of the validation of synastry (chart comparison) I've ever seen.[1]

Unlike my father, I'm not an expert in statistics or probability, but I know enough to know that the probability of these three tight conjunctions occurring by chance is one in a very high number: what my father would call the "surprise index" would be very high indeed. Allen Ginsberg was born the day after Jack's brother Gerard died. What some would dismiss as "coincidence" others might view in terms of pre-life planning, or "karma."

Speaking of synastry, I've always been struck by the fact that not only Jack and Allen, but Helen and I as well are all connected by close conjunctions in Pisces, the sign of poetry, spirituality— and drugs. Helen's birthday was just two days after Jack's, and her Pisces Sun-Mercury conjunction is within orb of my Pisces Ascendant and Allen's Mars, as well as of Jack's Sun.

1. Allen Ginsberg's birth time was given to me in conversation with his father, Louis Ginsberg, sometime in the seventies, and Helen Elliot's in conversation with her some time in the nineties. My own time came from my mother, who stated I was "on hand by midnight," and was later rectified by the distinguished American astrologer Charles Jayne.

Conjunctions between charts bring people together through common interests, lessons to be learned, or work to be done. Jack and Helen were drinkers; Jack, Allen, and I all experimented with drugs, all wrote poetry, and were all attracted to Buddhism in varying degrees. Jack, Helen, and I lived together, an arrangement that was the result of Allen's suggestion on the morning the boys arrived in the city.

Jack and I had other close connections in our charts. The

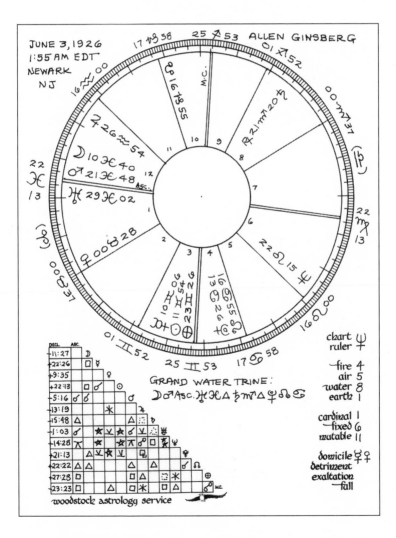

Sun represents one's work in the world, the Ascendant the physical body. Not only was my Pisces Ascendant conjunct his Sun—I was impressed by the fact that he was a published writer—but it opposed his Virgo Ascendant. In astrology as in life, opposites attract. Ascendants in opposite signs can be the astrological signature for physical attraction. In this case, with the opposition within four degrees of orb, it was love at first sight.

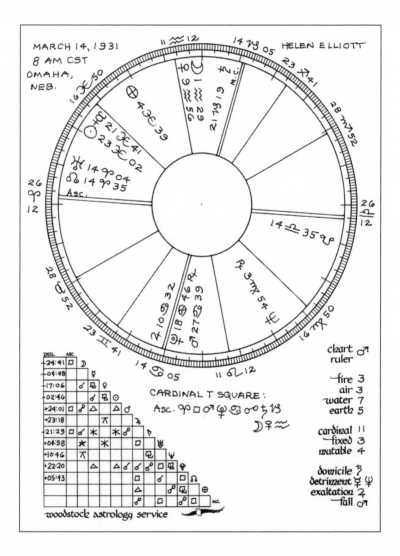

All things being equal, our Ascendants in opposite signs
would have made a good foundation for marriage, but of course
all things were not equal. The Moon rules our relationships with
women, and Jack's Moon was heavily afflicted. Its square to Mars
in Sagittarius and its opposition to Sun, Venus, and Uranus in the
mutable sign of Pisces made it difficult for him to have healthy
relationships with women or to remain with one woman.

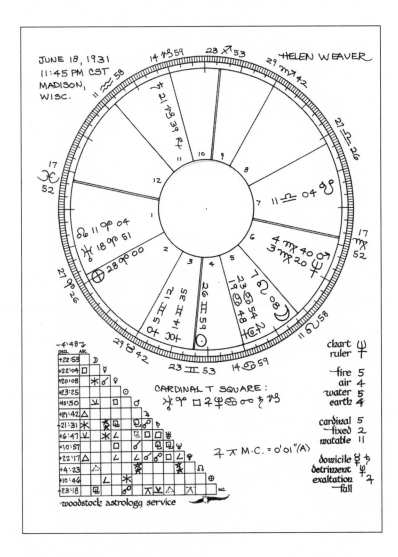

The problems weren't only on Jack's side. My ambivalent Venus-Mars square is not a good omen for lasting relationships either; my Uranus rising in the first house is the signature of a rebellious, independent nature; and many signifiers of loner tendencies in my chart all counteracted that initial physical and spiritual attraction. Astrology is just as complex as life, and there were too many other aspects working against us.

Astrologers have much to learn from studying the charts of geniuses, because geniuses are extreme beings and tend to live their charts to the full. Kerouac was an incredibly complex person, full of contradictions, paradoxes, and extremes between which he alternated, finding resolution only in the one constant activity in his life: writing, and in the one relationship he was able to sustain: his bond with his mother. Here are some of the ways in which the central dynamic of Jack's chart, the Mutable Cross and especially the Full Moon on the horizon, manifested in his life, and some of the opposites he struggled to resolve:

Born to French-Canadian parents and raised in a Franco-American community in the mill town of Lowell, Massachusetts, Kerouac spoke French until he was six, when he began attending a bilingual parochial school. He was both fiercely proud of his ethnic roots and conscious that the patois he grew up speaking was regarded as inferior to Parisian French. The English he wrote in was a second language for Jack, and he studied it with the avidity of a foreigner, immersing himself in Shakespeare and the King James translation of the Bible.

He idealized and romanticized the Lowell of his boyhood, celebrated his life there in his books, and always wished he could return to it, but while living there, he dreamed of escaping its provincial confines and becoming a great writer in the world beyond.

After he left Lowell for New York City and met the men who would be his friends and teachers—Allen Ginsberg, William Burroughs, and Neal Cassady—and especially after his family left Lowell and his father died, Jack began a ten-year pattern of alternating between traveling across America and staying home with his mother. His life on the road was a frenzied kaleidoscope of drugs, alcohol, occasional women, and endless conversation with his friends in New York, San Francisco, Denver, Mexico, and points between. When he had had enough excitement and stimulation, he would retreat to a hermit-like existence with his mother and write down everything that happened, transcribing the contents of the little nickel notebooks he carried with him everywhere and weaving them into the ongoing autobiographical saga he called "The Duluoz Legend."

He invented a technique of composition he called spontaneous prose, using words the way a painter uses paint or like a jazz musician blowing a riff. Yet *On the Road* went through at least four drafts: the master of improvisation did revise.

He had a deep respect for simple working class people like his parents, yet most of his friends were alienated, rootless urban types. John Clellon Holmes said that "he lived simultaneously in both worlds—a tremulous bridge between two realities bent on denying one another." Wherever he was, he wanted to be somewhere else: an easterner, he was drawn again and again to the West, literally following the setting Sun of his nativity. The Full Moon lying across the horizon of his chart was the cosmic signature of his restless shuttling across America.

Pisces is the sign least at home on this planet. From the time his beloved brother Gerard died at age nine when Jack was four years old, he lived haunted by a profound sense of impermanence and an ever-present consciousness of death. At ten or eleven, he saw the watermelon man drop dead of a heart attack on the Moody Street Bridge. As a young merchant marine on the *SS Dorchester*, he watched men drown when her sister ship, the *Latham*, was torpedoed and went down in Arctic waters.

Two years later, at twenty-four, he watched his father succumb to cancer of the stomach. His father's death helped him to focus on and complete his first published novel, *The Town and the City*. He decided that "the only true subject of poetry was death." When he was writing, the Pisces visionary was grounded by the Virgo workaholic who knew that "life is in the details." And the alcoholic whose consumption of liquor was so prodigious that it was a miracle he survived for forty-seven years carefully recorded how many words he wrote each day and kept his manuscripts and correspondence neatly organized in impeccable files.

The list of Pisces-Virgo contradictions goes on: his unstinting generosity in keeping his promise to his dying father to take care of his mother was equaled only by his legendary cheapness. Jack himself said that his saving grace in the eyes of certain friends was "the materialistic Canuck taciturn cold skepticism all the picked-up Idealism in the world of books couldn't hide."

Fundamentally heterosexual, he was incapable of a lasting relationship with any woman except his mother; he put down homosexuality, yet flirted with it, and two of his closest friends, Ginsberg and Burroughs, were homosexual.

At the end of his life, when he was lonely and ill, he could be paranoid, bigoted, and irascible, but Joyce Johnson, Carolyn Cassady, and I all remember his sweetness, his kindness, his disarming openness.

The media image of Kerouac (which confused the author of *On the Road* with its hero, Neal Cassady) was of an amoral, semiliterate barbarian who used and abused drugs and women, condoned petty thievery, and threatened "family values." The real Kerouac was shy, vulnerable, reclusive, a highly literate and serious person who admired Neal's apparent freedom from Catholic guilt and inhibition but was himself fundamentally conservative.

The most famous picture of Jack, which appeared in *Mademoiselle* shortly before *On the Road* was published, shows him with tousled hair and a checked shirt open at the collar. What it doesn't show is that he was wearing a crucifix that Gregory Corso had just put around his neck. Every newspaper and magazine that reprinted the picture, except the *New York Times*, cropped out the crucifix, which evidently did not accord with the media's image of Kerouac as *enfant terrible* and menace to society.

The media did not know, or care, that to Kerouac, "beat" not only meant exhausted, down and out, stripped bare like a Times Square junkie, with an inner knowledge that sees beyond the forms and conventions of the world; but also had the sense of "beatitude": that the Beat movement had a spiritual dimension.

Even these two meanings of Beat, the exoteric and the esoteric, reflect the underlying duality of Kerouac's nature.

Kerouac was a deeply spiritual person, and nowhere is this fundamental duality of his nature more apparent than in the question of his Catholicism vs. his Buddhism.

In the late nineteenth century the English poet Rudyard Kipling wrote: "Oh, East is East, and West is West, and never the twain shall meet, Till Earth and Sky stand presently at God's great Judgment Seat." Fifty years later the American poet Jack Kerouac, mainly to settle an argument about reincarnation with his friend Neal Cassady, went to the San Jose Public Library and checked out Ashvaghosha's *Life of the Buddha*.

The Buddhist model of the *bhikkhu*, or holy wanderer, which Gary Snyder introduced him to, helped to assuage Jack's guilt for the aimless lifestyle his relatives found irresponsible. Jack read and studied voraciously the few Buddhist texts that were available in English at that time and even translated sutras from the French. His understanding of the Dharma was immediate, subtle, and profound, and he was able to distill its essence in works like *Mexico City Blues* and *The Scripture of the Golden Eternity*. The impact of these and of his unpublished notes on Buddhism, originally written to explain it to Allen Ginsberg, earned him a respected place in the American Buddhist lineage.

Jack's Buddhism was authentic, but his Catholicism had been instilled in him from childhood, and eventually he returned to it. Catholicism, a religion based on an ideal of sacrifice, triumphed over Buddhism, a philosophy based on a practice: Pisces and Virgo again.

William Blake wrote, "Without contrarieties, no progression." The multiple contrarieties of Kerouac's Mutable Cross, which he carried for us, motivated him to explore the limits of his being and to turn his experience into art. Kerouac's struggle with opposites was a rich source of creativity, the shifting ground on which he was able to arrive at symmetry or balance in his art. We reap the fruits of his struggle.

ACKNOWLEDGMENTS

Heaven keep me from ever completing anything. This whole book is but draught–nay, but the draught of a draught. Oh, Time, Strength, Cash & Patience!

–Herman Melville, *Moby Dick*

This book has been in the works for nineteen years and it's been in the back of my mind for fifty: ever since that day in November 1956 when Jack and his friends landed on my doorstep and he entered my living room, my bedroom, and my life. When I finally got started in 1994 its birth contractions had to be sandwiched between the death throes of my mother. After she died there were other upheavals.

The Kerouac file sat on my computer for years pending the courage to complete. Residual anger at Jack, perfectionism, fear of hurting people's feelings, fear of failure, fear of success, innumerable false starts, genre confusion (is this an autobiography or a memoir?), and just plain laziness: all these have exerted the necessary pressure to keep this story from being told.

I had to lose my innocence of death. I had to discover Jack as a writer. I had to read all of his books. I had to read him aloud! And maybe I had to become a Buddhist, maybe I had to develop a little more patience and compassion before I could find my way to the final structure with something approaching clarity.

Waiting for "perspective" is all very well, but there comes a point where perspective is all you have left: it's all atmosphere and no details, like the Earth from space.

Through it all I never stopped feeling that I had a responsibility to present my little slice of history to the world, that, like Jack, I had a duty to record my experience to the best of my ability. And through it all I was cheered on by the belief and encouragement of my family and friends.

There's no way I'm going to remember all the people who have helped and supported me along the way, either in person or through their writing, but I have to at least make a stab at it, in the hope that anyone I leave out will forgive me.

My father, my mother, and my brother were all excellent writers and I grew up in a house full of books. I wouldn't be a writer myself if it weren't for them, so they go at the top of my list.

Don't let me forget my high school English teacher, Frances Bartlett, who sent one of my poems to Robert Frost and who taught me how to write prose. Or Archibald Byrne, who had the unenviable job of teaching freshman English Composition at Oberlin and who taught me to think like a writer.

Right after them comes my great friend and teacher the late John Button, a tragically underrated artist who knew I was a writer almost before I knew it myself.

My heartfelt love and gratitude to two dear friends who have a special connection with this book, the late Allen Ginsberg and my fellow survivor Dan Wakefield, for believing in it from the beginning and for the constant inspiration of their work.

I am graced with an extraordinary group of friends both clever and wise. Linda Baker, Miriam Berg, Sarvananda Bluestone, Annie Buck, David De Porte, Melissa Dunning, Gerald Fabian, Bob Gottlieb, Michael Korda, Marcia Newfield, Enrique Noguera, Cynthia Poten, Dan Wakefield, Sally Weaver, and Clarisse and Rob Zielke all read early versions and gave invaluable encouragement and advice.

Joe Lee, the soul of generosity, has been a kind of one-man fan club.

For years I worked with a version of the book that sagged badly after a promising start. Freelance editor Deborah Straw recommended drastic cuts which I initially resisted but ultimately accepted–especially when Dan Wakefield said the same thing. At last the book had the right shape!

I am grateful to Jon Graham of Inner Traditions, whose early enthusiasm meant a great deal to me.

Bob Gottlieb, Michael Korda, Dan Wakefield, and Mary van Valkenburg went out of their way to assist this agentless author. Joyce Johnson opened the door to City Lights. Chris Ammer at the National Writers Union was very helpful with contract advice.

I particularly value the help and support of Beat scholars David Amram, Carolyn Cassady, Ann Charters, Joyce Johnson, Dave Moore, Bill Morgan, and Bob Rosenthal.

It's been fun getting to know Carolyn via e-mail. Among her other kindnesses, she sent me that gorgeous picture she took of Jack in 1953 when he still looked like a movie star.

My old friend John Hollander supplied me with the complete lyrics of his immortal "Mandrill Ramble" and even put up with my abridged version.

Mikhail Horowitz kindly let me quote his eloquent tribute to Allen Ginsberg in the *Woodstock Times*. When Allen died I couldn't say a word because Mikhail had said it all.

Heartfelt thanks to Bill Belmont of Fantasy Records for his generosity in letting me quote excerpts from Lenny Bruce's routines.

Special thanks to Al Goldman for writing *Ladies and Gentlemen, Lenny Bruce!!*; to Martin Garbus for his ongoing support of Lenny's cause and for his book *Ready for the Defense*; and to Ronald K. L. Collins and David M. Skover not only for writing *The Trials of Lenny Bruce* but for the part they played in securing Lenny's posthumous pardon. All three of these books helped to jog my memory of Lenny's New York trial.

My thanks to Martha Mayo at the Mogan Cultural Center in Lowell, Peter Hale at the Allen Ginsberg Trust, Cynthia Zeiss at the *Washington Post*, and Norman Podhoretz at *Commentary* for help with research problems and in tracking down old documents.

Computer whiz Jonathan Delson has rescued me from more than one disaster. Rob Shear at Catskill Art and Office made copies of the text through a zillion revisions. Karin Peters has been my rock for over a year now and has helped me in more ways than I can say.

Great thanks to John Sampas for providing me with copies of letters I wrote Jack fifty years ago and to Luke Elliott for letting me use his mother's photographs.

And of course my eternal gratitude to Helen, without whom there would be no story; to Jack, Allen, and Lenny for the courage of their hearts and for sharing their amazing energy with me; and to Marcel Proust for showing us all that the past can be recaptured.

Finally, I want to thank Lawrence Ferlinghetti for founding City Lights; my editor Robert Sharrard, for his sensitivity and patience; Yolanda de Montijo for her great cover design; Linda Ronan for a book design that is true to the spirit of the fifties; Stacey Lewis and Sarah Silverman for getting the word out; and everyone there for helping to turn my dream into a book!

Helen and Brindle Weaver in Woodstock, 2008.

As a professional literary translator Helen Weaver has rendered some fifty books from the French. Her translation of the *Antonin Artaud: Selected Writings* was a finalist for the National Book Award in 1977. She is co-author and general editor of *The Larousse Encyclopedia of Astrology* and author of *The Daisy Sutra: Conversations with my Dog.*

Weaver lives in Woodstock, New York with her whippet mix Brindle. She is at work on a book about her scientist father, Warren Weaver, and their dialogue about astrology, tentatively entitled *Translation of Light.*